State Secrets by Lynette Sowell
Tara Whitley, an assistant White H
to become an amateur investigator. Then
operative Jack Courtland steps back into her life and recru
her to help uncover a plot to sabotage the next State Dinner.
But she doesn't expect Jack to uncover feelings for him she
thought had long since died. Can she trust him with her heart,
or will secrets separate them again?

Dying for Love by Cara C. Putman
Attorney Ciara Turner discovers the body of a judge on what
was supposed to be a routine morning at court. Daniel Evans,
a man she clerked with and now clashes with routinely, asks
her to help him bring justice to the killer. The more time they
spend together, the more Ciara wonders if she can ignore her
feelings for Daniel. But can Daniel prove he's not the rogue
she believes him to be?

Buried Deception by Gina Conroy
Archaeology intern and widow Samantha Steele wants to
provide for her children—alone. Security guard and ex-cop
Nick Porter is haunted by his past and keeps his heart guarded.
But when they discover that a broken artifact is a fake, Nick
and Samantha must set aside their stubbornness and rely on
each other—or the results could be deadly. Will they both
allow God to excavate their hearts so they can find new love?

Coffee, Tea, and Danger by Frances Devine
Susan Holland, proprietor of Coffee, Tea, and Sweets, likes her
life the way it is. Uncomplicated. Then at the age of forty, she
inherits a run-down mansion from her late ambassador uncle
and "accidents" begin to occur. Vince Martini doesn't need a
woman in his life, or so he thinks. But when danger threatens
Susan, his protective side kicks in. Will love overcome the evil
that is trying to control their lives?

CHERRY BLOSSOM CAPERS

CHERRY BLOSSOM CAPERS

FOUR-IN-ONE COLLECTION

GINA CONROY, FRANCES DEVINE,
CARA C. PUTMAN,
& LYNETTE SOWELL

BARBOUR
PUBLISHING

ISBN 978-1-61626-646-2

Cover design: Kirk Dou Ponce, Dog Earred Design

Published by Barbour Publishing, Inc., P.O. Box 719, Uhrichsville, OH 44683, www.barbourbooks.com

Our mission is to publish and distribute inspirational products offering exceptional value and biblical encouragement to the masses.

Member of the
Evangelical Christian
Publishers Association

Printed in the United States of America

STATE
SECRETS

by Lynette Sowell

Dedication

To my coauthors, Gina Conroy, Frances Devine, and Cara Putman, because of our little idea that finally came to life. "No" isn't always no forever. I'm so thankful we had the chance to write these stories. Working with the three of you has been a joy.

To my husband and kids, and the most memorable family vacation we ever had to Washington, DC. I will always cherish our adventures together.

There is nothing concealed that will not be disclosed,
or hidden that will not be made known.
LUKE 12:2 NIV

Chapter 1

Just before Jack Courtland entered 1600 Pennsylvania Avenue, he adjusted his tie and tried not to tug on the cuffs of his jacket.

"You're sure about this?" he asked fellow FBI agent George Clements. "Here, the White House?" His pulse thrummed in his ears. Once, on a grade school field trip, he'd toured the executive mansion. Now, he'd get to see areas off the main tour.

The older man with salt-and-pepper hair nodded. They walked toward the office of the chief usher. "Yeah, you lucky stiff. The intel's good, and you're the one they're going to want on the inside."

"It'll make our job easier if I end up here. We need eyes on the inside."

Their first contact, Chief Usher William Kanaday, had been part of the White House staff for several administrations, and had agreed to cooperate as much as possible, so long as it didn't interfere with any of the day-to-day functions of the executive mansion.

"Good morning, gentlemen," said Kanaday as he rounded his desk after shaking hands. "Now tell me exactly why you think there might be a planned attack on the White House."

"Attack is a strong word, Mr. Kanaday. We don't have actual word that the house will be under attack. However, we've encountered warnings of an imminent threat within the next two weeks."

The chief usher folded his wrinkled hands and leaned on his desk. "Any threat to the house is a threat not just to the current administration, but to the great line of safety that's surrounded this home. We've made sure that it won't be attacked and burned again."

No, it wouldn't. But today's enemies often worked more subversively, unlike during the War of 1812, when Washington fell and the White House burned. And today's enemies were out for blood, not just destroying real estate.

Jack glanced at George before continuing. "We believe the main target is the State Dinner on February sixth."

"We'll be your main points of contact during our investigation," said George.

Kanaday nodded. "I'll count on you for help, but I know every detail of the dinner, and I know every person who has a role, from florists to chefs."

At the word *chef*, a face immediately sprang to Jack's mind. Hazel eyes framed by dark hair, a messy cut that made its owner's slightly upturned nose and sprinkle of freckles all the more appealing.

Where was Tara now? Somewhere on the ground floor of the White House below him, maybe? George once mentioned her promotion to assistant executive chef at the White House.

"Hey, didn't you run around with her when we were in Paris?" George had said.

Run around with. Like a casual acquaintance. In the end, he'd treated her that way, tossed her heart to the side like a book he'd grown bored with.

Live and learn, Jack Courtland. Live and learn.

With the more than one hundred workers associated with the executive mansion, not counting the First Family's staff and appointees, Jack figured the chance of seeing Tara would be extremely slim. He was here to do his job and remind his superiors that giving him a position in the DC bureau was a wise move. He *deserved* to be here.

"Right, Agent Courtland?" George was asking. Both he and the chief usher eyeballed him.

"I'm sorry, Agent Clements?"

"We're ready for our tour. We need to walk the layout, especially of the ground level and State floor." George rose from his chair.

"Of course we do." He hadn't seen Tara in three years, but even now her memory rattled his brain like a jackhammer.

The chief usher escorted them from his office and back into the hall. "Just past this entrance hall and to the right is the State dining room." The soles of his shoes swished on the red carpet that led them through the Cross Hall and into the State dining room.

"Here we have the dining room, where the State Dinners are held." The man walked the perimeter of the room. "We expect to have at least fifteen eight-tops here."

Jack didn't care about table setup at the moment. He strode to the nearest long window that stretched nearly to the ceiling, and pushed a tied-back drape farther back for a better view outside. No one would have a good chance at a shot into the room. If there was a particular target, they couldn't know the seating arrangement. "I don't think anyone will take a shot. It wouldn't be impossible, but there would be more effective ways of attacking."

"You're right, especially with extra security for the event." George trailed along in Kanaday's wake, reminding Jack of one dog trailing another.

"Chief Usher Kanaday," Jack said as he looked the man straight in the eye, "I don't believe the attack will come from the outside. It'll come from within. Someone will bring something into the building, something that doesn't belong yet could look extremely routine."

Kanaday nodded. "I'll show you the ground floor next. Deliveries come through there, near the kitchen."

Once on the ground floor, the atmosphere changed. The belly of the executive mansion hummed with life.

"Here's the kitchen, this way," Kanaday said.

"One moment, Mr. Kanaday," said George. "I need to converse with my colleague here."

"Certainly," he replied, and stayed a discreet several paces away.

"Courtland." The force of George's gaze struck him, but he didn't flinch.

"Clements." Jack returned the look.

"I need you one hundred percent here. Right now."

"Understood."

"You've worked in Europe. You've seen dignitaries before. You choke on this, they'll shuffle you to the bottom of the pile here in the Washington bureau. You won't have time to get a lungful of air before you go down."

"It's not being around dignitaries. I'm fine with that. I'm not going to choke on this." Even as he said the words, a lump threatened to lodge itself in his throat. At the end of the hall, by what he assumed to be the kitchen entrance, a lone figure clad in dark pants and a chef jacket stared at him, arms crossed in front of her.

Tara Whitley felt the air leave the ground-floor hallway with a whoosh. Every nerve ending on her arms tingled, and she rubbed the sleeves of her chef's jacket.

"So after we meet with the First Lady, we need to talk with the distributor about a delivery date for the beef. I'll let you do that," Adelaide Montanez said. The chief executive chef, in her usual bundle-of-energy manner, buzzed away from Tara and into the White House kitchen.

All thoughts of the upcoming State Dinner prep had flown from Tara's brain. Instead, she felt the cold iron railing of the Eiffel Tower under her fingertips again, the wind on her face, and the hollow laughter and chatter from tourists echoed in her ears once more.

Jack Courtland. Ten yards away, standing with the chief usher and another guy in a suit. One of Jack's fellow agents, probably. Agents had a look about them, even when standing in plainclothes at a barbecue. Now, wearing their dark suits, standing in the ground floor hallway of the White House? Something was up.

"Jack," she heard herself say. She almost cringed at the sound of her voice, sounding almost as pathetic as poor Rose did on the movie *Titanic*, as she released Jack's frozen form to the depths of the North Atlantic. Her own heart had released Jack Courtland years ago. She'd had to.

Maybe Jack didn't hear the squeak in her throat. He had no reason to speak to her, and she had no reason to approach him. Those six months in Paris might as well have been a lifetime ago.

She'd been kidding herself to believe the whispered promises would mean anything now. People changed. People moved on. So had she, until now. Jack had moved on a long time ago, in Paris.

Tara fled to the security of the kitchen, its usual hum of activity, pans clattering, the voices of sous chefs and prep cooks bouncing off the walls. She caught up with Adelaide who was already at her computer, plugging in the rough menu for the State Dinner in two weeks.

"Tomorrow we have the Governors' Lunch," said Adelaide.

"I'll pull the list and make sure the prep work is under way." Tara reached for a folder on Adelaide's desk. Finally, the head chef had included Tara into more of the planning and supervising. She loved coordinating the meals. Not that she wanted her knife skills to suffer, but there was something to be said for orchestrating a meal for governors and other heads of state. Her job involved simpler events, such as planning a birthday party for one of the president's sons, who celebrated his tenth birthday on the South Lawn last summer. The day had made her miss her nephews in Texas.

"Yes. Mr. Kanaday has already confirmed the table setup for eleven tomorrow morning." Adelaide looked up from the computer. "Hey, you here with me?" She moved her hand in a slow wave.

"I'm here." Tara opened the folder. "I got distracted for a second. So the barbecue's already been pulled?"

"You bet. Maybe I can finagle a seat for you at lunch." The head chef's tone held a teasing note. "You want to meet the Texas governor?"

Tara shrugged. "It might be fun. I wouldn't dream of crashing the lunch, though."

Adelaide glanced past Tara. "Excuse me, may I help you?" Tara turned to see Jack strolling into the kitchen. He pulled out his badge in a fluid movement. She used to tease him about the stance.

"Chef, I've been working with Mr. Kanaday on the State Dinner preparations." He nodded at Adelaide. "I need to speak with Chef Whitley." He stared at Tara, who bit her lip and pulled a strand of hair over her right ear.

"I think I can spare her for a few minutes." Adelaide's eyebrows shot up, her eyes full of questions. "Go ahead, Tara."

Tara wanted her to say, "I'm sorry, we're busy. I can't spare Tara right now. We have a lot to do." Moments were ticking by, and they'd end up on the prep line themselves making up time for the Governors' Luncheon tomorrow for twenty-five. Then there was the president and First Lady's anniversary dinner. Just the two of them, candlelight, with pizza for the kids in their room.

"I'll be back as soon as I can. You can count on that." Tara ground out the words and followed Jack from the kitchen. No one else seemed to notice them leave, and Adelaide had already turned her focus back to the computer. People came and went all the time from the White House, and whoever came through the halls had a good reason to be there. So why was the FBI talking to Chief Usher Kanaday?

They entered the hallway, and Jack faced her. "We need to talk."

"I don't think there's much we have to talk about. You told me what I wanted to know in Paris."

She couldn't help but take in the sight of him. He still kept his dark hair trimmed close. Salt-and-pepper strands mingled at his temples. Stress did that to a man, turning his hair gray before its time. How old was he now? Thirty, with fine lines etched around his eyes. Jack, all business. The Jack she used to laugh with was gone forever, and he'd become the man he once told her he feared he would.

Now, he looked at her with those tired eyes and continued. "This isn't about Paris, Tara. It's about now. I need your help."

"Aren't you one of the experts? I'm a chef, not an investigator." Her words came out more sharply than she intended. Really, if she was over the man, his being here shouldn't affect her one bit. Someone she used to know, like receiving a friend suggestion on Facebook of someone from the good old days. Jack wasn't part of her life now, and she didn't need to show him anything but cooperation.

He reached in his pocket, pulled out a card, and handed it to her. "As I said, I need your help. I wouldn't ask if it wasn't important."

She nodded slowly. Her remark about Paris hadn't helped any. She wished she could take back the words, but then, you couldn't put toothpaste back in the tube once it was squeezed out. She studied the card, giving his address at the Washington, DC, bureau.

"All right, what is it?"

"We're investigating a possible threat to the White House, specifically at the upcoming State Dinner." His glance snapped up and down the hall, then back at her. His dark eyes held a once-familiar expression. She cleared her throat.

"I don't know how I can help. Chef Montanez has asked me to provide a backup role for her, but as far as a guest list or anything, I don't have that information." Her ire had cooled just a bit. Time to remember where she was and that this current situation had nothing to do with the past, nothing at all.

"Can you come to my office? We can talk more freely there."
He touched her arm, causing a shock of static electricity. Both
of them stepped back simultaneously.

Tara rubbed her sleeve again. "Why not here, now?"

Jack moved closer and lowered his voice. "If this is an inside
job, we don't want to alert anyone to our investigation. We want
to catch them, to show people that you can't plot to strike the
White House and get away with it."

"Inside job?" Now he was making her cranky again. "The
idea is ludicrous. I've been here for three years, and the staff is
almost like family to me."

"Well, they're not family to me," said Jack. "Right now, only
you and Chief Usher Kanaday and the Secret Service know
about this threat. No one else is to know."

"I don't like it. I don't like it one bit." Tara shook her head.
"A threat? On the White House dinner?"

"What time are you off tomorrow?"

She had the Governors' Lunch, but after that she was free.
"About two, I believe."

"Come to the bureau, and we'll talk."

"All right. I'll see you tomorrow."

"Thanks, Tara." He gave her a nod accompanied by a half
grin, and he walked off down the hallway.

Chapter 2

Tara detested that dimple now, as much as it used to drive her crazy way back when. Its memory followed her home that afternoon. She nibbled on her lip, exited the Metro train car, and entered the white-and-gray world outside. January snow held little of the magic of Christmas snow. After the latest snowstorm, Tara was ready to book a plane ticket to Florida for a good week. Or two. Maybe she'd job-hunt in the Sunshine State.

Then she thought of her dream job, right here in the DC area. She remembered the first day she'd walked the halls, feeling the weight of history made and still being created. And how proud her parents had been when they learned about their only daughter's appointment to the White House kitchen.

Back in Bastrop, Texas, they ran a legendary diner, the Blue-bonnet Café. Tara still remembered the pride in Daddy's voice when she told him about her new position in Washington, DC.

"Baby girl, God has rewarded your hard work. Like in Proverbs, where it says, 'Do you see someone skilled in their work? They will serve before kings.' And so, now you are. For such a time as this. What an honor."

She'd been nervous then at the idea of preparing food eaten

by leaders from around the world, as well as her own country's president and his family. She smiled at all the "helpful" letters she received from relatives, begging her to give the president advice on how to set the country right.

Her cell phone buzzed as she crossed over the pavement and headed for the Metro parking lot. A text, from her neighbor Ciara Turner. WE STILL HAVING MOVIE NIGHT?

Ack. Movie night. She'd forgotten, sort of. She had some leftover salmon puffs, an experimental recipe she planned to run by Adelaide for a future White House event. Plus, she had enough hot chocolate mix and tea for the three of them. Every day, she thanked God for her neighbors Ciara and Susan Holland. Her parents had never liked the idea of a young woman living alone and working in major cities like New York, where she attended culinary school, then Paris, and now DC. Each time, God had answered their prayers by sending Tara friends who made her feel as if Texas weren't fifteen hundred miles away.

She found her car, started the vehicle, and let it warm up. She peeled off her gloves before she replied to Ciara's message. YES. IS 6 TOO EARLY? ASK SUSAN, TOO. THX.

During the wave of snowstorms they'd had since Christmas, the three women had taken to having a movie night each week, classic films of the silver screen. They would take turns scurrying across the courtyard lined with cherry trees and over to one of their condos. Tonight's movie was a surprise, Susan promised. Last week's treasure from the film vault had been *North by Northwest*, starring Susan's heartthrob, Cary Grant.

Her phone buzzed a few seconds later. SIX IS FINE. SUSAN SAID THAT'S GREAT, TOO.

Tara's fingers flew over the smartphone keyboard. GOOD. I'VE GOT TO TELL Y'ALL SOMETHING.

Oooh. Big news?

Yes. No. Not really. Depends on how you look at it. Jack's in town.

You mean Paris FBI Jack?

Yup.

Oh wow. Tell me more when you get home.

K.

Tara looked at the simple words on the phone screen. It was a simple thing Jack asked of her, really. Help him with a case. Nothing about getting back together. No explanation of why he never showed up for their last date. Of course, she'd looked like the fool bringing it up in the first place.

She set her phone on the console between the front seats and put her gloves back on, the steering wheel still chilly to her fingers. Cherry Blossom Estates was a short ten-minute drive from the Metro station. On days like today when temperatures hovered in the twenties, her car barely warmed up by the time she reached her condo.

Six o'clock came soon enough and Ciara and Susan arrived at Tara's townhouse. Ciara wore an apologetic look as she carried a plastic box of cookies from the grocery store bakery. Susan brought a plate of scones, still warm. They shed their coats and exchanged hugs.

"Paris FBI Jack is *here*?" Susan asked as she set the plate of scones on Tara's kitchen counter.

"Yup. Never thought I'd see him again, and here he comes, strolling down the hallway toward the kitchen." Tara shook her head. "Oh, Suz, I put the kettle on if you want tea."

"That would be lovely." Susan's brown eyes sparkled but held a measure of concern. "Maybe I shouldn't have brought the DVD I did."

"Why not? You always pick good movies," Ciara said. She set the cookies on the counter beside the scones.

"I brought *Casablanca*. It's such a romantic classic, star-crossed lovers, him sacrificing his love for her safety. Sometimes a real hero steps back, when he knows he's not the one." Susan shrugged. "We can watch something else if you'd like, Tara."

"I'm okay with that. Really."

"I can't help but think of that one line, 'We'll always have Paris.'" Susan frowned.

"Don't worry about it. I don't mind watching," said Tara. Maybe tonight, she could purge these surging emotions and be done with them.

"So." Ciara put her hands on her hips, as if beginning her cross-examination. "Jack must be in the Washington bureau if you say he's in town. So why was he at the White House? Did you even get to talk to him?"

"One question at a time, Counselor Turner." Tara grinned at Ciara's stance. "He's working on, um, an investigation. And yes, we talked. In fact, after we saw each other in the hallway, he came to the kitchen and asked to talk."

"So, what are you thinking?" Ciara's gaze probed Tara's face.

Tara sighed and glanced at Susan, then back to Ciara. "I thought I was over him a long time ago. And then when I saw him, it all came back to me. All I want to know is. . .why? He could have just told me it was over back then, and I would have accepted that. It would have hurt, yes. But for him to disappear, without a word?"

"Maybe there's another explanation," said Susan. "Maybe he was called away by the FBI and couldn't call you."

Tara nodded. "I thought of that, back then. But to hear

nothing at all? I mean, ladies, it's been four years." She was fine. Just fine. Tears stung her eyes.

"Oh, sweetie, you go ahead and get him out of your system for good." Susan enveloped Tara in a hug. She smelled like lavender, and the scent brought Tara back to her parents' porch in Bastrop, sitting on the porch swing and telling her mom about her first crush. Susan wasn't nearly as old as her parents, but Tara found her sweet, warm nature a reminder of home.

Tara blinked until the stinging in her eyes went away. She pulled back from Susan and gave Ciara a grin. "Sorry. I'll be okay. I don't want to put a damper on our night. C'mon. I made these salmon puffs I want you to try. They have a texture like a meringue. I put them on a crostini, but maybe they're better on their own. You tell me."

Tara went to the oven and pulled out the tray. She inhaled. First Lady Franklin would *love* these. The woman ate fish so often, it was a wonder she hadn't sprouted gills. Or so she herself said.

"You're avoiding the issue," said Ciara. "Are you going to see him again? That's the next big question."

"Yes. Tomorrow after work." Tara held up her right hand. "But strictly business. Like I said, he asked for my help on a case. If it wasn't important and if he could get someone else to help, I'd say no."

"What's the case about? A matter of national security?" Ciara asked.

"I believe so. I really don't know much about it." Tara shrugged. "I know the White House gets threats from time to time, many of them blowhards spouting off, but this is the first time I remember the FBI coming in. That I can remember, anyway. Maybe I haven't really paid attention."

"Well, we know how you are when you're in your chef zone," Susan teased.

"Thanks for listening. Enough about Jack, though." Tara smiled at her neighbors. She'd deal with Jack tomorrow. Tonight, she'd bury herself in the movie and enjoy it. *Casablanca* might not have a happy ending, not happily ever after. Life often didn't either.

Jack stared at the text on the computer monitor as voices echoed around him in the office. They'd split up elements of the investigation, and house employee profiles fell to him, from Chief Usher Kanaday all the way to Estella Greene, one of the women who worked in the laundry.

He had a stack of files to work through, so he and George started plowing through the names. Another set of agents worked on the staff appointed directly by the president and First Lady.

Tara's earlier irritation made him smile even now. Her Texas twang emerged as her temper rose. Life had a funny way of coming up and chomping you on the ankles with unfinished business. He should have called Tara back then. At first he'd had a good excuse, but then he kept putting it off.

"So have you looked at that list of retirees?" asked George.

"Retirees?" he parroted back.

"We can't rule anyone out." George tapped the top of a file. "Not even your lady friend who works in the kitchen."

"She won't be a problem on this case." Jack glanced at the file. "In fact, she'll be an asset."

"How?"

"She can go where we can't without arousing suspicion. She's good with people, and she's good at reading them. I plan to get her help on this."

"Are you sure that's a wise idea?"

"It is if it'll help us catch these people. Like Kanaday said, we don't want to scare them off. We want to get close enough to get enough evidence and snag them. If they even suspect that someone's onto them, they'll fold up and we'll be back where we started." Jack saved the file and closed it.

"I'm cutting out. I'll be working later from home, though," said George. The lines around his eyes looked a little deeper.

"You okay, man?"

"It's been a long day." He steepled his fingers under his chin. "Sometimes I wonder if this is all worth it in the end."

"It has to be; otherwise we're doing it for nothing. Someone has to keep up the fight."

"Sometimes I wonder how long we each have to fight. Marcus is graduating in June. I feel like I'm running out of time with my family."

"No. Marcus can't be graduating." Jack tried to think. "Isn't he only in junior high?" George's oldest was only twelve, right? He'd first met Clements back in the day. Jack was only twenty-four himself, a new recruit fresh out of the Academy. The elder agent reminded him of a grouchy old bulldog who already knew everything.

"He was in junior high when you and I first met. It's been that long. And I've missed it, lots of it." George's voice bore the weight of years, countless hours of flying, stakeouts, endless interviews.

Jack didn't have words for him. Truthfully, George's own admission made him want to grab the nearest set of files and get to work.

"Maybe you just need a good night's sleep. A weekend off, even," he said. Hollow words. Right now, this newest case at the White House would claim the bulk of their attention.

"Maybe." George sighed as he studied the file in front of him. "Never mind. Forget I said anything."

"You got it."

An hour later, Jack called it quits. He wasn't a paper kind of guy. Never had been. Get him with people, talking face-to-face. He learned more that way than by reading the printed page. Maybe his idea of working his way up in administration wasn't the best. Now, George, he was good with the facts. George was also one of the reasons Jack now called the Washington bureau his home office.

He drove home along streets banked by heaps of snow pushed back by the snowplows. Darkness had fallen already, and Jack's mood sank on a level like George's had. He found his parking space empty tonight, for a change.

Yellow squares of comforting light glowed in his neighbors' windows. The young family that lived across from him was probably sitting around the table, finishing the last of their supper. He didn't know their last name, but the mother had hollered at the kids enough for Jack to know they were Katie and Caden, little tykes not even in school yet.

The father looked to be about Jack's age. He usually had a loosened tie and a strain in his voice when they passed in the covered breezeway that blocked their front doors from the elements.

Jack paused as he unlocked the door to his condo. It was a rental. He always rented, and this was his first rental since returning to the States six months ago. So far, so good. He scanned the hallway before entering the dark living room.

He flipped on a light, ignoring the pair of cardboard boxes next to the built-in bookcases that flanked the fireplace. They'd sat beside the bookcases for almost six months, and they could wait a little longer. With a flip of the switch, the gas fireplace ignited and yellow flames danced, the only source of warmth in the room.

Jack tossed his keys on the end table beside the phone and pushed the voice mail button. Maybe it was redundant having two phone numbers, a landline and a cell phone line, but if the cell phone towers ever went out, he'd still have a connection to the outside world.

He could still hear his father's voice: "Be wise, son. Be wise as a serpent, harmless as a dove." The memory made him smile. He ought to call home tonight and see how his parents were. Now that he was stateside again, he knew the barrage of phone calls would come. *When are you coming to Missouri for a visit? What about Easter weekend? Do they ever let you take a vacation?*

"Jack, it's Momma." His mother's voice echoed off the bare living room walls. "I just wanted to hear your voice and see how you were doing. I wish you'd get on Facebook so we can keep in touch. I know all the younger ones are doing that now. Well, I hope to hear from you soon. Love you."

Nope, no way was he getting on Facebook. That was all he needed, another distraction and possibly a threat to his personal privacy and security. His parents exchanged photos and news with his brother and sister, and Jack was the solo family holdout.

Something, though, in his mother's voice made him play the message again. Her voice was usually energetic, lilting notes. But this tone was more forced, as if she'd practiced the words. Usually, too, his dad would pop in with a greeting in the background. He could usually picture his father hovering over

Momma's shoulder while she spoke.

Something was wrong.

He dialed their number in a flash, and his dad answered the phone. "Son, good to hear your voice. I'll get your momma on the line—Bertie!" Dad's voice boomed through the phone.

"I got Mom's message. I had a late night at the office." The words tasted like an excuse.

"I know you're busy saving the world. Don't worry about us. Sure hope you can make it home for a visit this summer."

Jack took off his jacket and loosened his tie with one hand. "I need to. Maybe in June or July I can come for a week." He had no idea what he'd do with so much free time.

"Jack! You called us back." His mother evidently had taken the phone from his father.

"I just got home."

"Listen, I need to tell you something." Her voice kept cutting in and out, and Jack pictured her holding it on her shoulder; he heard footsteps and a door closing. "I wanted to talk to you without your daddy on the phone."

"What's wrong? I knew something had to be up."

"Your daddy—well, he's going blind." Mom's statement ended with a whimper. "Maybe by fall, the doctor's not sure."

Jack sank onto the leather couch and rested his head on one of his hands. "Why? How?" His parents had worked the land and now were enjoying a farmer's "retirement," which meant still farming, only smaller.

"It's degenerative. He had cataract surgery, but that was only putting off the inevitable."

"Oh Mom. I'm sorry. So sorry. Is there any possibility of more surgery, another procedure?"

"No, the doctor said there wasn't. I wanted your dad to tell you, but he kept saying he didn't want to bother you with it."

"You two are *never* a bother to me."

"I know, but you're so busy and we never hear from you."

"That'll change, now that I'm here in Washington. Tell you what. This next case wraps up, I'll be out there to see you as soon as I can."

"All right." Her unspoken sigh echoed over the line.

"I love you both."

"Love you, too." The line was silent between them, but his mother still remained on the phone.

"What is it?" Jack asked.

"I'm so glad your daddy and I have each other."

"I am, too." What was she being so philosophical about?

"One day, you're going to need someone, Jackson. What are you going to do when that day comes and you're alone?"

"I won't be alone." He figured he'd find someone, someday. But not now. Tara's face flitted through his mind. "Don't worry about me. You and Dad just take good care of each other."

"I can't help it, son. I'm a mom. Well, I'm praying for you."

"Thanks." Praying was something he hadn't done in, well, way too long. The job sort of swallowed up his personal life. If he tried praying tonight, his words would likely not rise above the ceiling.

They ended the call after some small talk, news about his nieces and nephews. Between his brother and sister, they more than made up for his lack of contribution in the grandchild department.

Jack put the phone back in its place and went to reheat some leftover takeout. An idle thought drifted into his head: *What is Chef Tara having for dinner tonight?* A memory flashed into his head, of an impromptu picnic in Paris. Tara had dragged him into her idea, along with a baguette, cheese, fruit, and smoked meat. They had lain on a blanket in a park, and for once he'd shoved his job away for a few hours as they talked and soaked up the romance of Paris and shared kisses.

He should have called her. He should have admitted to her the truth then. His job was his true love; it claimed his time and his attention and his devotion. Downright cruel, to lead her down a road of disappointment. It hadn't been fair to Tara then, and it definitely wouldn't be fair to her now.

Chapter 3

D elivery truck's here!" Adelaide called out to the kitchen staff. Two of the sous chefs sprang into action. "Chef Tara, here's the inventory we're expecting. Oversee and verify."

"Yes, Chef." Tara went to fetch the clipboard Adelaide held. "Let's go, y'all."

They walked outside to meet the truck from Capital Produce. Friday morning, last delivery before the weekend. Tara expected to hear songs in Italian on the crisp January air, but only heard the idling of the truck's engine.

A different deliveryman hopped down from the driver's seat. "Good morning."

"Where's Tony?" Tara asked. Tony Caproni always sang opera while making the fruit and vegetable deliveries. Old enough to be her father, yet still charming enough to make her giggle every once in a while. Harmless man, and he brought a smile to everyone who talked to him. She missed his deliveries during the summer, when the White House's garden was giving them its bounty.

"Hello to you, too, Chef." The dark-haired driver, younger than Tony, sauntered to the back of the truck. "Tony's not with us anymore."

"Oh. I see. Did he move?" Tara watched as the driver hopped onto the rear fender of the truck, then slid the door up.

"I don't think so." He moved to the nearest crate of produce. "Okay, I've got potatoes, snap peas, kale, and leeks on my list. Plus strawberries and mangoes."

"Right." Tara nodded. "Tony didn't tell us he was leaving y'all. He didn't even say good-bye."

Really, she sounded like a three-year-old, but she missed the early morning serenade. And surely the kind of man whose wife made cannolis and brought them as a Christmas gift for the White House kitchen staff would tell them good-bye if he was leaving.

"He always made us smile in the morning," said sous chef Ken. "Unloading a truck isn't usually much fun."

"You guys really don't want me to sing," said the driver. He picked up a pair of red cabbage. "I could juggle for you."

Tara laughed. "No, that's okay. Thank you anyway. I'm Tara Whitley."

"Heath." The driver hopped from the back of the truck back down to ground level. "Heath Smallwood. Nice to meet you. Next time, I'll bring a few kiwifruit and amaze you with my juggling skills. I can whistle, too."

The sous chefs busied themselves with loading the produce onto a wheeled cart as Tara checked items off the list. Heath leaned against the back of the truck, then tilted his head back to look at the building.

"Wow. It seems a lot bigger up close." He squinted at the windows.

"Yeah, doesn't it? Your first time here?" Tara asked.

"Yup. I was so nervous at the gate, I dropped my ID on the floor of the truck. Had to ask the guy at the guardhouse if

I could get out and pick it up. Couldn't reach it." He shook his head, a quirky grin on his face. "I tried not to crack jokes, but the old guy looked pretty serious."

"That would be Buzz. And yes, he takes his job very seriously." Tara watched the sous chefs wheel the heavy cart down the ramp and into the building. "I had my job interview for the position here, and when I left, I found the nearest bathroom and lost my lunch. Oh sorry. TMI."

Heath glanced at his watch. "No problem. Glad I'm not the only one. See you next week?"

"I'll be here." She smiled at him as he turned and gave her a nod before returning to the driver's side of the truck. Heath opened the door, then climbed up into the truck's cab.

She'd miss Tony Caproni and his cheerful disposition. But Heath Smallwood seemed a decent replacement so far. Definitely a morning person. No crabby delivery people, thank you very much. Sometimes bad moods could be contagious. Tara caught up with the sous chefs as they negotiated the cart into the kitchen and headed for the pantry.

Before long, the Governors' Lunch would be over, and she'd be on her way to meet Jack. The girls had warned her to be careful with him. Oh, she'd be careful all right. She wasn't about to be let down again. Besides, she had no idea how much Jack had changed since Paris.

Tara tried to smooth down her windblown hair as she entered the J. Edgar Hoover Building. She hoped she didn't smell like kitchen. She probably did. She unbuttoned her winter coat and sniffed, then yawned. Not too bad. Her eyelids fought to stay open as she went through security before stopping at the reception desk.

Last night, her bedroom clock had read 3:15 right before her mind finally quit racing and she fell asleep. "Don't count sheep; talk to the Shepherd," Mom always told her. And so Tara had, which helped. She didn't know what the next days held for her, between now and the State Dinner. She knew two things for certain: she'd be crazy-busy with menu preparation in addition to her regular duties, and she would have to steel her heart against Jack.

Silly really, she reminded herself as she smiled at the receptionist and showed her identification and Jack's card. She honestly wasn't sure what she could do to help him, but despite her personal political views, she'd grown to care for the First Family. She saw a side that the media didn't.

"They're just a family in the house," one of the maids had told her right after the inauguration. "They're part of history, and by serving them, we're helping create that history."

The receptionist gave her a visitor's pass and directed her to the elevators. Tara walked along, feeling out of her element as other workers passed. She shared the elevator with an older gentleman who busily tapped on his phone. Then she reached the floor where Jack's office was.

Men and women in suits talked on phones or studied computer monitors, and a few were gathered by a whiteboard covered with lists. Jack's head and shoulders emerged from behind a monitor, and he waved her in his direction.

"Glad you made it." He stood and moved as if to shake her hand, then reached for a notepad and a manila folder on his desk instead. Nope, they hadn't done a lot of handshaking in Paris. Just that first meeting in a café, as a couple of lonely ex-pats.

"I came right after work." She ought to have bought new insoles for her work shoes. Her feet screamed at her after the walk along Pennsylvania Avenue.

"We'll use one of the interview rooms. It'll be quieter there. This place is a zoo right now." He touched her elbow and led her toward one of a series of doors on the far wall of the office.

The room he took her to looked more like a living room, with a love seat and a pair of soft chairs. Two lamps flanked the love seat and a reading lamp on a pole stood between the pair of chairs. Nice. Tara hoped she didn't start nodding off once she sat down.

"This is one of our soft interview rooms." Jack motioned to the love seat as he took one of the chairs facing it.

"I hope it's not too soft. It's been a long day," Tara admitted as she sank onto a soft cushion.

"I know. I don't plan to keep you long." He opened his notebook. "I just want to talk to you about the staff, your impression of people. One thing I always loved about you was your honesty, and your keen perceptions of people."

Loved. Past tense. *Get a grip, Tara. He's old news.* If this affected her any more, she could always request to talk to another investigator on the case. Maybe the guy who had shown up with him at the White House yesterday. He sort of reminded her of her uncle Greg, her dad's younger brother.

Tara cleared her throat. "Well, thanks. I'll do my best to help."

"I know you will." Jack kept staring at the page in front of him. It was blank; Tara had seen that much when he opened the notepad. Maybe this encounter was affecting him as well.

She waited for him to say more. After all, he'd been the one to invite her to come. This was his show, and she was just a player in everything to come.

"All right." At last, he looked up at her. "We have a long list of people to sort through. We have the guest list for the State Dinner. We have the list of the White House employees, including the administration's appointees. We also have the list of waitstaff who've been hired for the event. They've been screened already, so that helps us, too."

"Explain to me exactly how I'm helping with this."

"The regular staff. You've been with them for a few years now. I know that yesterday you were pretty resistant to the idea that one of them could be planning something. What I need to know is, has anyone acted out of the ordinary? Have you heard anything?"

Tara fumbled her thoughts. "I don't know. Honestly. I know they're not perfect people, but I don't believe they'd do anything to harm anyone, especially at the White House."

"I see that there haven't been any new staff hired in the last nine months, and no one's left recently."

"Not yet, anyway." She regretted the comment immediately.

"What do you mean?"

"Mart Welch's last day is February seventh." Tara followed that up with, "But that doesn't have to mean anything."

"Do you know why he's leaving?"

"He, um, honestly? Well, it's because he didn't get the promotion he was hoping for. I doubt Mart is really that upset about it, because he's going to New York to work for Eric Ripert." She'd almost turned the hue of a frog herself at the idea of working for one of America's most renowned chefs.

"So who got the promotion Mart wanted?"

"Uh, that would be me. But that happened a few months ago."

Jack set down his notepad and opened the manila folder.

"Martin Welch has been employed there longer than you, according to his record."

"Chefs know how competitive the culinary world is, and you learn to deal with that. Otherwise, you're in the wrong business if you hold grudges for very long." Tara felt herself oozing deeper into the love seat cushion. Then she yawned. "I'm sorry."

"Don't be. You've already put in a full day's work. As for Martin, if he's in the clear, we'll know it. Would you rather us check someone out and have them be clean, or ignore someone because they might 'seem' innocent and turn out to be the conspirator?"

"You're right, Jack." She realized she still wore her winter jacket and shrugged out of it, placing it on the cushion beside her. "I would make a lousy FBI agent. I always try to assume the best about people." Just like she had about him. She picked at the stitching on the edge of the cushion.

Jack placed the folder on the other seat and leaned forward in his chair. "Tara, I should have called you. In Paris. You deserved more than silence."

"So"—she fought to keep her voice from shaking—"you were still around."

He shook his head and stared at the floor. "No. I was called away to South Africa for a few weeks, then spent a few days back in Paris before I was off again. Then I got the position with the London bureau then here."

Tara nodded. "I figured as much. Well, it looks like things have worked out for you with your job. Same for me."

"I'll say—the White House?" Jack's tone brightened. "I'm not surprised, though."

The door to the room flew open, and the older man she'd seen with Jack at the White House leaned into the room. "We have a new lead. The CIA shared fresh intel about Anqara."

"We're almost through here," Jack said over his shoulder. Tara couldn't read his expression to tell if that was relief or irritation on his face. His fellow agent nodded and shut the door.

"Anqara. The Anqara royal family is going to be at the State Dinner," Tara said. She sat up straighter.

"What do you know about Anqara?" Jack faced her again, all business.

"It's a small Middle Eastern nation-state, sort of tucked near the corner border of Syria, Jordan, Iran. Kind of like Monaco. I actually looked up Anqara when we started dinner planning, because I'd never heard of it." Tara chuckled. "Um, their crown prince is looking at colleges in the U.S., which is why they're here, visiting schools. You think the threat might be because of him?"

"I don't know. Either that, or whoever's behind this is using Anqara's presence here as a cover-up for what they're really planning."

He'd said too much. Jack had felt his guard slipping with Tara, ever since his admission that he should have called her. He'd been warned that he shouldn't share too much with her, since after all, she was on that list of employees. Of course, she'd come out clean so far, according to George.

Jack studied her now, seated on the love seat and looking like she'd rather curl up in a quiet corner and go to sleep. Still wearing her chef's jacket and cotton pants, a thin gold chain and a simple tiny cross that lay just above the rounded neckline of her white T-shirt. The gold winked at him when the light caught it.

Maybe he could keep the personal and the investigation separate. "Don't be worried. I won't let anything happen to you."

"So what exactly do you want me to do now, in the meantime?" She shifted on the cushion and it squeaked.

"Be my eyes and ears. Talk to Martin, find out what's going on with his new job. See if there's anyone or anything unusual going on. If there's a new employee or someone's out of place from where they usually are. Like a maid hanging out in the kitchen."

Tara nodded. "I'll do my best."

"Would you like to meet me for coffee sometime?" The impulsive question startled him and made Tara snap to attention.

She regarded him like a cornered cat. "Um, okay."

"I don't regret Paris, just so you know." He sounded like he'd developed a sudden case of laryngitis. "I regret not calling you, but not Paris."

"Me either." She brushed her hair over one ear. "But we're at different points in our lives now. Our careers have really taken off."

"They have. I finally made it here."

"You sure did." For the first time, she smiled at him. It had the force of a punch.

Beautiful Tara, and picnics, walks on rainy evenings along the Seine, kisses to warm up under the umbrella. Tara's blush, saying she never kissed in public. And coffee. The best coffee. But that was Paris, and he'd found himself tugged along into the current.

"So, do you need anything else today?" She reached for her coat, breaking the moment.

He snapped himself back to attention. "No. I'll call you about coffee. And you call me right away if you learn anything that might help us."

"I'll do that." She stood, picking up her coat.

"Here." Jack reached for the coat, helping her put it on. She flipped the ends of her hair out from behind the collar. As she lowered her hand, it brushed his.

He grasped her hand. "Tara—"

She tugged her hand from his grasp. "I'll let you know what I find out."

Of course he deserved that. "Thanks. I can walk you to the elevator."

"Don't worry about it. I can find the way." With that, she smiled at him and left the interrogation room, her posture straight and her eyes bright.

He'd tried to sound casual, friendly, genuinely sorry. Part of him was. He wanted to admit his cowardice to her, but knew it wouldn't change anything. George was right. Tara was ripping his focus from the job right now. She was a great resource, though, and if they could have at least a tentative friendship, he could get through this investigation.

Jack picked up his notebook and the file on Martin Welch. The guy had had a string of jobs since culinary school, staying in none of them for much more than a year, until now. He'd been at the White House for four years, securing his employment one year before Tara signed on.

Another memory rippled across his mind. Standing on a bridge in Paris, they'd looked out over the river drifting below them and talked about dreams. His was to go on to FBI's Washington bureau. Tara wanted her ultimate chef's job—to work at the White House. Something about Paris had made them both feel they were invincible, as if anything were possible.

His faith had been a lot stronger back in Paris, too. He'd thrived because of weekly Bible study with a small group of ex-pats. Friends who worked for the State Department had paved the way for that. Not only had he tossed Tara away for his career; he'd also let his relationship with God slip to the side, then out of his focus at all. *Lord, I don't know where to begin. . .I hurt Tara. I was such a wimp, no matter how big and bad I thought I was, or am.*

Here in the quiet atmosphere of the little room, Jack saw the brisk pace of the office outside move in its chaotic dance. George had said something about new intel coming in about Anqara. He'd better get out there and see about it. Plus, he had a whole stack of employee files to work through still. He made sure, though, that George would see to Tara's.

He entered the busy office area. His tie had somehow grown tighter in the last half hour or so.

"What's the latest on Anqara?" Jack joined the others at a desk.

Steve Durbin, another colleague, pointed at a screen. "The royal family will be arriving in three days, not seven days from now as we originally thought. Prince Ahmed has added Georgetown University to his list of colleges to attend. Plus there's murmuring among the Muswali in Syria, who are against Anqara's friendly relationship with not just the United States but with Israel. If there's an attack against the White House while the royal family is visiting, that won't change."

Jack thought for a moment. "But if the royal family arrives sooner, that means any threat will follow them."

Steve nodded. "And it might tick off our conspirators enough to step up their plans."

Which meant that Jack needed to get through the employee files as soon as possible. Determine if any of them had connections to Anqara at all. It seemed unlikely, but then he reminded himself of the unlikelihood of seeing Tara again. Yet here they were, paths crossed.

"Hey, Courtland. Over here." George motioned Jack in his direction. "You need to see this."

Jack strode over to George's desk. "What is it?"

"You're not going to like it." He tapped on the screen. "It's about your pretty chef friend."

Jack tugged a stray chair over and sat down beside George. "What are you talking about?"

"We just got this in from her e-mail. Did she mention anything about a Trevor Bradshaw back home in Texas, coming to Washington in a week, ironically, at the time of the State Dinner?"

"No, she didn't tell me anything. She agreed to keep an eye out for something suspicious."

"Look at this e-mail from her cousin." George pulled some pages from the printer and handed them to Jack.

He scanned the first page.

Hey, Cuz,

I'm comin' to DC. I'll only be in town for 1 weekend, but I was hoping we culd see each other. Its been awhile. I know your working a lot at the white house. Maybe I can get a tour. It wuld be wild to meet the president. I culd give him a piece of my mind since he aint got one of his own. Sometimes a southern boy needs a butt-whoopin' to set him strait, know what I mean? LOL TTYL

Trev

"Okay, so the guy can't spell and his grammar stinks. What's wrong with that?"

They saw their share of wackos who talked big, yet nothing ever came of it. The silent ones who slunk around on the fringe of things—they were the ones to worry about and much harder to crack.

"We've run a tail on Trevor Bradshaw and started pulling his financials. He's been buying materials that could be transported easily enough without suspicion, but could be assembled on the other side to make a bomb."

Chapter 4

Tara's foot slipped, and she skidded into a pile of slush as she trudged into the entrance of Cherry Blossom Estates. *That's it.* She was going to use some vacation time after the State Dinner and fly home to Texas for a long weekend. At least there was no snow there and she could maybe break out her sandals for one day and let her feet breathe.

In a couple of months the cherry blossoms would be the first heralds of spring. Tara could hardly wait to resume her outdoor three-mile runs every morning. Her treadmill wasn't the same. The scenery never changed, the air not as fresh.

Tonight wasn't movie night, but she almost considered calling Ciara and Susan to see if they'd like to come over anyway, especially after her meeting with Jack that afternoon. She wanted the support of her friends. Nah, she'd be fine. There were other more pressing needs in their neighborhood.

She squinted over at Mrs. Bickler's brick condo, where a light shone in the window. EMS had taken the elderly woman to the hospital not long ago. She'd had a stroke. Tara shuddered at the idea of what might have happened if Susan hadn't noticed Mrs. Bickler's change in routine and checked on her. The sweet woman likely wouldn't have survived.

The door to Mrs. Bickler's condo opened and a brunette with long hair, a sweater bundled about her, emerged.

"Hello!" the woman called, her breath making puffs in the air. She held up a covered dish. "Tara, isn't it?"

Tara paused and tried not to shiver. "Yes, that's right." Oh. Her storage container.

"Thanks a million for that casserole." The woman crossed the space between them, minding the occasional slick patch. "I've been too busy to cook lately."

"You're definitely welcome. Samantha, right?" Tara hoped she hadn't guessed the woman's name wrong.

"Yes, Samantha Steele." Samantha handed Tara the glass dish with its lid.

"How's your grandmother doing?" Tara should have asked sooner about Mrs. Bickler's condition, but with her schedule being so crazy, she hadn't noticed if anyone was home.

"She's doing well. The doctor's really happy with how well her function is coming back so far."

"I'm glad to hear that. So how much longer do you think you'll be here?"

"I'm not sure. I've actually applied for an internship at Mount Vernon, so I may be back with my kids as early as this summer."

"Super. Well, keep in touch. Susan and Ciara and I will be glad to have another friend in the neighborhood."

"Will do."

Tara waved as Samantha trotted back to the other townhouse. Maybe what Jack asked of her wasn't such a hard thing. Just as Susan had noticed the change in Mrs. Bickler's routine, she could keep an eye out for anything out of the ordinary at the White House.

But what could she do? And she didn't like the idea of ferreting information from Mart. Jack did have a point. When she'd learned that she'd been given a promotion instead of Mart, he'd dropped their friendly banter and had turned to clipped responses. However, why wait until now to get revenge, especially if he was leaving to work for a chef and restaurateur like Eric Ripert?

She continued along to her back door.

A pair of men emerged from around the side of the townhouses. Both wore nondescript coats of dark gray, one taller and stocky, the other man barely as tall as she.

"Ms. Whitley." The short one held up an identification. "Agent Smith, FBI. We need to ask you a few questions about your cousin Trevor Bradshaw."

Tara gripped the casserole dish like a security blanket. But she'd given up Blankie, her flowered patchwork quilt made by her nana, years ago. "Right now?"

"Right now. I'm Agent Durbin." The tall one flashed his own ID, his voice reminding her of Darth Vader. A cold breeze sliced through her coat.

"Do—do you mind if I call my friends to join me? They—they both live just across the way, and I'd feel better if at least one of them were here." She tried to suck in some of the cold air, but she felt like she was breathing in through a straw.

The shorter agent spoke first. "Go right ahead."

Did these men know Jack? Why wasn't he here, if he was on the investigation? She set the casserole dish on the step and peeled off her gloves.

She called Ciara first. "Ciara, I know it's almost suppertime, but could you come by for a few minutes? The FBI are here—and they want to ask me some questions."

"I'll be right over. Don't say a word to them about anything until I get there." The line went dead, and Tara stared at her phone.

The click of a door across the way made her, and both agents, look in the direction of Ciara's townhome. Ciara scurried off her small deck and headed across the courtyard in their direction.

"Here I am." She wore a skirt and nylons, making her fuzzy slippers look out of place. Her silk blouse was covered by a turquoise blue cardigan. "I just got home not too long ago."

"Thank you." Tara owed her, big-time. She'd definitely make Ciara a batch of her gourmet brownies as a big thank-you.

"Not a problem." She faced down the agents. "Ciara Turner, attorney at law. Do you have a warrant?"

The tall agent's lips twitched as if he were stifling a grin. "Ms. Turner, Ms. Whitley's not been charged with anything."

"Ciara, it's okay. I don't mind talking to them. Agent Durbin, you said something about my cousin, though. Trevor?" Tara pulled out her house keys, then took the casserole dish from Ciara.

"We'll talk inside, if you don't mind," said Agent Smith, motioning for the women to proceed ahead of him.

Tara's heart beat a staccato rhythm in her chest as she tucked the dish under one arm, then unlocked her door. "Please come in." She snapped on the light as they entered the living room. Definitely not how she expected to kick back tonight and try to relax. Plus, she was due for her weekly phone call home. If she was late, Mom would worry.

The pair of agents settled themselves onto each of her wingback chairs. Ciara took one end of the love seat. Tara went to the kitchen counter to set down the casserole dish along with her purse, then returned to the living room.

Tara nearly offered to make them coffee, but thought better of it. "So, you mentioned my cousin."

"Have you heard from Mr. Bradshaw recently?" asked Agent Smith. His even gaze almost made her feel guilty.

"Yes, I have. He's going to be in town. A convention of some kind, for a history club. He's into Civil War reenactments. I told him if I was free, I could maybe meet up with him and show him the sights." Although truthfully, she wasn't sure how well that was going to work.

"When was the last time you saw him?"

"At our last family reunion about seven years ago, not long before I left to work in Paris in 2005. I haven't seen him since. My dad and his mother are brother and sister. But you probably know that already." A light clicked on in her head. "You're working on the case with Agent Courtland."

They exchanged glances. "Yes, we are," Agent Smith said, pulling some papers from a file he carried. "During our background checks, some interesting information has come to light about your cousin. We read the e-mail he sent you."

"My cousin? I figured I'd be screened, but my family members, too?" Tara stood, then accepted the papers from the agent. She scanned the e-mail. "Trevor's, well, sort of a conspiracy theorist. He's not a fan of the current administration, from what you can see. He thinks that President Franklin and his policies are being disloyal to the South. But is this enough to be considered a threat? If you could hear some of my family members start talking politics at a barbecue, you'd know everyone has some kind of an opinion. It's the Civil War debate all over again."

Oh great. They couldn't possibly think that her cousin was going to try something at the White House. She continued. "I mean, *I* didn't vote for the president and I disagree with some of his policies, but I love my job. I love where I am. Just because someone disagrees with someone else doesn't make them a threat." She glanced down again at the e-mail. Insulting the president's brain, or lack thereof. Oh boy. . .and mentioning a "butt-whoopin'"?

"Ms. Whitley, he's been ordering a number of materials online, enough to make a small explosive unit. He can transport these items with him and obtain the rest of the ingredients locally."

The skin on her arms prickled. "You're not serious. Trevor?"

"We're completely serious," Agent Durbin said.

All this time, Ciara sat beside her, but her gaze bored into both agents, then snapped over to Tara.

"What—what am I supposed to do?" Tara asked.

"Let us know when he contacts you again, especially if he gives you any flight information or where he plans to stay while in the area." The short one's expression thawed a few degrees. "Courtland's told us you've been giving your full cooperation and assistance, and we appreciate that."

She nodded. "I will."

"Our cards. Call us anytime." The short one stood and glanced at his compadre.

"Anytime," echoed Agent Durbin as he stood.

Tara stood as well, pocketing the cards they gave her. She'd gathered quite a collection of FBI business cards in the past twenty-four hours. The idea would have made her chuckle, but for the expressions of the agents standing not three feet away.

"Well, um, thank you. I'll definitely let you know." She assumed the interview was over. They acknowledged her, then Ciara, with a pair of nods before leaving out the front door.

Ciara turned to face her as the door clicked behind them.

"First FBI Jack, and now these guys. You're under their microscope for sure."

"I know. Trevor is a goober and has a mouth on him, but he wouldn't build a bomb." Tara shivered again. "And even though I haven't done anything illegal, nor am I about to, I can't help but feel nauseous at the thought of being under surveillance. Big Brother, watching me. Reading my e-mails. Showing up here now. What if they've bugged my home?" She glanced around the room, looking at the wingback chairs, the eclectic mismatched end tables and lamps.

"Well, next movie night's at my place," Ciara said. She raised her head and followed up with, "You hear that?"

Tara burst out laughing, even while her stomach wound itself into a slipknot.

Some guys kicked back with a cold one after work, but Jack preferred spending an hour or so at the firing range. When it was just Jack and his Glock, facing a target from ten yards, everything else seemed to vanish. Rounds weren't cheap, but it was better than drowning his sorrows like a few people he knew along the way.

He'd recently been contacted by an old buddy of his from their college days as criminal justice students. Nick Porter was a security guard at Mount Vernon now, of all things. What had happened to the street cop he'd known? Working security, telling people to please not touch the antiques. They'd lost touch until Jack came to the Washington bureau.

In the years since they'd known each other, Nick once had a wife, a kid, had done the entire family thing. But not anymore.

Jack couldn't imagine the knife gouge to the heart that losing them must have been for Nick. Being a police officer, or any law enforcement officer, came with a measure of risk. Another reason Jack had pulled away from Tara. That, and he didn't want to have regrets like George.

His feelings for her had scared him worse than any horror movie. Not since his days in the Academy had he felt something—no, someone—consume him. While in Paris, he could see it, see them together, as long as he blinded himself to the reality of the danger he'd put her in, and himself. He used to pray to find a wife, someday, in the right time. But maybe for some, it would never be the right time. Like him. In the end, he'd told God he wouldn't do that to a woman and walked the other way.

Sure, plenty of guys in the FBI were married. But Jack had seen the toll the job could take on a relationship. Saw it now, in the agent across from his desk.

"Did Natalie call you back?" he asked George.

"Nah." He shrugged. "But it's all right." Their targets returned to them on mechanical arms. George reached for the paper to see where he'd hit.

"You can always call her." Ironic, him giving Clements suggestions to help patch up his marriage.

"I told her the ball was in her court. She wants me back, she can call. Guess I got my answer."

Jack frowned. The older man had a soft spot, and that was his wife of nearly twenty-five years. Stubborn, stubborn man. "You've got a lot invested in your marriage, though."

"Maybe. People change, though. She's tired of the badge. I told her, give me five more years at the Bureau before I call it a day." George pushed a button and sent a fresh target back to the end of the firing lane.

"Well, I hope you work it out. I would, if I were you." Jack popped a fresh clip into his Glock. One more round of shots, and he was about done here. He was heading back to work some more on leads for the State Dinner conspiracy.

"Gun!"

Pops of gunfire sounded from shooters in the other lanes, and the smell of sulfur tickled Jack's nose. He chambered the Glock, aimed, and fired in quick succession. Two of his shots went wild, away from the center. George's shots looked like a new shooter was trying to get the handle on the gun. What a mess.

"Take your own advice," said George as their targets zoomed toward them on the line.

"What?"

"Your pretty little chef. Fix whatever you need to fix with her. If she's the right girl, she won't just take you—she'll take your job, too. Can't have one without the other, you know. Besides, you're a man of faith. I respect that. But if your God is so powerful, can't He take care of you two?"

Jack swallowed hard. Ouch. George wasn't a believer, but the two of them maintained a respectful tone when it came to faith. He'd seen George listening more when he spoke of his faith. Now, he was using his own words against him. Maybe he trusted God to a point, but not enough. He looked down at the Glock in his hands.

True, too, his job was part of him. Most people clocked out from their job at the end of the day, but Jack Courtland never stopped being who he was. But then, that was Tara, too. Her passion for showing love through good food spilled over into every area of her life. Or, it had in Paris. She understood that much, and had even said so.

This afternoon, though, the hurt in Tara's eyes said far, far more. She'd been forthright at the office, willing to help. If she was up to the job of loving Jack Courtland, that was one way to show it. Trouble was, he didn't know if she'd trust him again. He didn't blame her. Relationships took work, and he didn't want to commit to something if he wasn't all-in.

His pager started buzzing on his hip. George touched his pager as well. "Something's up."

Jack holstered his Glock and grabbed his jacket. George was already calling.

When he hung up, his face was grim. "Local police made a number of arrests at a demonstration near the Capitol last weekend. A homeland extremist group called Soldiers of the Way. And guess who was with them?"

"One of the names on our list, a guy named Antonio Caproni, a driver for Capital Produce, who makes deliveries to the White House at least twice a week. Interesting, he didn't show up for work this week."

"Wonder if he's one of our conspirators."

"Don't know for sure, but it doesn't look good. If he's got friends helping him, they're not going to be happy."

"I can't let Tara do this on her own. I need to get in there."

"It's done. Smith also said you're now on the White House rear delivery gate. Effective immediately. Whoever goes in, and whoever goes out, you'll see 'em."

"You heard Tony got arrested?" Mart asked Tara as they were prepping for the First Family's Saturday evening meal.

"Produce Tony?" Tara blinked at Mart. She looked down

at the cutting board in front of her, minding the sharp knife. "Unbelievable. Really. I don't believe it."

"Yeah, that's what I heard. Some new guy made the delivery. You should have heard him. I think he wanted me to take his picture by the side door or something."

"That's Heath. He's working Tony's shift for now. He was in awe of the place. I told him about when I interviewed here." She sliced the fresh pineapple into small chunks. "I still remember my first day on the job."

"Me, too. You were as bug-eyed as a brand-new culinary school graduate." Mart's tone sounded teasing, but Tara glanced at him. His eyes weren't happy.

"I wasn't that bad, was I?" she asked.

Mart nodded. "It happens to everyone. I mean, look at where we get to work. Who we get to cook for. We go places that few people have ever been."

"We're doing prep work for the president's daughter's pizza night." Tara grinned. "But I just think about cooking good food for good people. A regular family."

"I'm glad you're satisfied with that."

"What?" Tara stopped slicing and stared at him. "This is a *dream* job."

"Well, I'm not going to bust my hind end working here in obscurity."

"Obscurity? You talked about how amazing it is that we get to cook for the leader of the free world, how we see things that people don't. I know you wanted that executive chef position." And it still probably got under his skin that she got the job he wanted.

"Maybe I did. Once." He continued slicing. "All I know is, the day after the State Dinner, I'm throwing my gear in the

SUV and heading for the Big Apple. Kissing these ridiculous politics good-bye."

"You know it's never about the politics here in the kitchen. It's about the food."

"Not always." Mart kept chopping.

What was with him? "I've got to admit I'm almost jealous of you. Working for Eric Ripert."

"You'll see. In five years I'll have my own restaurant after I'm done at Eric's."

Mart didn't sound like he was plotting anything. She kept slicing peppers, then started shredding a block of mozzarella cheese. A moment ago he'd sounded jealous that she'd gotten the position. Maybe he was just getting in a last dig on the way out. Strange, too, that Mart should suddenly grow so chatty.

Two of the sous chefs were preparing a soup across the way, and Adelaide was busy at her computer, going over menu plans. Nothing seemed out of the ordinary, yet Tara found herself questioning motives behind the simplest statements.

Did Jack and his cohorts know about Tony's arrest? They probably did.

"Yep, I'll be out of here soon enough. They'll be sorry. Especially Chief Usher Kanaday."

"Why's that?" She blinked at Mart's sudden change in tone.

"He'll see what a mistake he made."

"What do you mean?"

Mart cocked his head to the side a little and held up his knife. "Success is always the best revenge. Served up hot. Kanaday had better watch it."

Chapter 5

H ere's some of the kitchen staff now," said Marine First Sergeant Beaumont Decker, longtime guard at the White House. He flagged down the neat little blue sedan that approached the guardhouse. "They usually get here early, especially so with today's snow."

Jack tried not to yawn. His uniform felt stiff, fresh off the hangers. He'd arrived here shortly before 6:00 a.m., just ahead of the first stream of employees making their way to the White House.

"Always check ID. I don't care who it is or who they say they are," Decker said as he slid open the guardhouse window. "Morning, Chef Montanez."

"Morning, Buzz," said the petite Hispanic woman behind the wheel of the car. Jack remembered her from his first day when he and George had checked the place out. Tara's boss. "I've got an extra one today. Tara Whitley's with me."

"Hey, Buzz." A familiar voice and motion in the front seat made Jack duck his head to see into the vehicle and catch Tara's expression as she handed her ID to Chef Montanez. Her eyes widened, and he winked at her.

The chefs continued on their way, windshield wipers

swishing away the gentle snowfall. Decker slid the window shut. "It's been a wicked winter, Courtland."

"I hear ya on that one." Jack watched the vehicle head to one of the coveted parking spots. "So everyone stops here?"

"You bring a vehicle onto the property, you stop here." Decker took a sip from his covered paper cup. "Otherwise, no one gets in. I don't care if I've seen them fifty-two weeks a year, they stop. I see ID."

This was good to know. But would he get a chance to see anything beyond this small guard shack? He squinted out at the sky, now a dark gray instead of the ink black he'd seen when he'd first awakened. Dawn wasn't too far off, but today would be cloudy with snow flurries.

Beaumont Decker, or "Buzz," as he liked to be called, had been appointed to the White House for nearly fifteen years. Already he'd told Jack stories of the past as they sucked down their hot coffee.

"Has anyone ever tried to make it past you?" Jack asked him.

"Once, in ninety-eight." Buzz chuckled and shook his head. "They received a welcome from the Marines. Nobody's tried since, at least not on my watch."

"I imagine people would think twice after hearing about that." The Marines kept a twenty-four-hour watch on many parts of the White House. Sealed as tight as the proverbial drum, nothing would seep in—or leak out—unless it was someone on the inside.

These employees were screened to an extent that many companies didn't screen their workers. Even Tara, with her completely benign record, had a red flag with her cousin, simply by the fact that he'd made contact with her.

He imagined she probably freaked out the other day when

Smith and Durbin showed up on her doorstep. It had been three days, and he hadn't seen nor heard from her since. But here came Monday morning, and he was in an ideal position to see and hear, at least to some extent, everything that was going on in and around the executive mansion.

"You're thinking some pretty deep thoughts there for a Monday," said Decker.

"I guess so." He looked along the winding driveway at the house that had withstood wars and changes in government and American culture. "Hard to believe I'm here."

"Well, Chief Usher said you were part of a new security effort with the State Dinner coming up. I tell ya, I'm on top of things here."

"I don't doubt that you are."

"So why *are* you here, then?"

The man didn't miss a thing, and if someone were to get in during his shift, it wouldn't be because of Decker's lack of observation.

"I'm consulting. Always a good idea to evaluate what we do, to see how we can make it better."

"If you want my opinion, the heater in here works fine, but you should be sitting out here in July. I think I lose ten pounds of water weight every week, much as I sweat."

"Duly noted, sir." Much as he'd dreaded the guardhouse, at least this guy was good for a laugh.

Buzz looked at him with narrowed eyes. "But in all my years here, I've never seen a 'consultant' show up here in my guardhouse, thinking they know how to do my job better than I do."

"Not at all. I'm here to learn from you, actually."

Buzz slapped Jack on the back and took another swig of coffee.

By the end of his shift, Jack knew that the produce arrived early, the secretary of state had bad breath even from three feet away, and the secretary of the interior drove a vehicle older than his Camry. The delivery route of the White House wasn't easily accessible. Definitely an inside job somehow. Jack also knew, though, that Buzz would kill for the sake of his country and to protect those he served. Fresh after his service in the Gulf War, Buzz joined the security staff and had stayed ever since.

"This is my family now," Buzz said.

Jack kept hearing the White House workers were like a family. Even Tara's hackles had raised when he brought up the idea that maybe an insider was trying to sabotage the State Dinner and attack the nation's home for the First Family.

He sent her a text message. I'M FREE AFTER 2. COFFEE?

Tara checked her phone as she and Adelaide walked along to their meeting with the First Lady. Someone had sent a message. No, two someones.

Trevor: HOWDY CUZ. SEE YOU SOON? CALL ME. BIG STUFF COMING UP.

And even better, Jack: I'M FREE AFTER 2. COFFEE? In spite of her resolve, her heart gave a happy hop inside her chest. Then she clutched her clipboard a little more tightly. Jack had been wearing a security uniform and greeted her in the guardhouse with Buzz this morning. The wink he'd given had warmed her to her toes, once her head quit hurting after she cracked it on Adelaide's rearview mirror.

Was there hope for them? Would there be a *them*, eventually? Tara had lain awake last night, praying for an answer. No handwriting appeared on the wall, saying, "Yes, Jack is the one for you. True love will overcome all." She half grinned at the idea. In the Bible, the handwriting on the wall hadn't been a harbinger of good news.

"Perfect love casts out fear," the Bible taught her. No wonder she feared for her heart. Her love for Jack, and certainly his for her, hadn't been perfect.

Adelaide had kept talking about the menu and the seating arrangement she had from Chief Usher Kanaday, and now she stopped outside the First Lady's office and faced Tara.

"Yoo-hoo, Tara?" She snapped her fingers a few inches from Tara's nose.

Tara shook her head. "I'm sorry."

"Just making sure you're with me." Adelaide gave her an elder-sister smile. "I'm not running this show. Your role is just as important as mine. This is going to be the best State Dinner ever."

"You said that about the last one."

"Of course I did. And so it was." Her round brown face crinkled in a smile.

The door to First Lady Franklin's office swung open, and her assistant greeted them. "Please come in. Thank you for coming. I know you've been very busy. But the First Lady wanted to touch base with you again."

Tara smoothed her chef jacket, the one she kept on hand for special occasions. Her everyday jacket was downstairs in the locker. They entered Beverly Franklin's office.

She rose from her desk chair, her crisp red linen jacket topping black slacks. Simple gold bangle bracelets matched her hoop earrings. The lady had style, her red-haired bob the hottest new hairstyle since the campaign and inauguration.

"Chefs, thank you for coming," she said in her soft Southern drawl. They'd dubbed her the "Steel Magnolia" on the campaign trail as she supported her husband on his journey to the White House. "I'm passing along more information for you about the menu. I decided I'd like to add a course with Middle Eastern food to honor the Anqaran royal family, besides giving them a sampling of our American cuisine."

Tara followed Adelaide's lead and took one of the chairs in front of Beverly Franklin's desk. She glanced at her boss, who started writing on her notepad.

"We can do that," Chef Montanez said. That was always her response. "Don't tell them you'll see about it," she'd told Tara once. "Tell them you can. Then make it happen."

Thankfully, no one had ordered sushi yet.

"Do you have any idea about the protein you'd like to serve?" Tara asked, finding her voice around the bump in her throat.

"Lamb, something spicy," the First Lady replied. She reached for her printer and handed a paper to Adelaide.

"What's this?" Adelaide asked.

"The royal family's chef sent this recipe, so I'd like to duplicate it, or come as close as we can."

Tara wrote *LAMB* in all caps and nodded. No pressure. It would be like making her grandma's chicken fried steak and serving it to Cat Cora. Or even Paula Deen. Some chefs didn't consider Paula legit, but as far as Tara was concerned, Ms. Deen definitely knew her Southern cooking. She didn't want a poorly executed dish to be the cause of any issues between Anqara and the U.S., no matter how amicable their relationship seemed.

Adelaide passed the recipe to Tara. It was a list of ingredients for a simple meatball and sauce. "Will this come before or after the beef course?" Tara asked.

"I think it would do nicely after the salad, something warm, to remind them of home," replied First Lady Franklin. "I'm a firm believer in food bringing people together."

"Us, too," Tara said. She passed the recipe back to Adelaide. They had most of the spices on hand. They needed a garnish, though. One more thing to add to the produce list.

"If you could make a test batch and have it ready for me tomorrow?" The First Lady rose from her desk chair.

"Of course. I'll make sure of it," said Adelaide. They both shook hands with her, and Tara followed Adelaide from the office.

Once they left the administrative wing where the First Lady had her office, Adelaide's stroll kicked into a top-gear walk. Although taller than the executive chef, Tara had to keep her own pace quick.

"Do we have enough lamb?" Tara asked.

"For now. For the samples, anyway. Call Capital Produce. We need some extra greens for garnish—and I'm making that tomato sauce from scratch so it can blend overnight. But we'll need more tomatoes for the sauce. Get an extra ten pounds." Adelaide scribbled on her notepad.

"Will do. Sounds like a great recipe."

"I'll make enough for the whole crew to try. Might as well, since it's a last-minute addition to the menu." Adelaide slowed down once they reached the stairs. "Oh, and a Girl Scout group is coming through tomorrow morning. Plus a news team from CNN. They want to cover dinner prep."

Tara nodded. "It sounds like we'll have a three-ring circus going on." Especially now since Jack walked back into her life and her job, she realized how busy the White House was, with all the coming and going. Carefully screened, of course.

She shivered, remembering her parents' phone call a little

more than two years ago, about the shootings on Fort Hood, just over an hour from where they lived. The shootings rocked the military base, echoed through the country. What would prevent a shooter from doing the same here, someone who *belonged* in this environment? Surely there were warning signs with the shooter on the base. The news had painted a picture of a disturbed individual who still had access and people either missed or ignored important clues. She thought of Mart, disgruntled. He was moving on, but what would prevent him from giving a departing jab to the White House on his way out?

Were they missing warning signs here, even now? *Lord, I surely hope not*, she prayed silently as she headed back into the kitchen with Adelaide. *Guide Jack. Guide me. Protect our First Family and the ones who lead us. No one is in office that You didn't allow to be there.*

Before she called the produce company, she took out her own phone and sent Jack a message: Coffee sounds great. C U then.

A brisk wind blew through Farragut Park. Jack gritted his teeth. Sometimes winter liked to hang on, and on. The park probably wasn't the best suggestion to share cups of coffee. But it was close to the White House, and both Jack and Tara were free.

"Maybe we should go somewhere warmer," he offered.

"Sounds good to me. Although the cold air feels great after being in the kitchen most of the day." Tara walked beside him, a tote bag slung over her arm, her boots with secure footing on the pavement.

"How do you do early mornings like that? I'm not a fan,

myself." Of course, being up late working didn't help either.

"I'm used to it, I guess." She smiled at him, pink tingeing her cheeks. "Where do you want to go?"

He pulled out his phone and searched on the map. "Fifteenth. There's a café."

They ambled along, a block over until he led her to a place called Simone's. Ironic, the closest place was a French bistro. He glanced into the front window. Mostly deserted.

Jack held the door for Tara as soft violin music filtered past them. Soon the hostess had them tucked into a corner booth that formed a semicircle and bordered on making Jack feel claustrophobic. He set his phone down on the table. They settled into the seat, facing the front of the café. Neither one of them wanted their backs to the window. Not in Paris, and not now.

"You were in the guardhouse this morning," Tara said. He'd wondered when she'd ask.

"Yes, for now. Probably until the dinner." He studied the menu, but he didn't want to eat. "If you'd like to order something besides coffee, go ahead. My treat."

"I'm fine right now. I'm just getting coffee. A big, strong coffee." She arranged the flatware in front of her into a more orderly appearance instead of askew.

"Any news I should know about?" he asked after they ordered their coffees.

"Mart actually started talking on Friday about how he felt about leaving, and not getting the position. It sounds like his beef is more with Chief Usher Kanaday. I didn't call you about it, though, since you're already looking at him."

He bit back his words. True, they were looking at Chef Welch already. "You know about the produce deliveryman being arrested."

"We're shocked. I find it hard to believe. Plus, Adelaide heard that Tony claims he was framed."

"He was right there with the people who started throwing bottles over the White House fence. They didn't respond to security so they were taken into custody."

"Tony Caproni is a sweet man. I've seen him three mornings a week for the past three years, more or less. I couldn't imagine him doing such a thing."

"Which gives him a perfect opportunity to try something. If not him, then someone coercing him."

"What are you talking about?"

"Tony has regular access to the White House and drives a large van. He brings produce that the First Family and others attached to the White House consume. Why not target him?"

"But he was arrested. How can he do anything now?"

"We're watching him all the same." A warning signal flashed in his mind's eye. The barista appeared with their coffees.

"What's wrong?" Tara studied his face as he took his first sip of coffee.

"Look, we shouldn't talk about the investigation anymore," he managed to say. "I don't want to tell you anything you shouldn't know."

"So what should we talk about? The reason you asked me for coffee is to talk about this case, right? I might have some information you can use. Remember, *you* invited me for coffee." Tara poured cream into the cup, then followed it with a generous spoonful of sugar. She stirred with enough vigor to slosh a little of the coffee onto the tablecloth. She frowned.

"Yes. No." His own demeanor baffled even him. "Tara, ever since I saw you last week. . ."

She shifted on the booth's seat to face him. He couldn't

guess how many times he'd thought about this very scenario, what he'd say if he could be the better man and not just walk away because it was the easy thing to do.

He cleared his throat. "Ever since last week, all I can think about is how foolish I was. No. A fool and a coward."

Then Jack allowed himself to do what he'd promised himself not to. He pulled Tara close and kissed her.

Chapter 6

Any minute now, Tara knew she'd wake up. Her pulse roared in her ears as the kiss continued. To be in Jack's arms again, to hear him say he'd been a fool. This was the stuff of dreams. Dreams she'd finally quit having. She'd moved on with her life until last Thursday, when Jack had literally walked back into her kitchen.

She pulled away first, not as gently as she'd hoped. "Jack—"

He touched her cheek. "All the time I wasted."

"I know."

He chuckled. "Don't be so quick to agree with me."

"Where do we go from here?" She didn't want to pin him down. Men like Jack Courtland, if they even suspected anyone was hemming them in, would run the other way. Even now, she suspected the booth felt too confining to him.

"We get through the State Dinner. After that," he said, reaching for her hand, "I want to see you again. As often as possible."

"Well, that sounds romantic. Are we on the schedule for Monday, Wednesday, and Friday, then?"

"Ouch, don't shoot me down when I'm trying."

"Sorry."

"I mean, Tara. . .I remember what my life was like when you were in it. You added something. Something that's been missing since Paris."

She'd never heard him talk like this. "I don't want us to go down the same old road, Jack. I can't do that again. You missed dates. Because of work, I know. But then, when you finally left. . ." She shook her head.

"George said something to me the other day. He basically said that I need to be willing to trust God enough and work on our relationship enough to make it work. And George isn't a believer." Jack flipped the knife back and forth on the tablecloth. "I was trying to do it all on my own the last time."

"George is pretty smart." Tara sipped her coffee and looked toward the front of the restaurant. Foot traffic had picked up on the street outside. Another couple entered the restaurant and stopped at the hostess desk.

"I'm working on it, Tara. I haven't depended on anyone else in a long time. If I don't make something happen, it doesn't happen. It's hard for me. I see George's marriage on the rocks, and I see my own parents' marriage that's been going on for over thirty-five years. One side of it, and the other." He shrugged. "I can't promise you, though, that I won't break your heart again. And you don't deserve that."

Tara nodded. "I'm glad you're being honest with me. I tell you what. You figure out what it is exactly that you want. One kiss and a heart-to-heart talk aren't enough. You have a lot going on now with the case, just like I do."

He stared at her like she'd just slapped him. "Aw, Tara—"

She reached into her purse and found a five-dollar bill. "Let me know in a week where you are. You know where I'll be."

Thanks to Tara's simple text message on Tuesday, giving Jack a tip about Trevor Bradshaw's travel itinerary, they hauled Trevor in for questioning as soon as he arrived at Reagan National on Friday, and Jack almost didn't care. Of course he cared. He had to.

Like Tara suspected, Trevor's mouth was bigger than his resolve to hurt anyone or make any "statement" of how he felt about the administration. The fertilizer he'd bought was for their acreage and was back in Texas, as was all the other paraphernalia he'd purchased.

"I can't believe y'all are dragging in a red-blooded, all-American citizen like this." Trevor Bradshaw sat there in a chair, scowling. "I ain't against our president. He can have his fancy-shmancy dinner party—I don't mind."

"We had to be sure, Mr. Bradshaw," said George.

"I'm only against socialism. We don't need the government trying to make our decisions for us. Really, I'm sure y'all don't want that either. I don't like the philosophy of President Franklin, that he and Congress can think for us better than we can."

Jack had to admit the guy had a point. "You're free to go. But I'd avoid asking your cousin for a White House tour. You need months' notice for that anyway."

Trevor nodded. "I found that out. I got a Capitol tour scheduled with my congressman's office. After the tour, I'm having lunch in the House of Representatives cafeteria."

"You enjoy your stay in Washington, Mr. Bradshaw. We'd put you on our tour schedule here, except we're not conducting tours currently," Jack said.

He left after asking if he could get his picture taken with "two real FBI agents," and George turned him down. "That's all we need, us popping up on Facebook," he said as Trevor headed for the elevator.

"What about the dinner staff, the servers?" Now that they'd spent their time working through the employees, there was the matter of the servers appointed to work the State Dinner. Most of them were college students or interns of some type.

"Working on it. Only one red flag," George said. He pointed to a name.

"Lilith Mansour?" Her info said she was twenty-one, the daughter of physicians from Richmond, Virginia, in her final semester of undergrad studies at George Washington University, pre-law.

"Her parents fled Anqara when she was two years old. It seems back in the early nineties, the present king of Anqara and his brother were battling for the throne, so to speak. Her parents were big supporters of his brother. So it was either leave town or put up with a man they hated."

"I don't remember hearing that in the news."

"Probably not," George said. "The world was busy watching the Persian Gulf instead."

"So Ms. Mansour snags a recommendation to serve tables at the State Dinner." Jack rubbed his chin. "We have a tail on her now?"

"Already done. So far, she's keeping a low profile. Staying out of the cold, going to the library, to a few restaurants around the university."

"Good. Does Kanaday know about this?"

"He knows."

Try something, just try it. Jack said, "Get a server's uniform from Kanaday. I'm going to be there, too."

Chapter 7

Tara's feet hurt, and it was only eight in the morning on the day of the State Dinner. She'd been dog-paddling through the past week with dinner preparations, had seen glimpses of the floral arrangements, and had even oohed and aahed over the place cards penned by the chief calligrapher.

The kitchen was already hot, so she fled to the hall for a breather. She gave herself a mental pep talk. She hadn't let the kitchen's heat get to her in years, even with the sweat-soaked bandanna she wore on her head during eighteen-hour days like today.

Adelaide had already launched a tirade in Spanish when sous chef Ken dropped a pan of dough for the flat bread, and the dough tumbled across the tile floor. Tara interpreted about half of Adelaide's stream of speech. Her mother would've washed her mouth out with soap for that spiel.

"C'mon." Adelaide appeared at the door. "I know it's been a hard week for you, but you can do this. One day, my job could be yours."

"Really?" If Adelaide had so much faith in her, she couldn't cave.

"You've got what it takes. I know so. Chief Usher Kanaday

thinks so, as does Social Secretary Brinks. I'm not going to be here forever." Adelaide nudged Tara's shoulder. "I'll be ready to slow down sometime in the next five years or so."

Tara straightened her posture. "I'm good. I just needed a minute."

Adelaide paused before they reentered the kitchen. "If that man is worth it, he'll show up for you."

"Thanks. I hope he decides to show up, once and for all." She drove thoughts of Jack from her mind.

The phone rang, so Tara grabbed it. "Kitchen, Chef Whitley speaking."

"Delivery, Capital Produce," said Buzz.

"Got it, Buzz." She hung up the phone. "I'll go meet the truck." She grabbed a wheeled cart.

The Capital Produce truck came to its usual spot. A driver jumped down from the seat, singing in Italian. "Here we are. Got your leeks, endive, more strawberries, mangoes, blueberries, and pineapple."

"Tony! You're back." Tara couldn't help but run toward the driver's side of the truck to hug the older man. "What happened? You were arrested?"

Tony shrugged. "Call it the wrong place at the wrong time. My daughter sent me a message that said, 'Dad, meet me downtown.' So I do. But it's not her. There was a big group. Next thing I know, I get hauled in with a bunch of protestors. I'm cleared now. I'm okay." He shook his head.

"Wow. Well, we missed you. We were worried."

"You wipe away that frown, Miss Tara. Tell you what, I get Sofia to make you all some cannolis. Is this everything you need?" He gestured to the crates.

Tara scanned the produce. "That's it."

"I give you a hand." Together, they wheeled the produce to the kitchen. "Oh, it's good to be back, Miss Tara."

"Heath was nice, but he's definitely not you." At that, they both laughed.

Jack straightened his tie and tried to look relaxed. *Relaxed* wasn't a word in his vocabulary most of the time. Every nerve ending on his skin tingled underneath his tux. George had done one step better than get him in as a server; he was set to shadow Chief Usher Kanaday, who at the moment looked like a skinny penguin bouncing from table to table, checking place cards and tweaking floral arrangements.

They'd already had the State arrival ceremony that morning on the South Lawn. Although the Anqaran royal family had been in the DC area since Thursday and it was now Monday, this was considered their official welcome to the country.

The servers were scheduled to arrive within the next thirty minutes and receive instructions from Kanaday and Chef Montanez. Jack was ready to meet Lilith Mansour.

He hadn't seen Tara, and didn't expect to. She was likely in the belly of the White House, scurrying around with the rest of the kitchen staff. Up here, guests had started to arrive in all sorts of tuxedos and gowns in every color of the rainbow.

Jack had made up his mind about Tara. He only hoped she'd really listen to him. He didn't blame her for being gun-shy, for lack of a better term.

"All clear on the South Lawn," a voice crackled into his earpiece.

"State Dining Room clear," Jack said.

"Maxwell's downstairs, Courtland. Do a walk-through instead of hobnobbing."

"Going now." Jack headed toward the elevator that would take him to the ground floor.

Tara stepped into the walk-in and inhaled the scent of fresh produce. Before long, they'd be plating the salads. A mix of arugula, romaine, and iceberg lettuce. Sous chef Ken had slaved over his vinaigrette until it sang on the taste buds.

Best chopped fresh, the salad had to wait until the last possible moment. Already the hors d'oeuvres had gone upstairs to the dining room to be served to the guests as they waited to be seated.

"Chef Whitley." The voice made her freeze.

"Hello?" She knew the voice but couldn't place the owner.

Heath Smallwood stepped out from behind the rack of produce and pointed a gun at her.

"I think it's time for you to help me prepare a special course." He pointed at a bowl heaped with green leaves of spinach. "Try a sample. *Now.*"

"What are you doing here?" *Oh Lord. He's got a gun. Jack.* Her phone was in her pocket. Maybe he had his phone with him. He had to. She moved her hand toward her pocket, but Heath gestured to the bowl.

"Eat this, or I shoot you. Then I move on to others. I'd rather you cooperate first. It'll work much more smoothly this way."

"What's wrong with the spinach?"

"Not much other than a little salmonella, some E. coli. You'll get sick. Probably won't die. I don't think. It can happen in extreme cases." He gestured with his head to the box. "And now it's all in that salad mix you're getting ready to prep. Nice, huh?"

"Why are you doing this? *What* are you doing?" The walls of the walk-in closed in around her like a trash compacter. "How did you get in here?"

Heath glanced down at his chef jacket. "A truck can hold more than produce. You and Tony, the brainless driver, were too busy chitchatting while I walked right in with these crates of spinach and lettuce."

The elevator was out of order, so Jack took the stairs, after yet another person checked his credentials. He figured extra security on the ground floor.

He took the hallway slowly, glancing into doorways. A buzz of activity at the end of the hall told him the kitchen was in full banquet mode.

His phone buzzed on his hip. Tara's number.

He pushed a button. "Tara?"

A clattering noise, an echoing voice. *"You stupid woman— don't make me shoot you."*

Heath yanked Tara's hand from her pocket and snatched her phone. "One phone call, and I send people to your townhouse. They know which ones are your friends, the lawyer and the tea shop lady."

She wanted to scream, but she didn't want anyone else to stumble onto this scene. Which they would, soon, if she didn't get out there with the lettuce and spinach so they could prep the salad.

"The king of Anqara is ill, very, very ill, which many people don't know. Catching E. coli or even salmonella would be deadly for him," said Heath Smallwood. "His brother, shall we say, is eager to set things right in the nation-state again. They're prepared to align with Iran and give them cooperation and funding instead of being a pebble in the shoe of their efforts."

"How does this help you? What do you get out of this?"

"I get plenty. Normally I'd rather shoot people, but this is paying me enough so I can disappear for a while."

Tara started to reach for the nearest crate of spinach, then stopped. "I need to start prepping. They're going to wonder where I am."

"Try anything and I mow down this kitchen one by one." He lowered the gun a fraction. It had a silencer on the end. He could pop off a shot and no one would know.

Did her phone call go through? She wasn't sure.

"Kitchen—now—it's going live—" Jack hollered as he ran down the hallway. "Backup, now!"

He flew into the kitchen and saw the head chef. "Montanez—where's Chef Whitley? She's in danger."

"In the walk-in—in the back— What?"

"Chef, who's that new chef that brought in a big crate of produce?" asked a slim young man wearing a chef's jacket. He pointed over his shoulder.

Jack left them and ran for the walk-in, his gun drawn.

"Everybody down." He yanked open the door.

The door opening made them both turn.

"Down on the ground! Down now!" Jack growled.

Tara glimpsed Jack in the doorway, gun aimed. She grabbed the nearest crate and yanked it onto both her and Heath. Produce and plastic crates tumbled on them.

"On your face, on your face!" Jack was shouting.

Tara scrambled away from Heath, toward the doorway and safety.

"Move, Tara!"

She flopped onto the spinach scattered on the floor.

Heath rose up on one knee, gun in hand.

Two pops, one loud and one soft, echoed inside the walk-in.

Tara screamed and crawled to where Jack lay on the floor.

"I'm hit—" he whispered.

Chapter 8

W e did it." Jack tried to move on the hospital bed, but another mind-searing bolt of pain shot through his shoulder. He grunted and finally sat up.

"No, you did it. And you're gonna yank something loose and end up in the ICU if you keep pulling stunts like that." George stood by Jack's hospital bed.

"What, and leave all the work to you and the rest of the crew? Nah." Jack shook his head. He glanced at the clock. His parents were arriving any moment. Once they'd heard the news, Dad booked the first flights they could to Reagan National. "How's Smallwood?"

"ICU. He'll live, though. We've already traced the deposits in his bank account to Switzerland, and then to Anqara. He'll face so many charges he's not going to see the outside of jail for a long time," George said. "Your chef is a scrappy thing, pulling that crate onto Smallwood. If she wasn't a chef, I'd recommend we recruit her."

Jack couldn't imagine the thought of Tara packing heat instead of wielding a chef's knife. "I hope she keeps doing exactly what she's doing now."

"Son! We're here." His parents entered the room. Dad

looked grayer, and Mom had a few more lines on her face than he last remembered.

George stood. "I'll leave you three to catch up." He nodded at Jack's parents before stepping from the room.

Mom reached his bedside first. "Oh, my sweet boy. I've always been afraid of this happening to you." She clamped her hand onto her mouth and a few tears trickled down her cheeks.

"I'm okay, Mom. I'm going to be back out there in a couple of months." Of course, there'd be physical therapy and another shoulder surgery. "I'm thankful, though, it wasn't my right shoulder."

"Son, we are so proud of you." Dad's eyes were bright. "I don't think we tell you enough."

"Thanks, Dad. I know you are. But you didn't have to come. Airfare is expensive, and it looks like I might be able to fly home sooner instead of summertime."

"We needed to be here," his father said. "Not every day is our son a national hero, even though nobody knows about it."

"It's not important for people to know." Jack squeezed his mother's hand. "Mom, don't cry. I'm okay. Really. It hurts like anything, but it'll be fine."

"Do I need to get the nurse?" she asked, dabbing at her eyes.

"No, Mom, but thanks."

"Speaking of thanks, well, I'd like to give thanks," Dad said.

"Go right ahead, because I would, too." Jack closed his eyes and listened to his father's voice.

"Lord," his father said, "thank You for keeping Your hand on our son. We know that even though he's hundreds and sometimes thousands of miles away from us, he's not outside of Your reach. We don't know where he is sometimes, but we know You do. Nothing happens to him that You don't know about or care about. So thank You again for preserving his life. Now, I ask that You touch his heart, his mind, and strengthen him. Help him make wise decisions in the days and months and years ahead. In Your Son's name I pray, amen."

Jack blinked. He'd forgotten what it was like to hear his father pray. A simple Midwestern farmer whose faith ran as deep as the trees on his land. "Thanks, Dad."

"Well, I meant to tell you. There's a pretty lady outside the door who insisted we see you first."

Tara—

"Send her in, please."

"We'll be right outside if you need us, hon." Mom gave him a smile before they went into the hallway.

Tara entered the room with a wave at his parents. She was at his bedside not soon enough, yanking a chair to sit close to him.

"You're okay—"

"I'm perfect right now." Heat swept through him at her nearness, and not because of his arm. With his good arm, he pulled her closer and gave her a lingering kiss. "You did good, Special Agent Whitley."

"I'm not packing my knives away and heading for training at Quantico anytime soon." Her smile was brief, then faded. "When I saw that gun, and what he was trying to do, I kept trying to think about how I could stop him, how I could let you know. Because I knew you had to be there somewhere at the dinner."

"I heard you. I came as soon as I did."

"About last week, at the café."

"I deserved it." He knew he did. It had been a long time coming. He shouldn't have thought that one kiss and apology would make up for the past. *But Lord, I don't want to lose her again.*

"Give it time."

"Maybe," Tara said, sitting up a little straighter. "And even now, I don't want us to make any decisions in the heat of the moment—whether it's because of a kiss, or gunshots—that we aren't prepared to back up later. I love you, Jack Courtland. I knew it when you hit the floor of that walk-in, and I thought about what life would be like without you, alive or dead. I didn't like either. But I'm not going to give you an ultimatum. That's not fair. The State Dinner is over, and I know we still don't have our answer. Not just yet. Or do we?"

She had a point. He really just wanted to kiss her again, and then spend the afternoon in the hospital channel surfing, since the docs weren't ready to let him go just yet. He had a ton of reports to write, and it would all be waiting for him. For now, he just wanted Tara to be with him.

"Give it time."

"You're right, an emotional moment isn't the time to be making big decisions." Jack swallowed hard. "I tell you what. Let's see each other again—next Tuesday."

Tara nodded. "Valentine's Day?"

"That seems appropriate. You name the place."

"The Washington Monument reflecting pool. Six o'clock."

"You're going to freeze," Susan Holland said as Tara put on her gloves.

"I need to go. If he's not there, I'll know. Just like Paris."

"Honey, it's not a movie. It's real life. And Jack Courtland is just a man."

Yes, he most certainly was.

After the shooting in the White House kitchen, the news media ran an interesting story. Evidently a worker slipped in the kitchen during the State Dinner, struck his head on the counter, and had to be medevaced from the White House with a head injury. Funny how a gunshot wound turned into a kitchen mishap.

"Y'all are sweet for thinking of me." Tara glanced from Susan to Ciara. "I'll be okay. I'll call you if everything goes south."

"You sure?" Ciara asked.

"I promise."

Tara hurried away from Cherry Blossom Estates in the dusk. This was crazy, heading into the city's downtown on Valentine's Day. She found a parking place not far from the Washington Monument reflecting pool.

Her feet took her, too swiftly, to the walkway. A figure in a dark coat waited.

"You came," Jack said. His left arm was in a sling.

"Yup," was all she could manage. She refused to let herself step into his arms, at least into the circle of his one good arm. "So where are we?"

"I love you, Tara Whitley. I once thought I'd forget about you, but I couldn't," Jack said. He held a square box. "And I'm here. I'll keep showing up, every day, for as long as we live. If I can't find a way back to you, I'll keep working at it. But I'll never let you forget who you are to me."

If he whipped a diamond ring out of that box, she didn't know what she'd do. They still had a long way to go. He opened the box. Inside was a gold heart pendant.

"It, uh, should go nicely with the cross you always wear. I thought they'd look good together on that chain. I mean, I didn't want you to not wear that, since. . .well. . ." He bumbled with the box lid, and Tara almost laughed. She'd never seen him fumble with words or babble.

"I love it. And I love you." She touched the heart, about the size of a dime. One side had simply "Jack" engraved on it. "It's perfect."

"This is our beginning. Well, I want it to be." Jack cleared his throat. "I don't want any enemy in the world, or otherwise, to come between us. Never again. I want a life with you, to build a family with you, Tara. I work hard at being a good agent. But I plan to work just as hard at being the man that God, and you, want me to be. Please say yes, Tara. Tell me that's what you want, too."

"Yes, yes, a million times yes!" She leaned closer and he pulled her to him and kissed her as the city lit up for the night.

LYNETTE SOWELL is an award-winning author with New England roots, but she makes her home in central Texas with her husband and a herd of five cats. When she's not writing, she edits medical reports and chases down stories for the local newspaper.

DYING FOR LOVE

by Cara C. Putman

Dedication

Many thanks to Becky Germany for the opportunity to write a novella for this collection along with three stellar authors and friends. Gina, so delighted to get to write this with you—your first book! Lynette and Frances, it's been worth the wait to get to share this experience with you.

Additional thanks to Casey Herringshaw, Ashley Clark, and Sue Lyzenga for loaning me their eagle eyes and serving as first readers for me. Appreciate you!

Also a big thank-you to my George Mason Law School classmate Amy Mirabile, who helped me nail the details about Alexandria courts. Any errors are mine.

To Linda Adair, my amazing paralegal, who makes me a better attorney than I am alone and is a good friend I cherish.

My kids are amazing. Thanks for always having bigger dreams for my writing than I do, even when the hours are long and my sleep non-existent. I couldn't write without you.

To my husband, Eric, for the early years of our own "Cherry Blossom Caper" in Fairlington Village inside the Washington, DC Beltway. God graced us with a great home—that looked an awful lot like Ciara's—and a group of friends as incredible as Ciara's. I treasure those years and you. I can't wait to see what chapters God writes next in our love story.

Thank you, Jesus, for the gift of story and for the opportunity to write stories for You. May they always glorify You!

Chapter 1

Ciara Turner sucked in a breath, trying to calm the adrenaline-addicted hummingbirds filling her stomach as she straightened her shoulders and adjusted her grasp on her attaché case.

She pasted on a smile and pushed into Judge Banter's still-dark anteroom. The judge had issued one of his infamous pre-hearing orders on Friday, so she'd rushed to the office extra-early for the first-thing-Monday-morning appearance. His secretary's desk stood abandoned, but the judge would expect her to enter anyway. She strode to the judge's office door and glanced down the short hallway to the clerks' desks. Based on the silence, neither of them had arrived either. It looked like she'd even beat opposing counsel, Daniel Evans, to court. That in itself made the day an unusual one. They'd raced each other in when both clerked for the judge, a race that continued when they found themselves on opposite sides of a case like this one.

Ciara shifted her hold on her briefcase and rapped on the judge's door.

"Judge Banter? It's Ciara Turner." She pushed on the cracked door and stepped just inside. "Sir?"

A rustling sound reached her, and she stepped deeper into

the darkened room. She frowned. Usually by this time in the morning Judge Banter would have opened the curtains and filled the room with sunlight. Most in the legal community knew Judge Banter usually arrived by 6:00 a.m. so he could capture the early morning peace. He liked to attack whichever legal puzzles waited on his desk with the windows thrown open, no matter how cold. He'd always commented on how healthy sunlight was for a person.

With spring giving hints it had arrived, he should have the windows open. She'd worn a cashmere sweater under her suit in anticipation of the chill.

The door to his private restroom stood cracked with fluorescent light spilling onto the carpet and the walnut desk. The rows of bookshelves behind the desk were as crammed with books and papers as they had been during her clerkship. It all looked as she'd expected, except the judge wasn't sitting on his towering leather chair.

Ciara glanced over her shoulder at his assistant's desk. Still no sign of the woman. Guess she might as well pull out the motion she wanted to file. Daniel wouldn't like it, but she didn't care. Virginia still required alimony, and his client would not get away with the paltry amount he offered. If it took filing a motion for an accounting, then so be it. The cuckoo clock perched on the shelf behind the judge's desk wound into its song and dance. Now the judge and Daniel were both late.

Where was Daniel? He knew Judge Banter's intolerance for anyone arriving late for a hearing. The judge insisted each counsel be present when speaking to him about a case. Ciara set her bag on one of the wing chairs, then startled when the outside door opened. She jerked to attention. Maybe Judge Banter had returned after stepping out.

The strong strides of a man approached the chambers. "Ms. Glenda?"

She closed her eyes as Daniel's smooth baritone called for Judge Banter's assistant. While she'd relished her clerkship with the judge, Daniel Evans was the do-over she longed for from that two-year stint. With his all-American looks and smile that could twist her insides into knots, she'd fallen head over heels the moment she walked into the tiny office and found him at the desk next to hers.

"Anyone here?" Daniel's steps approached the door.

She turned, pasting a smile on her lips. She refused to let him know that five years later he still made her heart somersault. "Good morning, Mr. Evans."

His slow, lazy grin stretched across his mouth as he took her in. She resisted the urge to shift under his inspection.

"Is my dad here?" He looked over his shoulder then caught her gaze as she shook her head. "I always look for him when someone says Mr. Evans." He shoved his hands in his pockets, his stance relaxed. "Now this is the way to start a Monday morning."

"I'm sure you say that to all the girls."

"Only the ones who bring a ray of sunshine with them."

Ciara bit her lower lip to hide an answering smile. "Are you ready to get to work?"

"Sure." Daniel examined the room. "Where's the judge?"

"I haven't seen him or a clerk, but someone must be here since the door's unlocked."

Daniel frowned. "That's not like him, especially when he issues a summons like this. He would have made us come in early with him for these command appearances."

"I know. But I haven't seen Glenda or a clerk." Ciara

shrugged. "Maybe he's loosened up since we clerked."

"Doubt it." Daniel walked toward the judge's large walnut desk. Stacks of legal treatises and briefs covered the surface, except for the desk calendar. "This doesn't show anything but us until a ten o'clock hearing."

Ciara followed him to the desk, then glanced at the bathroom. She froze when she saw a shoe. "Daniel—"

He glanced at her, a question in his eyes.

"Is that Judge. . .Banter?"

The next moment Daniel inched the door open, then eased to the floor. "Judge?" He touched the judge's neck, then stiffened. "Call the sheriff's office downstairs and ask for an ambulance and officers." Without glancing at her, he started chest compressions.

She froze, her gaze captured by the image of Judge Banter's lanky Abraham Lincoln frame splayed across the cold tile floor.

"Ciara."

She jerked to attention, reaching for the phone on the judge's desk and sending a pile of briefs cartwheeling from the top. Her fingers fumbled as she dialed. "This is Ciara Turner. I'm in Judge Banter's chambers, and he's unconscious on the floor. Please send an ambulance."

She stumbled as she remembered Daniel's other request. She looked at him, still kneeling next to the judge. "Daniel Evans says we need officers, too."

The deputy on the phone barked at her. "You need what?"

"Medical help and officers."

"In Judge Banter's office?"

"Yes, sir."

Muffled shouting filled the background as she waited for the deputy to come back on the phone. "Your name again?"

"Ciara Turner. C-i-a-r-a." She rubbed her temples trying to stave off the building pressure.

Daniel Evans leaned over the judge, praying he'd feel a puff of breath or a flutter of a pulse. Instead, his mentor lay too still. Daniel fought to control the anger that rolled over him like a rogue wave swamping his sailboat. What cases did the judge have now that would cause someone to kill him? Child support and custody didn't usually lead to more than violent words.

Daniel glanced at Ciara. Her quiet voice filled the space, soothing even as she played her thumb back and forth across her fingers—a nervous habit when she felt out of control. She had no idea it was her tell that would ruin her chances in many card games. He'd never told her about the gesture because he needed every advantage he could wrangle when fighting her in court.

He pressed two fingers against the judge's carotid artery again, then held his breath. What was that? The faintest flicker seemed to pulse beneath his fingers. He inhaled sharply and checked for breath. Maybe he'd written the judge off too quickly.

In a rush, the outer door banged open and soon paramedics pushed him out of the way. He eased back, relieved to let someone else worry about what to do and how to save the judge's life. If it could be saved. . .

Not long after the paramedics, a couple of Alexandria City sheriff's deputies and someone in street clothes walked into the chambers. Soon the time rushed past in a flurry of questions, few of which he could answer. A detective took Ciara across the room. Daniel tried not to concentrate on her instead of the officer in front of him. He needed to focus, intent on giving answers that might help them find whoever attacked the judge.

"All right." Detective Middleton flipped his notebook shut and reached into his pocket. "Here's my card. Call me if anything comes to mind. I'll be in touch."

Daniel slipped the card into his breast pocket, then glanced at Ciara. Her cheeks were pale as she accepted a card from the other detective. The two conferred in a corner of the judge's chambers, so Daniel moved to Ciara's side.

"Hey."

She glanced at him, then down at her hands. The knuckles were white from the way she clenched her fingers. "Can you believe this?"

"No." Daniel ran a hand across his hair. "I've tried to think who would do this."

"And why. I saw him last week at Inn of Court, and he didn't mention any cases that bothered him."

Daniel wasn't surprised Ciara was active in that monthly professional gathering. "He didn't sound any different from normal when he called us in early either."

"I know." Ciara bit her lip. "But someone didn't want this."

He frowned. "What do you mean?"

"What if it was someone involved in our case?"

"Over custody?"

"Your client seemed pretty intent."

"He's the dad. Of course he's intent on doing what's best for his kid. It's what dads do." As soon as the words slipped out, Daniel wished he could yank them back. Especially when Ciara's face shut down and that old, familiar companion of distance erected its wall between them. Why did he have to poke at her today of all days?

Ciara fought to keep from lashing out at Daniel. Of course he'd start his familiar refrain about how all fathers were perfect and deserved full custody of their kids. She couldn't go there.

Not today.

She wanted to pray the judge would be okay, but he'd looked so pale and still. And Daniel's client had jumped a witness during the last hearing. She'd decided to file today's motion in part to rein him in. Sometimes hitting people in their pocketbooks reminded them a lot more was at stake.

How had Daniel ended up on the wrong side of these cases?

When they had clerked, they both had been passionate about protecting children, and family law was the best way to do it. They'd seemed on parallel tracks as their clerkships wrapped up. Then Daniel decided to start a firm on his own. His ability to care for the children seemed to evaporate with his responsibility to pay the bills. After that, she'd ended their relationship. She couldn't pretend a future existed with someone who saw the world in such a different vein than she did.

If only he still cared. But he didn't, so today she'd fight the attraction and focus on what thrust them together.

The clients who brought them in front of the judge.

Hopeless. That's what she was.

"Come on, say it." Daniel's words pulled her from her thoughts.

"Say what?"

"The words on the tip of your tongue. The ones that paint me with the same brush as the evil fathers I represent."

"You aren't the same."

"You don't believe that." A flash of something appeared on

his face. "We used to think we could fight together, Ciara."

As she met his gaze, that old attraction exploded through her chest. She tried to erect a shield between them, but failed. Instead, the same feeling returned. The one that made her wish they could be something more than adversaries. That they could reclaim the easy friendship they had as clerks. No, she had to steel her heart and order herself to treat him as the enemy. Otherwise, all she got was the sense she could spend the rest of her life with him and she'd never find anyone else to compare. If only he didn't specialize in tearing families apart—and she got stuck trying to salvage something from the wreckage. Not what she'd imagined when she invested years in law school.

"Look, I'm sorry about that." Daniel sighed and shoved his hands in his pockets. "I'm a little rattled."

Ciara considered him, as if weighing his words. He could feel the scales tip against him. Sometimes he just wanted to ask when she'd decided to hate him. They'd left their clerkships eager to tackle the legal community. Somehow their paths had diverged, and he stumbled around whenever they worked a case from opposite sides. It was hard to pay attention to a client when advocating for them required calling her and bearing her scorn.

Why couldn't she accept every story had two sides? Nobody was 100 percent right or wrong when a marriage fell apart. And like it or not, if either party wasn't committed to saving the marriage, there wasn't anything he could do to change that person's mind.

He glanced at his watch and straightened. "I've got to get to Arlington."

"Hearing?"

"Meeting with a client." His gaze swept over the judge's chambers. Several officers and plainclothes detectives worked the room. He prayed they found what they needed to nail whoever attacked the judge. "Guess they're done with us now. I'll call you later."

But the rest of the day sped by without even five minutes to follow through on the call. He could just imagine how she'd take it when he did snag a few moments.

Ciara stared at the phone, then wanted to lecture herself. Some things never changed, from her willingness to believe Daniel or her insane longing to hear from him about something other than a divorce.

Case files lined her desk, each representing a wife or child who needed an advocate. She had to direct attention to their cases, but each time she picked one up, she saw the judge.

She'd checked online news services repeatedly, but hadn't found anything about the morning's events at the court. She played with the card one of the detectives had given her. Should she call him? See if he would update her?

The thought was ridiculous. He had to have a zillion more important things to do than answer inane questions from someone who found a half-dead man.

She dropped her forehead on her arms. *I have to focus.*

"You all right, Ciara?" Linda Troxel, her paralegal, stood in the doorway when Ciara looked up.

"Just grand."

"Then get moving. You'll miss your meeting with opposing

counsel in the Forsythe matter if you don't hoof it."

Ciara groaned. "Any way to postpone that one?"

"Only if you call. I'm not telling Ms. Snooty Pants her matter's been delayed again. You know she's hot to trot to Vegas with that boyfriend of hers. What was he? The pool boy?"

"Cliché, Linda."

"It's the truth."

Ciara laughed at the expression on Linda's face. The woman kept Ciara's spirits lifted with her running commentary on their clients. Especially when she laid on a heavy Southern accent like she just had.

"Can you do a favor for me?"

Linda shrugged. "Sure. What do you need?"

"Call this man." She handed the card to Linda. "See if you can find out how the judge is."

"I'll do one better and call Judge Banter's assistant. She'll know everything."

"Great idea. Thanks." Ciara grabbed her trench coat, briefcase, and the file Linda handed her as she rushed from her office. If she hurried, she might arrive in time since Mr. Forsythe's attorney's office was only two blocks away.

As soon as she exited the town house where she worked, she lifted her face to the sky and let the sun warm her face. Spring hinted at its impending arrival with the soft scent of tulips and the cheery faces of pansies lining the flower beds of the storefronts she passed. She slowed long enough to wait for the WALK signal, then picked up her pace again.

The meeting went well, and she headed home after it. She drove until she reached the end of a line of town houses in Cherry Blossom Estates. Then she pulled her sporty BMW convertible into her parking spot. She bounded up the couple of steps to her porch and unlocked the front door. As soon as she entered the living area, her shoulders slumped from the fatigue pressing against her.

Her knee-high boots clicked against the wood floor as she crossed the living room. She placed her briefcase on the dining room table and then shed her trench coat and hung it on the coat tree in the corner. Her answering machine blinked a message from its spot on the kitchen pass-through. She hit the button and waited for the message as she flipped through the mail, tossing half of it into the kitchen trash can.

"Ciara, this is Linda. I finally reached Glenda. I don't know how to say this." Linda paused after sounding choked on the last few words. "Judge Banter didn't make it." The message continued in silence for a few moments, then ended with a beep.

Ciara startled, then hit the button again. Nothing changed the second time she listened. She stumbled backward and sank onto the nearest dining room chair. "Poor Judge Banter."

Did Daniel know?

She reached for her cell and dug it from her purse with trembling fingers. As she scrolled to his number, she tried to frame what she'd say. How did one tell someone his mentor had been murdered?

Chapter 2

Daniel wiped a band of sweat from his forehead and dropped back to a crouch. Across the racquetball court, Tom Newman pointed at him with a cocky grin. "You're going down if you can't focus, old man."

Usually, Tom's good-natured banter would cut through the stress of the day as it had throughout law school. But today, Daniel's thoughts kept drifting back to the judge. "Maybe I should concede."

"And rob me of the opportunity to beat you fair and square? Won't let you."

"Really, Tom. I need to go. Before I get hurt." Get away and think about what had happened.

Tom frowned then nodded. "I guess I understand. Next week, same time?"

"Yep." If he didn't get hit by a truck or jumped by who knew who at his office.

As he cleaned up in the gym's locker room, Daniel tried to imagine who would want to hurt Judge Banter. The man was firm but fair from the bench. Parties could find themselves in front of much worse judges. Sure, there were always those who believed the world was out to get them. But that wasn't the judge's fault.

His phone sang an old country tune from somewhere in the depths of his bag. He sifted through the corners until his fingers clamped around the small piece of metal. He pulled it out and unlocked it. "Hello?"

A shuddering breath echoed in his ear.

He glanced at the phone's screen. It showed an unknown number. "Can I help you?"

"Daniel?" Ciara's voice didn't have the strident tone he hated in the courtroom. "Have you heard the news?"

"News?" Why did the woman speak in riddles? A thought struck him, and it was his turn to haul in a rough breath.

"Judge—Judge Banter didn't make it. Linda just called, and. . .I thought you should know."

Daniel eased onto the bench. Lockers clanged open and shut around him, the aroma of dirty socks and sweaty bodies adding to the surreal backdrop. "Dead?"

"Whoever attacked him succeeded."

"Okay." His mind spun with images from that morning. "I'm headed over." He hung up before she could sputter any type of protest. Whoever did this would pay. A good man had died. Someone who strived for justice in all Daniel did. Who made the hard decisions. He hoped one of those decisions hadn't led to his death.

"Everything okay?" Tom asked.

"Yeah. No. Judge Banter died."

Tom sucked in a whistle. "That's nuts. The guy never hurt anyone."

"I'm sure some of those who appeared before him don't agree. Still. . .murdered." Daniel couldn't shake the image of the man sprawled across his bathroom floor, the back of his head coated with blood from some kind of wound. "I've got to run."

"Sure." Tom shook his head. "Sometimes I don't understand this world."

"Makes two of us." Daniel grabbed his gym bag and hightailed it to his car. Tom hadn't clerked out of law school, so he wouldn't understand the bond that developed between a clerk and judge. Ciara did. On the phone she'd sounded as shaken as he felt.

Ciara turned on the burner beneath the teakettle. She couldn't get warm and needed something hot in her hands. What if she had arrived at the courthouse a bit earlier? Would she have seen the murderer? If she'd been a few minutes earlier, could she have prevented the murder? Since she discovered the body, would the police think she'd somehow been involved? She tried to remember. . .what happened in all those crime shows?

Outside of a criminal law and a criminal procedure class in law school, she'd avoided that area of law. She purposely built her practice around helping the defenseless. And now she wondered what it all meant.

She might need to cancel her next couple of days' appointments. Tomorrow would be soon enough to make a decision. A soft breeze fluttered the curtains at her front window. Even the sound of her neighbors returning home from their evening's activities couldn't distract her from the questions racing through her mind.

Maybe she should go outside. Join them in an attempt at normalcy. Ciara opened her front door and stood on her stoop a moment. Having the end townhouse allowed her to observe the activity without joining in.

"Ciara! Where have you been hiding, girl? You should have heard the buzz all over the White House. A judge was murdered."

Tara Whitley, the adorable gal who owned a condo across the cul-de-sac from Ciara, barely paused to take a breath before she covered her mouth. "Did you know him?"

"Yes."

"I'm so sorry. There I go again, speaking before I think." Tara heaved a dramatic sigh, smoothing out her white chef's coat. "Like most things, it leaked in the cafeteria first. A couple of Secret Service agents."

"I was there when his body was discovered."

"Oh Ciara! That's horrible!"

Ciara swallowed against the lump the size of a dollar coin that seemed lodged in her throat.

Tara squeezed Ciara in a tight hug. "Let me know if you need anything."

"I will." Tara hurried to the main door of the building housing her condo before disappearing. Ciara considered following her. Being alone didn't seem right. Maybe she'd take a walk instead. The neighborhood lawns and trees had begun to show evidence of spring. Any day now the cherry blossoms would erupt alongside the pansies and daffodils. Then it would be official. Spring had arrived, only shrouded with a tinge of black.

She shoved her hands in her jeans pockets and hunched her shoulders. The breeze seemed to whisper in her ears— if only it would whisper who had killed Judge Banter. Ciara exited the cul-de-sac and headed up the slight hill through the neighborhood. A car pulled to the curb, but she ignored it.

"Ciara."

Daniel? She turned around. "You came."

"I told you I would."

"Sure, but why?"

He stepped on the sidewalk next to her, and suddenly she didn't feel so alone. She almost stepped closer before remembering nothing had changed. They were still going different directions in life. Opposing directions. Diametrically diverging directions. She stepped back and tried to find neutral ground.

"Can you believe it?"

Daniel fell into step next to her as she started up the block. "It's surreal." Daniel rubbed his head roughly. "I don't want whoever did this to get away with it."

"I'm sure the police or whoever is investigating will find the murderer."

"They don't know the judge. We do. We can catch things they might miss."

Ciara stopped and stared. "We're just former clerks. We'd get in the way. Muck things up."

"Not when we can tell them what's different. If anything's odd."

"Don't you think Glenda will take care of that?"

Daniel studied her, darkness shadowing his gaze. "This murder makes me angry. You know Glenda. She's a great assistant, but she'll fall to pieces over the judge's death. You and I can move past that."

He stared at her, and she felt like she could see through him. "The judge gave me a chance no one else would. Even after clerking for him, no one would take on the young attorney from the wrong side of the tracks." He snorted. "Can you believe there's still such a thing? But there is."

"So? I still run into the good-old-boys club."

"This is Virginia." He shrugged. "Do you know why I started working with the deadbeat dads? Court appointments. Clear and simple. I had to pay the bills, and Judge Banter knew it. He helped me the only way he could. . .sending me those who qualified for free attorneys."

"I wish I'd known that."

Silence settled between them, and it felt good. Not awkward like when they'd landed in elevators together. Was Daniel still the same underneath everything? Maybe working with him on his wild-goose chase would give her a chance to find out.

The silence felt heavy. Did Ciara think he wanted to take a fool's mission? Probably. But he couldn't sit back and wait to see what happened. Not when anyone who worked around the law or read a crime novel knew those first few days were critical. And if the detectives missed something he could see. . . He wouldn't let that happen.

"All right. I think you're nuts, but as long as we don't get in the way, I'm in."

At Ciara's quiet words, he rallied. They could do this. Together. Just like when they worked for the judge and plotted grand strategies to take over the legal community.

"Where do you want to start?"

"I don't know." He'd never claimed he had a plan.

"I can touch base with Glenda tomorrow. Try to find out if anything unusual has happened."

"Maybe I'll track down his son." Daniel wondered if the college kid would take his call.

"It's worth a try. I got the sense after Mrs. Banter died they drifted apart."

"Alexander still might know something."

"The poor guy is all alone now." Ciara shuddered.

Daniel couldn't imagine missing Sunday brunch at his parents'. A command performance for all seven kids and, for those who had married, their families. And now Alexander wouldn't even have a father to call.

"Maybe you could offer to help him plan the service." Ciara's voice was so soft, he took a half step closer.

The service. He hadn't thought about a funeral yet. He stifled a groan as he considered what might be involved in planning it. "I'm glad the judge knew Christ."

"Me, too." This situation would be more terrible if the judge hadn't been a solid believer. Ciara shivered next to him. "Should we head back?"

"I guess I should have grabbed a jacket before heading out." She stopped and looked at him. "Do you want to come in for coffee?"

"Sounds good." The walk back to her town house was silent. He left his car where he'd parked. She walked in without unlocking the door. "Don't you lock the door?"

"Don't need to. See all the curtains fluttering?" She pointed back in the courtyard. He bit back a laugh as several flapped. "Those would be my girls. They watch my back and I watch theirs."

"That's great."

"You have no idea." She turned back to the large room. The walls were painted a vibrant salmon before melting into a bluish color that worked. It made him think of a vivid sunset and the rainbow of colors she usually tucked into her outfits even when wearing a stern suit in the courtroom.

A faint whistle sounded from around the corner. She bolted toward it before coming back around with a kettle. "Guess I forgot to turn this off."

"Don't do that often, do you?"

"Just days like today. Good thing it was full when I turned it on." She led him to the narrow galley kitchen. "I have tea or instant coffee."

Instant? He might have to rethink drinking anything. He must have wrinkled his nose or something, because she laughed.

"How about French press instead?"

"That sounds better."

She measured grounds into the press then added the water. They were quiet as the water darkened. She grabbed a couple of mugs from a cupboard and filled them. "Sugar or milk?"

"Still take it black."

"Guess I should have remembered."

He tensed. "Sorry. Black is great. And you'll have two teaspoons of sugar and some milk. And when you're done it's not really coffee anymore."

Color flooded her cheeks. "I add syrup now. Peppermint."

"Isn't that a Christmas flavor?"

"Only if you don't stock up."

She slipped past him and headed to a small love seat tucked under a window. The seat had a feminine print of some sort and, based on the books and coaster piled on the table in front of it, was her preferred place to relax. He glanced around but didn't see a TV anywhere. Not even a cabinet that could hide one. Instead, a solid walnut bookshelf filled the nook, every square inch lined with titles.

"What you expected?" She smiled over the top of her mug

at him. Guess he'd been busted.

"It's you."

"I like to think so. Where do you live?"

"A condo downtown."

She stopped drinking and stared. "DC?"

"Nah. Old Town Alexandria. One of the run-down town houses. Probably hasn't been renovated since the war."

"World War Two?"

"Civil. The only good Yankee is. . ."

"A dead Yankee."

Tears filled her eyes. "Judge Banter said it with teasing, but I always think of him when I see art from *the war*." She bracketed the words with her fingers. "Which side was the artist on?"

"He loved the Civil War. Did you know he was researching for a nonfiction book he wanted to write?"

She shook her head. "I didn't. Guess you were closer."

"No. Just interested." He had thought the judge was on the right track. More than revisionist history, his theories would transform the way the Battle of Manassas was interpreted. Could his death be related to his research? He took a swig of coffee and grimaced as it burned a track down his throat.

"That bad?" Ciara's eyes twinkled as she looked at him. "I offered sugar and milk."

"No, just had another thought." But as he met her gaze, he decided he wanted to make the most of this opportunity to show her they could recover what they had as young law school grads clerking for the world's best judge.

Chapter 3

The next morning Ciara sat at her desk, reliving the prior evening. After they talked a bit, a switch flipped and Daniel shifted from the murder into a charming companion. She'd laughed as he told stories about a client who brought his kids to the office. Each time the client did, Daniel found colored crayon gifts all over his walls.

She couldn't pull her thoughts back to work. Between Judge Banter's murder and Daniel's charm, she felt distracted and out of sorts. Maybe staying at work had been a mistake after all.

Linda hurried in with a stack of files, but slowed when she saw Ciara. Her sky blue eyes softened. "Are you okay?"

"I will be." She nodded to the pile. "What have you got for me?"

"A stack of new motions filed by opposing counsel in these matters. The most important is this file." Linda handed it across the desk. "The dad's moving for a reduction in child support. Claims his income has decreased 25 percent so his support obligation should, too."

"Is he represented?"

"Your favorite."

Ciara groaned. "And I was just starting to like him again."

"Not sure I'd waste the energy. Why does Mr. Evans always end up with the deadbeats?"

"He told me last night Judge Banter routinely fed those types of clients to him. All in an effort to help him build a practice."

"Humph. Not sure that helped him much. I never could understand why a guy as smart as him didn't land with a firm. Must not interview well."

Ciara couldn't stifle a laugh at the thought. Daniel's charisma should pull in whoever interviewed him and leave them begging for more. He had the engaging smile and direct gaze that made a person want to like him. In fact, if he practiced on her side of the cases, they'd still be friends. She was sure of it.

"Well, here you go." Linda patted the stack and moved to the door. "Let me know if you need anything. Oh, and your appointment is running behind."

"Will do." Ciara grabbed the top file and read through it. Another sob story from a father who claimed the world had collapsed on him. Sometimes it did. Even she could admit that. But sometimes, the dad resented his child support obligation and stopped working to avoid paying. She'd have to scan the file to determine this father's category.

Funny how one conversation could tilt her perspective about a man she'd thought she understood. Guess she'd jumped to conclusions. Though one good night didn't erase years of courtroom drama. Did it?

Ciara pulled up Glenda's number and waited for the call to ring.

"Hello?" The hollow voice sounded nothing like the usually vibrant Glenda.

"Ms. Baxter?"

"Who's this?"

"Ciara Turner. I'm so sorry about Judge Banter."

A soft sob filled the line. "You found him?"

"With Daniel, yes."

"I don't understand how something like this could happen. He never mentioned anything to me."

Ciara doodled on the legal pad next to her phone. "Did you notice anything unusual? People he saw, blocks of time he asked you not to schedule?"

"You sound like that detective." With Glenda's tone, Ciara couldn't tell if it was a compliment or not. "Each day was busy and full. You know the drill. Judge Banter packed every moment. That's why he came in so early. Especially since his wife died, he worked hard to get out of the court at a decent time. No more late nights since Alexander needed a parent."

"What happens to Alexander now?"

"The kid started college last fall. I imagine he'll stay in college, though I'm not sure I could hold it together. All alone at eighteen." Glenda's sigh mirrored Ciara's. "Why all the questions?"

"Daniel and I talked last night. I can't shake the image of the judge on the floor. Guess I feel a need to wrap my mind around what happened."

"If you figure it out, let me know. This is one event I'll never understand. I'm adding it to that list I'm taking with me to the Pearly Gates."

They chatted a couple more minutes before Linda tapped the edge of Ciara's door and pointed at her watch. "Glenda, gotta run. Client just arrived. Please let me know if you need anything."

Ciara tried to switch gears to custody matters and brace for her client and whatever stories she brought. A glance out the window had her wishing for time to escape outside for a quick walk in the spring air. Maybe with a certain someone at her side.

This tale would never end. Daniel was absolutely, completely convinced his client would never run out of terrible things to say about his ex. Days like this, Daniel wished he'd stayed in Leesburg to run his family's restaurant. Even days spent with clothes soaked with the aroma of grease would be better than listening to Ralph Manchiso spew this garbage.

He held up a hand, and his client sputtered to a stop. "I get the picture."

The burly guy crossed his arms and clenched his jaw. "I ain't done."

"I can continue to sit here, but you will get a bill for each minute. Or we can move on to what, if anything, you can do."

Ralph shrugged. "I ain't done."

"It's your money." Daniel sat back and tuned the rest of the words out. This guy didn't need an attorney. He needed a therapist. Too bad Daniel got to fill that role today. As he half listened, his thoughts wandered. He needed to track down Alexander Banter. Probably shouldn't call Glenda, since Ciara would contact her.

Last night had been good. Really good. Amazing how a short walk, a cup of java, and a little conversation could restart something he'd thought couldn't be resurrected.

"You listening to me?" Ralph thumped a fist on the table. "If you're gonna bill me, you oughta listen."

Daniel tugged his attention to the man. Better to concentrate and extricate the man from the building than get him riled. The man had the temper to back his restraining order. Finally, an hour later he escorted the man from the office. When he walked back in, his assistant—his "man Friday"—shook his head.

"That guy is the worst we have." Clive Tillman sank into his chair at the reception desk.

"Nice of you to conveniently disappear from your desk."

The kid looked unrepentant as he pushed up his shirtsleeves. "The guy gives me the creeps."

Daniel shook his head. "This is exactly why I don't have a female receptionist."

"You know that's discrimination."

"Nope. Protection. I wouldn't want a lady to have to deal with him." He eyed Clive's lanky form folded behind the desk. "You shouldn't have any concerns."

Clive reached for a stack of phone slips. "Here are your messages."

Daniel flipped through them as he took the few steps to his office. The small waiting area, his office, an office supply room doubling as a library, and a small kitchenette and conference room rounded out his space. Not bad for the few years he'd been in practice. It had taken hard work and long hours, but he'd turned the corner and could see some fruit. He just had to remind himself on days like this, clients like that last one were worth it only because they facilitated everything else he did.

When he returned to his office, Daniel sank onto his mesh desk chair and kicked back a moment. He needed to do a quick search for Alexander—he'd find something online. Every kid at a minimum had a Facebook or similar site. Then he could call later. If the kid was in college, he'd either be in class or asleep since it was before ten in the morning. He turned to his computer and started clicking away. Bingo. A blog. What did a kid have to share with the world? After scanning a couple of entries, Daniel realized Alexander had a unique way of looking at international affairs. He seemed to see everything through a different lens. Daniel clicked to the bio and grinned. Of course, the kid was a student in Georgetown's School of Foreign Service. Now his blog made perfect sense.

Daniel could track him down now, especially if Alexander lived on campus. A call to the switchboard, and he'd be patched through to the appropriate dorm room. Not as good as a cell, but it would start the connecting process.

As expected, he left a quick message. He'd bet pizza money the kid wouldn't return the call, but now he had a number. It wouldn't take much to get a room location either. Then he could stop by and see how the freshman was holding up.

A few more times over the course of the day, Daniel tried to reach Alexander. The result never changed. The same garbled answering machine picked up. When the day ended, Daniel hopped in his car and headed through traffic into the city and west to Georgetown. He'd love to leave the car, but without a closer Metro stop, he'd walk too far to reach the dorms. Instead, he spent time scouting for an elusive parking spot.

The kid lived in Village C, one of the residence halls in the heart of campus. Daniel couldn't imagine arriving unannounced at the hall, so he pulled out his cell and tried one last time as he hoofed it across campus.

"Hello?" It sounded like Alexander had a cold. His husky voice reminded Daniel of the somber purpose of his call.

"Alexander, this is Daniel Evans. I used to clerk for your dad."

"So?"

Daniel bit his tongue. He'd give the kid a little slack for the rudeness. "I was one of the people who found him yesterday. Do you need any help right now? I'm on campus and could meet you."

The husky tone of the kid's voice transitioned to hostility. "Look. I don't need strangers around or the media."

"I don't mean to intrude. Ciara Turner—she also clerked for your father—and I wondered if you had anyone planning the service. We could..." For someone who had a silver tongue, none of this came out as he'd imagined. "I don't know how you're doing, but I'd like to help. If I can ease some of the stuff you have to deal with, I'd like to." That was marginally better.

"You found him?"

"Along with Ciara. We were supposed to have an early meeting with him."

"I would like a cup of coffee." Alexander gave him directions to one of the student-run coffeehouses. Ten minutes later, Daniel waited at an outdoor table, the sun beginning to slip behind the skyscrapers surrounding the campus.

His phone rang while he sat, and he quickly filled in Ciara. They made plans for another walk. . .a chance to share what they'd learned. He closed his phone and turned his attention to the students filling the sidewalk. How would he know the right college student in the flood that was trying to reach their next class on time? He searched the foot traffic anyway. A few minutes later a lanky young man with a five o'clock shadow ambled to a stop in front of him. The kid's gray eyes were bloodshot and red-rimmed. Daniel imagined he hadn't slept much since his dad's death.

Daniel stood. "Alexander?" The kid nodded. "What can I get you?"

"A black coffee." He slouched at the table while Daniel

went in and got their drinks.

It felt awkward as the two sat at the small bistro table, the umbrella's edges flapping in the breeze. The scent of flowering trees carried toward them and mixed with feelings of somberness that draped Alexander like a coat he'd outgrown.

"So what did Dad look like?" Alexander studied his coffee as if expecting to find answers for the crazy events of the last couple of days.

"He was down on the floor. There weren't puddles of blood or anything like that. Almost like someone hit him on the head."

"The police aren't telling me anything." Alexander glanced up for just a moment. "I guess they're trying to protect me...but I want the truth."

"So do we, Alexander. So do we."

Chapter 4

Ciara sat on her front stoop as the day slid into dusk. The trees lining the sidewalks had erupted in blossoms and she let the image soak in, replacing the stress of the day. She'd learned early in her practice that she had to find a way to release each day's troubles. In the summer she used the community pool a few feet from her back door. In the spring, moments like this recalibrated her.

If traffic hadn't held him up, Daniel would arrive soon.

She wasn't sure what she thought of that.

The judge's murder had cast them together, put them on the same side for the first time in years. But she had to be careful. Remind herself how he'd broken her heart once. Everyone could call her a fool if she let him back in without any hesitation.

She sat on the border of doing just that.

Letting him slide back into her life as if nothing had ever changed. But it had.

She rubbed her temples and tried to think about anything else. Even one of her non-Daniel cases would work. She had to face reality. Once the police caught whoever murdered Judge Banter, things would return to normal. Daniel wouldn't call a couple of times a day and make plans to stop by in the evening.

They wouldn't share cups of coffee and strategy.

Instead, they'd return to being opponents, squarely defending the rights and needs of their clients. At odds with each other on multiple levels.

"Enjoying the evening?"

Ciara startled and dropped her hands in her lap as Susan Holland settled next to her. The woman looked as relaxed and neat as always, the picture of a woman at peace with her life. Bet she didn't see the beginning of crow's-feet when she looked in the mirror.

"Yes. I love this neighborhood and the way it explodes into spring."

Susan looked unconvinced, her brown eyes seeming to see through Ciara. "A case bothering you? That's usually what makes you all pensive."

"Not tonight." There were some things she couldn't share with her sweet neighbor. Not yet.

"Well, bring him by Coffee, Tea, and Sweets. I'll save some of my best scones for you if you call the shop ahead."

Ciara grinned. "I didn't say I was thinking about a man."

"What else would it be since it's not a client? And I'm glad to see it. You need someone who sees how special you are." The woman patted her hand then stood. "I've got to get ready for my book club. The girls'll be over shortly, and I still have cookies to make. I hope they like this new recipe I'm trying. Delores can be a tad picky."

"I'm sure they'll love them. Everything you make is delicious."

"You're sweet. Good night."

"Night." The sound of a man's shoes clomped in the growing darkness. Ciara peered that direction, then smiled when she spotted Daniel. She stood and brushed off her jeans.

"Still up for a walk?" Fatigue etched lines around Daniel's eyes as he stood in front of her.

"How's Alexander?"

"I'm not sure. He started out hostile, then turned really sad. Didn't want help, though. Seems determined to strike out on his own from the beginning."

"Can't blame him. Yet what a hard thing to do."

"He said the police haven't released the body yet, so he's not sure when the funeral will be."

"Surely they'll speed up the autopsy. He was a judge."

"It'll still take time." Daniel rubbed his head in a brisk motion, then pointed down the sidewalk. "Ready?"

"Sure." Ciara locked her door and then joined him.

They walked side by side as they retraced their route from the previous night. They stopped when they reached the bridge over I-395. Below, the headlights of cars raced, heading into the city and down into the Virginia suburbs. Daniel seemed lost in thought, not attempting to keep up banter. As the silence stretched, Ciara wondered why he'd bothered to join her. Being alone wasn't so bad in light of his brooding.

She bumped his shoulder. "What's eating you?"

He started and glanced down at her. "What?"

"You're a million miles away. Why come if you didn't want to? I didn't make you."

"I couldn't stomach going home to nothing."

The words branded her. "Thanks."

"Wait, that's not what I meant." Daniel stifled a groan. "Today everything's coming out strange."

"This from the guy who won every moot court competition he entered?" Ciara arched an eyebrow, and in the light of the streetlamps he could tell she wasn't biting.

"My wit abandoned me."

"That happens. But seriously, go home. I'm not someone to mark time with. Either be here or go."

Her words hit him in the chest like a line drive. He could remember every moment of the last time she'd thrown them at him. Still regretted walking away. Not fighting for her. Guess he had a choice this time. Would she let him make it? Her posture tensed as if she'd braced for him to stalk off like he had the last time. Instead, he forced his shoulders to relax.

"I'm not going anywhere, Ciara."

"This time?"

He nodded. "I've regretted leaving."

"Then why did you?" He saw moisture reflected in her eyes. "I stayed right here."

It had seemed the right choice at the time. Now he knew he'd turned into a coward that night and all the nights following. Ciara had paid the price. Maybe she'd give him a chance to fix it. Make things right. Earn the right to be with her again.

Maybe.

Daniel's eyes tried to send her a message, but in the shadows, Ciara couldn't read them. Just once, she wished he'd come out and say it. Whatever was on his mind, just spit it out. What made it so hard for him to own what he'd done?

He'd left.

She'd stayed.

And then they collided in court. Two planets destined to crash and explode whenever they intersected. She loved the attraction, hated the collisions.

She shoved her hands in her pockets and turned away from the traffic flying by below. It was time to head home. "I'm sorry, Daniel."

As she walked away, she listened. Would he follow?

The whizzing of cars threatened to overlay any other noise, but she couldn't hear him. She bit back a tear at the realization he wouldn't follow her tonight. She shouldn't have expected anything else.

Two days later, Clive buzzed Daniel. "Detective on the phone for you."

Maybe the man had news for him. Good news. Daniel desperately needed some as his thoughts continued to cycle back to the night he let Ciara walk away—again. "Thanks."

He picked up the phone and punched the blinking light. "Evans here."

"This is Detective Howard. I'm working Judge Banter's murder."

"Yes, sir. What can I do for you today?"

"Do you know if the judge had any health conditions?"

"No." Daniel scoured his memory. "He hadn't mentioned anything the last few times we met."

"All right."

"Have you talked to Alexander? He could at least tell you who his dad's doctor was."

"He didn't know. Typical kid. Out of touch with his parents' health. And there are no prescriptions at the house. We'll keep digging."

"Any suspects?"

"A few, but can't mention them in an ongoing investigation." The detective's voice indicated he thought an attorney should know that answer.

"Sorry I couldn't be more help."

The detective thanked him and hung up. Daniel's fingers hovered over the numbers, poised to dial Ciara. Had she received a similar call? Maybe if he hadn't let her walk away, he could call. Instead, it felt like the chasm between them had widened again rather than shrinking. He was a fool.

Ciara kept waiting for something—something she didn't want to define. But if she looked at her cell phone one more time, just to make sure she hadn't somehow missed a call, she would chuck it out the nearest window so the closest vehicle could run over it.

No man should have this much control over her thoughts, especially Daniel.

She groaned. She'd done it again, let her thoughts cycle around when they should be focused on her job.

Her clients added meaning to her days. If she could protect one woman and her children, she'd done something that mattered. But could she really do that anyway? She wasn't God. She could only do her best to provide some boundaries.

"Get up." Linda stood in the doorway, Vera Bradley bag hooked over her shoulder. "It's time to get you out of here."

When Linda had that look in her eye, Ciara hopped to attention. The woman's instincts had been aroused, so she might as well go along. Otherwise, she wouldn't hear the end of Linda's mothering. Ciara tugged her purse from her bottom desk drawer and stood. "Where are we going?"

"Somewhere we can clear your head." As soon as they exited the office, Linda made a beeline for King Street. She set a pace that made Ciara almost trot to keep up.

"Where's the emergency?"

"You need some ice cream therapy."

"I don't know about the therapy, but ice cream sounds good."

"Of course." Linda lowered her sunglasses just enough to let Ciara know how ridiculous her statement was. "Every girl needs it from time to time. Now spill the beans."

"I don't know what you mean."

"Don't play dumb. I may be your paralegal, but I've worked with you long enough to know when something is eating through you. I don't think it's a client situation this time. We haven't had an emergency in several weeks. So what is it?"

Ciara's steps slowed. Linda was much more than her assistant. The woman's kind care and concern had won her over almost from Linda's first day on the job. If anyone at the office really knew Ciara, she was the one. But that didn't mean Ciara wanted to lay everything out for inspection.

Linda slowed her pace as they neared Scoop's Grill and Homemade Ice Cream. The deep green storefront gave way to an inside with a refreshingly short line. Often the line would extend outside, and Ciara didn't have that kind of time for a quick break.

"So are you going to say anything?"

"Other than the Rocky Road, what looks good?"

Linda rolled her eyes, then chuckled. "All right. You don't have to say anything. But if you don't shake whatever's bothering you, the big boss is going to notice. I'm surprised you haven't yanked your cell out half a dozen times to check it for calls."

"Am I that pathetic?"

"Lately. . .yes." Linda placed her order then paid. "I know the judge dying shocked you, but that doesn't explain all this."

Ciara accepted her paper dish of gooey pistachio ice cream. "I know. Let's just say it's reopened old wounds. The kind I'm a fool to entertain."

"So why do that?"

Ciara took a bite, letting the creamy flavor slide down her throat as she bought time. "I'm a glutton for torture?"

Linda shook her head. "Try again."

"I'm a fool who believes true love exists." The moment the words left, she cringed. She had not meant to say those words out loud. Not even to Linda.

Linda scooped a bite into her mouth and dug out another. She pointed the loaded spoon at Ciara. "True love exists. But it takes a lot of work. The kind that doesn't run when something gets tough."

"Did you somehow join us on our walk?"

"Us? Meaning Daniel Evans?"

"Yeah." Ciara pushed back out on the sidewalk. "I told you I'm a fool. He's already hurt me once, and I let him walk right back in after one nice evening."

"But you walked away?" Linda's brow furrowed as she followed.

"I did." Ciara grimaced and pulled her shoulders up. "Can you believe it? We were talking, and I walked away like a fool. And I wanted him to follow me. What a waste of hope."

Chapter 5

A waste of hope. The words echoed through her mind as Ciara tried to focus on her job. When had romance and true love devolved to something too painful to risk? When she and Daniel first broke things off.

She'd been convinced they had forever in front of them. A bright future working together, righting the wrongs of their little corner of the world. That happily-ever-after never materialized, and she'd let the disappointment kill her hope of ever finding love. Working on so many broken marriages didn't help her perspective. It was easy to become jaded. To believe anything else came from watching one too many Disney cartoons as a kid. She'd bought into the whole idea that there was one man out there who would complete her and make her whole.

She knew better. Really she did. Life had shown her Jesus was the only One who would never leave her.

Where did one buy hope and learn not to spend it frivolously on people who didn't respond?

She pulled on her trench coat and added a stack of case files to her briefcase. Nothing like a little late-night reading to keep her occupied. Maybe she could make up for her wandering thoughts. She walked to her car and then drove up King Street to her neighborhood. When she pulled into the cul-de-sac, she slammed on the brakes.

What was he doing here?

Daniel leaned against his car, legs crossed and his hands crammed in his pockets. His sports jacket looked rumpled, and his hair mussed like he'd just run his fingers through it again. She eased the BMW into the parking spot next to his older sedan.

"You could get your car towed if you leave it here." What an opening line.

A tired smile lifted the corner of his mouth. "That's why I didn't leave." He studied her a moment. "I hope I won't have to leave it here long."

"What?"

"Join me for supper tonight." He glanced down at the pavement. "I want to make it up to you."

"Make what up?" The man didn't make any sense.

"Letting you walk away." He looked up, his gaze colliding with hers with such intensity she almost jolted. "Give me another chance?"

She searched his eyes. Could she open her heart again, risk him hurting her? She tugged her lower lip between her teeth. Everything in her screamed no, except for a small corner of hope that whispered it could be okay if she'd risk it all. "Okay. But don't do something like that again."

Daniel shoved his hands in his pockets to resist reaching out and touching the strand of hair that had escaped her ear. How like Ciara to agree, but then tack on her own stipulations. He'd seen that maneuver a hundred times. "Do you need a few minutes to get ready?"

"No more than five."

"I'll wait here." He gestured to his car. "Make sure this piece of metal doesn't get towed."

She studied him another moment, her hazel eyes probing his, and he wondered if she found whatever she looked for. Part of him questioned why he'd come. They seemed destined to act like two magnets, attracted and repelled all at the same time. It was a maddening dance, but one he had to try again. Maybe this time they'd get the steps right and avoid each other's toes.

He flipped around and placed his elbows on the roof so he could watch for her return. After another long day, he'd considered heading home, but the detective's call had made him reluctant to spend the evening alone.

All those meals by himself got repetitious. And while many women thought dating an attorney was great, many were reluctant to get too close to someone who specialized in the law of broken families. Didn't exactly feed their longings for happily ever after.

"Waiting for someone—or stalking her?"

Daniel startled and whipped around. A woman in her forties studied him. "Waiting."

"All right. Treat her gently."

"Do I know you?"

The woman laughed. "I don't believe we've ever met. But I have the feeling you're the man giving Ciara so much trouble. I'm Susan Holland. I live in that unit there."

"Daniel Evans. Nice to meet you?"

"Nice to meet you, but I'm serious. Be careful around her. She deserves someone who will treat her like a princess."

"Yes, ma'am." Daniel wasn't sure what else to say to an assault like that. He straightened with some relief when Ciara hurried from her town house.

"Hello, Susan. Ready to go, Daniel?"

"Absolutely."

"Have a nice evening."

Ciara slipped into his car then turned to him. "Did she give you a hard time?"

"No," he bluffed. "Why would you think that?"

"Something about the shell-shocked look around your eyes. Where are we headed?"

"Shirlington? I know it's close, but there are some great restaurants there."

"Sounds perfect."

Daniel pointed his car down the hill and, in a few moments, slid into a parking space in the parking garage. He opened the passenger door and waited for Ciara to slide from the vehicle. "Feel like the Carlyle?"

Ciara paused and looked at the cranberry red awning. The food was always excellent at the Carlyle, but did she think it was too formal for the night? "How about the Capital City Brewing Company? A burger sounds good."

Sound invariably ricocheted off the concrete floor while the high stools made it easy to mix and mingle in a group. It provided a casual atmosphere compared to the Carlyle, but Daniel didn't know if that was what he wanted tonight. Although, after his stunt earlier in the week, he decided to let her take the lead. This time he'd follow, even if it was to a nice burger joint.

She maneuvered among the tables set outside and into the restaurant. In no time, a hostess led them to a black Formica table in a corner. Daniel thanked her, hoping the location would give him a chance to actually hear Ciara. In short order, a waitress had glasses of tea in front of them and had collected their orders.

Ciara sat across the table, twisting the edges of the paper napkin wrapped around her silverware. Her jittery edge made him again regret letting her leave.

"I'm sorry, Ciara." He reached across and stilled her fingers. A jolt of electricity shot up his arm, and he pulled back. "Forgive me."

She considered him through glazed eyes. Had she felt the jolt, too? Then she seemed to snap out of whatever place she'd disappeared. "Yes." She glanced down and uncurled the napkin, settling it across her lap. "But I'm not sure how many more times I'll let you do that."

"I understand." What else could he say? It wasn't like they could launch any kind of serious relationship.

Ciara studied him. He still didn't get it. Didn't understand the hurt he'd inflicted when he hadn't fought for her. That was what the prince did. Battled for his girl, even if the fight was with her.

She needed to know she mattered. More than what, she couldn't say. Simply that she mattered more.

A throb pounded a steady beat in her temple. She resisted the urge to step away, protect herself, and abort the headache. "Daniel, what is it you want?"

"Sorry?" He leaned back and crossed his arms across his chest. Even in khakis and a polo, he had an air of authority that had the women at nearby tables glancing his way. He brushed a lock of wavy hair off his forehead, and Ciara could almost hear the collective swoon.

"Is friendship what we can attain?" She gestured at the space between them. "Or is there more?"

"I don't know." He looked like he regretted bringing her here.

How long until the appetizer arrived? They needed something to look at other than each other. How sad was that? Two adults who couldn't carry on a simple conversation. Discussing their jobs didn't work. Instant jump to conflict. What else did they have in common?

"So where are you going to church?"

Daniel's quiet question caught her off guard. "Me?" she asked.

He glanced around, a small smile on his lips. "See anyone else with us?"

"You don't have to use sarcasm." Yet she couldn't help a grin. "There's a community church right off King Street that's not too far from my neighborhood. It's a smallish congregation, but I like knowing most of those who call it home. Are you going somewhere?"

"Just switched to a non-denom in downtown DC. It meets in a theater, kind of different, but the pastor gets me every week. Being uncomfortable is a good thing."

Ciara had to nod. She loved that her pastor seemed to nail her each week with ways her life needed to change to better reflect Christ. "I don't remember you talking about church much when we clerked."

Daniel shrugged. "It wasn't that important. But I couldn't be around a man like Judge Banter without wanting to learn more about how life could be infused with Christ in such a natural way. More than Sundays, but not preachy, if that makes sense."

"It does." Ciara prayed her life contained that same natural fragrance of Christ. "How do you reconcile that—" She stopped short. She did not want to bring up work. Not tonight.

"With my job?" He leaned forward, closing the distance between them. "Can you believe that just like some attorneys are committed to every accused person having a criminal defense, I'm committed to men having an attorney even if they aren't great dads or husbands? Some have tried. Others don't care. But they all get their defense. Maybe you'll never accept that, but it's who I am."

"What if you could find a firm to work for?"

"Look at me. I don't want those strings. Sure, it's not easy being my own boss, but I control my schedule and which clients I accept. There's no pressure—" She quirked an eyebrow at him, and he continued. "Okay, no pressure, other than making payroll and rent, to take on every potential client."

"I don't know that we can reconcile that difference."

"Then we'll have to be acquaintances."

The thought left her empty and cold. She'd enjoyed spending time with Daniel over the last week. She'd missed his camaraderie, but this difference went to the core of who she was. To her sense of justice and right and wrong. She couldn't just walk away from what she believed. She swallowed as she searched her mind for another conversation topic.

The waitress saved her by placing the appetizer between them. Soon they dipped various fried delights in different sauces as they discussed the chaos on Capitol Hill.

After dinner they strolled the length of Shirlington, stopping to read the list of movies showing at the theater. The eclectic mix of first run and foreign films caught her attention.

Too bad she didn't have more time to see movies or someone to take her. She glanced at Daniel, but he studiously kept his attention on the board. Guess there was no chance this night would evolve into dinner and a movie. What did she expect when she'd so thoroughly shot down what he did?

This was why she remained single.

In a city filled with career-driven people, she shoved away the only man who'd held her interest. She should have focused on the way he brought up church and his faith rather than what he did Monday through Friday, but she couldn't divorce the two.

Her faith compelled her to work with the clients she did.

Could it be the same for him? Even if he worked for those wearing black hats?

"Let it go, Ciara." Daniel's voice startled her.

"What?"

"Quit analyzing everything. It might work well in the courtroom, but it doesn't work here. Sometimes you have to let go and have faith."

"Let go? With you?" She clamped her lips together before she started ranting. This coming from the man who couldn't decide what he wanted. "Thanks for the advice."

He stared at her, sadness clouding his eyes, until she felt heat rush up her.

"I'm sorry. Maybe you should take me home."

"Maybe I should. I wish things could be different."

As he left her at her front door, she longed to reach out to him. To call him back. To tell him that it didn't matter, they'd find a way to make things work out.

But she didn't.

Because it did matter.

Chapter 6

The days passed with no leads. Dignitaries and others packed Judge Banter's funeral when it was finally held two weeks later, but Ciara sat in the church alone. She tried not to search the crowd for Daniel, but she couldn't keep her gaze from traveling to the other side of the sanctuary where he sat. Then he stood and made his way to the front to give one of the eulogies. Tears collected in her throat as she listened to him recount the virtues of a man who gave them both a singular experience at a pivotal time in their careers. As he spoke, his eyes sought hers, and she felt mesmerized by the intensity in his. It felt as if a silent plea to understand who he was traveled across the chasm that separated them. The moment the service ended, she stood and skedaddled to her car, still shaken by what had passed between them in the church.

She sank into her car, then locked the door. The keys remained tightly in her grasp as she tried to understand what had happened.

What was left to know? They were too different.

No matter how much she felt the jolt of physical attraction each time they shared space in a building, she couldn't open her heart to the possibility that something could happen between them.

That night she pulled on a pair of yoga pants and a fitted T-shirt and scooped her hair back with a stretchy headband. She brewed a cup of tea and settled onto the love seat.

Any other night she'd find herself absorbed in the novel she'd started by her favorite suspense writer, but she couldn't get lost in the plot and pages.

She set the book aside. Was she wrong? She didn't like the thought. She prided herself on reading people well. That was what had stung with Daniel. She'd been so wrong. Right or wrong, she had to reach a resolution she could live with. Soon she'd find herself back at a table next to his in one of the area's courtrooms. They'd sit on opposite sides of a family crisis, and she had to find a way to live with that. She'd rather not be bothered by his presence at all, but for the moment she'd settle with not falling to distraction when she saw him.

Was that too much to ask?

The curtain fluttered against the back of her neck, bringing a kiss of goose bumps.

She picked up her cell phone and slid over to the calendar. Colored blocks filled the next week, a dizzying mix of client meetings and hearings. Three involved Daniel.

She set the phone down and wondered if she could declare a desperate need for vacation time. Surely she could claim the chaos of the prior weeks as evidence that her life hadn't filled normal parameters, and any woman would need a few days, maybe a few weeks, to reorient herself to the idea that she'd found the body of her mentor. The partners might argue she should have asked earlier, but she could always blame a delayed reaction. Surely things like that happened all the time.

A girl could wish.

Daniel waited for Alexander Banter to pick up the phone. He couldn't shake the kid from his thoughts, especially after the funeral. Someone needed to make sure Judge Banter's son held up okay, but Daniel couldn't trust others would do it. However, the kid never answered his phone the first or fifth time he called. Must have driven Judge Banter nuts.

If the kid didn't answer, Daniel would have to wait and try again after the next client meeting. He hoped Alexander would comply because he could use any reason to delay the inevitable meeting with Ciara and her client.

He couldn't shake the quiet desperation mixed with distance that had filled her expression when his gaze collided with hers at the funeral. Neither could he alter the reality that she had dashed out of the funeral before he could get out of his row. If that wasn't the definition of avoiding him, he didn't know how the dictionary would describe it. To her it might look like he'd let her leave. . .again.

Alexander's voice mail kicked in. "Leave a message for the man who is now free."

Huh?

Daniel hit SEND again and waited for the message to come up once more. Maybe the kid was in a weird philosophy class, but that message didn't make much sense. Daniel cleared his throat. "Alexander, it's Daniel Evans. Wanted to check in. Call if you need anything."

He ended the call reluctantly, then stared at a painting hanging across the office. Its rich frame hugged an image of an executive slumped in his office chair after a long day. Jesus knelt in front of him, washing his feet. Most days the image comforted him, especially the idea that Jesus saw how he worked for others, and that even when others didn't notice, Jesus did.

Today, though, he felt convicted. As if it reminded him he hadn't done enough.

Enough of what and for whom, Lord?

He kept reaching out to Alexander. He took on the clients others didn't want, often without regard for whether they'd pay his bill. What had he overlooked?

The silence didn't break as he waited.

The phone sputtered to life. "She's here. With a client." Clive's tone bordered on unkind and left no question who he meant.

"Show them to the conference room." Daniel should get up. He should grab his file and move across the hall. But he couldn't. Not with all the soul-searching still left to do when it came to Ciara. Had he treated her in an unChristlike manner?

He didn't want to think too hard about the answer, but she waited in the other room. Clive likely had grabbed a Diet Mountain Dew for her, one of the few Daniel kept stocked for the times she had to venture to his office. Did she notice the details? Probably not, and why would she? In this forum they were enemies, but he wanted to change that.

Clive's demeanor was cold as he led Ciara and her client Julie Stephens to the conference room and handed her a Diet Mountain Dew out of the small refrigerator.

"Thank you."

He nodded, then turned to Julie. "Anything for you, ma'am?"

Julie frowned. "A diet cola if you won't call me ma'am. Makes me feel ancient. My husband's already done a good job of that by trading me in."

Clive had the good grace to color as he retrieved the can. "Here you are, miss."

"Much better. Thanks." Julie sank onto one of the leather chairs pushed against the table. "So you think anything good will happen today?"

"Maybe we'll hammer out the settlement."

"I was still hoping for a miracle."

Ciara considered her a moment. While she wanted to believe in miracles, she hadn't seen enough of them for her clients. "It's possible, I suppose."

"Not exactly a ringing expectation."

"You know me, left-brain dominant, hard rule of my emotions." What a joke when it came to her personal life, but Julie didn't know that. Ciara popped the top of her soda and took a sip. And Julie never would understand, so long as Ciara could get firmly behind her wall before Daniel walked in. For once, she didn't mind waiting for him to wrap up whatever he worked on in the other room. She simply wasn't prepared to pretend his actions didn't wound her.

"Still carry a flame for this guy?"

Ciara spewed diet soda all over the table. She coughed and searched for a tissue in her pockets. "What?"

"Come on. Just because my happily-ever-after didn't work out doesn't mean I'm immune to sparks the size of the Fourth of July fireworks on the Mall. Watching the two of you skirt the obvious is the only thing making this hideous process bearable."

"Then I'm truly sorry." Ciara stood and grabbed some paper towels from a roll hanging over a small sink. She mopped up the mess, then wet a towel and wiped the table down again.

The door opened, and Daniel stepped into the room. In an instant the walls seemed to crowd around her, and she straightened, the limp paper towel dripping on the table.

"Place not clean enough for you?" Daniel's quirked eyebrow couldn't hide the twinkle.

Julie caught her gaze, a knowing light in her eyes.

And all Ciara wanted to do was crawl under the table, or better yet, out the door.

Daniel should have felt bad, but he didn't. Instead, he pictured a hundred and one different scenarios that left Ciara leaning over his table with a tattered paper towel, cleaning up some unknown substance. It was too fun not to poke at her.

"Where's my husband?" Julie Stephens skewered him with her eyes.

"I regret to inform you that he called to say he won't make the meeting."

Julie growled, then turned on Ciara. "I told you this was a waste of time. That man refuses to see how his childish actions impact anyone but himself."

Ciara turned on Daniel. "And you couldn't call us? Tell us not to bother coming here?"

Daniel held up his hands. "If I'd known, I would have. Clive just now handed me the message when I asked where Lawrence was." And he'd have to get on Clive for not delivering the message immediately. He couldn't blame Ciara and Julie for being irate. He'd feel the same if in their position.

"Then I guess we'll take this to the judge." Ciara tossed the towel on the table. "We'd like to resolve this without a nasty, long hearing, but if your client won't even come to a meeting, he's leaving us no choice."

"Now wait a minute. I'm sure he has a good reason."

"Like taking his mistress shopping," Julie muttered.

Ciara shot her a glance that told her to keep out of the fray. Daniel doubted it would do any good with Julie. The woman wasn't much easier to control than her husband, but at least she was here. "Look, I'm really sorry. I didn't know, and I will give my client a what-for about it. Is there anything we can accomplish without him?"

Ciara looked at him like he'd suddenly grown a unicorn's horn in the middle of his forehead. "I can't imagine what."

"All right. Meet you at motion hour later this week to schedule the hearing?"

"Thank you." Ciara grabbed her briefcase but paused as Julie brushed past her.

Daniel placed a restraining hand on Ciara's arm. "Do you have a minute?"

Ciara glanced from his hand to his face. "A very quick one."

Now that she'd agreed to hear him out, he didn't know what to say. Other than the vague impression he'd had in his office, nothing had changed. It was time to do something about that. He didn't like the status quo, so he needed to act. He took a deep breath.

"Would you go to dinner with me tonight?"

Now, he had no doubt she believed he'd grown a horn. "Dinner? Tonight? Are you crazy?"

"Yes, I'm going crazy not seeing you. Ciara, most of my best days involve you, and I can't just walk away like we've done in the past. I know I've somehow hurt you." He held up a hand as she started to sputter. "Give me a chance. You know guys stink at emotion." She closed her mouth and crossed her arms. "I don't want to let you slip away. I want to see if we have a fighting chance."

"We seem to do the fighting part well."

"Actually we don't. One of us walks away as soon as the other indicates there's something deeper to talk about. We have to stop that." He rubbed his hands over his hair. "Ciara, anything of value is worth a fight."

Chapter 7

How did one prepare for a dinner that might be a date, but shouldn't register as one?

She'd call Tara or Susan for advice if she had time, but she barely had time to freshen up as it was.

A date? Ciara sighed as she weighed what that would mean. Could she take that step?

After years of not trusting Daniel, she found herself ready to try. He'd shown his character to mirror that of the law clerk she'd fallen in love with. Maybe she'd been unfair to lump him into the same category as so many of his clients. He had a point that they deserved someone to protect their rights. . .she just wished he wasn't the one doing it.

She turned to her closet and stared at the clothes hanging neatly there, uncertain how to dress. Would a silk dress be too nice? Make it look like she cared what Daniel thought? But a pantsuit seemed too rigid; and a sweater set, while feminine, felt too casual. Dinner should not turn into a complicated wardrobe issue.

With a glance at her watch, Ciara grabbed a floral dress that swirled around her calves in frothy layers. She'd pair it with a rich aubergine cardigan—a compromise between too casual and too formal.

She hurried through a shower and blow-dried her hair. The soft blond waves framed her face as she added makeup. After a last glance in the mirror, she pulled on a pair of dark purple pumps and clomped down the stairs to the living room and her love seat. She adored her town house's wood floors, but at times like this, the noise made her feel as graceful as an overweight elephant. She plopped onto the cushion, then grabbed a magazine. Five minutes later, she couldn't remember a single word she'd read.

A brisk knock pulled her back to her feet. She stood, opened the door, and stilled at the expression that brushed across Daniel's face.

He whistled, low and a note that wrapped around her heart. "Wow! You look amazing."

Ciara swept a hand down the length of her skirt. "Thanks." She turned and grabbed her purse and beige trench coat. "Where to?"

"It's a surprise." He devoured her with his gaze for another minute, then offered her his arm. "Shall we?"

She nodded, and he led her to his car. Soon his sedan pointed down King Street, soft classical music filling the silence. She stared out the window, mesmerized as the Washington Memorial came into view, silhouetted in stark relief against the dark sky. It always struck her as the gate standing between Old Town and its neighbors. They passed the Metro station, and soon Daniel's head swiveled as he looked for a parking space.

"Here we go." He found a spot on Lee Street. Before she could open the door, he'd slid out and walked around. "My lady."

Ciara accepted his hand and tried to climb gracefully from the car. His hand slipped naturally to the small of her back as he guided her back toward King Street. This wasn't normal. She couldn't sink into the emotion and protection the simple gesture offered. She tried to add another layer to her wall, but couldn't.

Soon they were in the lobby of her favorite Italian restaurant. Its brick walls and wooden floor served as the perfect backdrop to the small tables covered in red-checked oilcloth. The waiter handed them menus, but she didn't bother opening hers.

Daniel arched an eyebrow. "Know what you want already?"

"Yes. The veal scaloppini alla picatta is one of my favorites."

"Still tend to stick with your favorites?"

"Yes, sir. Once I like something, why risk disappointment?"

"Not very adventuresome."

"I went to law school. That was enough adventure for me."

Daniel chuckled. His head swiveled slightly as he scanned the room. A cloud collected on his features as his gaze locked on something. He seemed to stare more intently, and Ciara sensed him slipping away from their pleasant evening. She started to turn to see what had captured him, but he squeezed her hand.

"What is it?"

"Who."

"Who?"

"The son of a recently deceased judge is over there having the time of his life."

Ciara didn't care what Daniel said; she pivoted and then felt her jaw drop. Alexander Banter sat at a table surrounded by a couple of college coeds. He looked like anything but a grieving son. Instead, he hefted a mug of beer high as if in a toast. Whatever he said, it made the girls laugh. A flush of heat raced through Ciara at the image. "What is he doing?"

"That's the question of the hour." Daniel pulled out his phone and hit some buttons. He flipped the phone around to her. "I'll take these photos to the detective tomorrow. Maybe they need to look into Alexander a bit."

Ciara swallowed back a wave of bile. "I can't believe Alexander would do something like that."

"Well, I know if I were the grieving son, I wouldn't be out partying days after the funeral."

"What's he supposed to do?" Her mind raced for a logical conclusion, one that would stand up in court and didn't involve the son murdering his father. "And why on earth would he kill his dad? It doesn't make sense."

"Maybe, but I'm going to dig."

"Daniel." She let the word draw out. "Don't go looking for a killer everywhere. Next thing you'll think I did it."

"Did you?" After a brief moment, he smiled, but it didn't quite reach his eyes.

She straightened and pulled back from him. "You know the answer to that, mister. Besides, I had nothing to gain. What does Alexander have to gain?"

"Freedom from a father with expectations?"

"Hardly seems worth murdering over. He'd already moved out of the house and into the dorms."

"Money. Maybe he wanted to do things Judge Banter wouldn't allow."

"Possible, but still, to kill over it? Eventually Judge Banter would have come around. He wasn't that hard."

The laughter behind her built. "To my father. May he rest in peace now that I finally have mine."

The laughter drizzled to a stop. Ciara gripped the edges of the table to keep from turning and staring. Half the room must have heard him.

"I can't say I'll miss him." The words slurred as a mug slammed against a table.

"See, he's drunk." Ciara shook her head. "Tomorrow he'll be embarrassed if anyone tells him what he did tonight."

"Maybe." But the look in his eye let Ciara know Daniel wasn't letting it go.

Daniel tried to pull his attention from the young fool across the room and back to the beautiful woman in front of him. He sat here for her. He didn't want more years to go by with this friction and distance between them. But if he kept pulling away to analyze Alexander, then his hopes for tonight would be aborted by none other than himself.

Time to multitask. He'd make a mental note to follow up on Alexander in the morning. But right now, he'd enjoy this time with Ciara. See only her and let her know that.

The waiter set plates piled high with Italian food in front of them. "Anything else right now?"

They shook their heads, and the next moments were quiet as the pasta disappeared.

Ciara dabbed the corners of her mouth with a napkin. "Will you let it go if the police can't solve Judge Banter's murder?"

He grimaced. "I don't want it to stay unsolved."

"But what if?"

"Then life will have to go on. What else is there?" He spun fettuccini around his fork and shoved it in his mouth. He studied Ciara while he chewed. What a complex woman, one he wanted to know. To understand. Deeply.

She shifted in the seat as if uncomfortable under his scrutiny. He swallowed and quirked a smile.

"What?" Her word had a timid edge to it, like she wasn't

sure she really wanted to know.

"Just wondering what motivates you. What gets you up and going in the morning?"

"That's not a small question."

"The best ones rarely are."

"True." It was her turn to look beyond him. He gave her the time to consider her answer. "I like to bring hope to women in crisis. Even when they think they want the divorce, it's a crazy process. And if I can help them reconcile, then I want to."

"It's not about the fee?"

"Never. Well, to the partners it is, but I've chosen not to take that track—at least for as long as they'll let me. I always want it to be about people first. About helping them through traumatic experiences. Especially the kids. I don't know how people can do it to children—" She held up a hand. "I know sometimes there isn't a choice, but I wish there was."

"Sounds like you've got a mission."

"I guess I do." She cut a piece of her veal. "Every choice we make is like this. We think it only impacts ourselves, but it spirals out. Touches all those around us. Some in visible ways, and others in unseen. I'll never forget how blindsided I felt when my parents split a year ago, and I'm around it for a living. Who'd have thought it would impact an adult child?" Her voice dropped. "But it does. I felt just as lost as that six-year-old who can't quite understand why Daddy left or Mommy's moving away."

"I didn't know. I'm sorry." The words felt awkward and inadequate.

"I don't tell many people. After all, I'm thirty. It shouldn't matter as much. But it's made me question a lot of things that I always thought were constant about my life. I've learned that only one thing is unchangeable and unshakeable."

"God?"

"Absolutely. I can always count on Him—even when I don't understand. I can't say that about most people."

Did he fall in that category? He didn't dare ask, because he knew the answer. One he didn't like. "I'd like to become someone in your life you can count on."

She smiled, but it held shadows. "You used to be."

The words pounded through him. Used to be. That didn't sound too promising for *and will be again.* Yet that was what he wanted. More than anything. To earn the right to be someone she could count on as a constant in her life. To stand there when the bottom fell out and her world shifted.

The waiter stepped up to the table in the silence. "Can I get y'all dessert?"

Ciara shook her head as she pressed a hand into her stomach. "Not me."

"I think we're ready for the check." Daniel wondered if she'd consider ice cream. Most women would jump at it, but Ciara wasn't like most. No, when he was around her, he wanted to be more than he ever did with others. He wanted to rise to the occasion. Be the man she needed. Would she let him?

As he held her coat for her, he wasn't sure, but he knew he'd do whatever he could to become that in her life.

The next night, the girls knocked on Ciara's door for their monthly movie night. The long-running marathon of Cary Grant movies tied them together. As soon as the girls arrived, they had an agenda.

Tara handed Ciara a tub of dip and a plate of chips.

"What are these?" Ciara held them up, knowing it couldn't be routine chips and dip.

"Mango salsa and homemade cinnamon chips. There's nothing to them, y'all." She grabbed the pitcher of tea and stack of cups before heading down the stairs. "But tonight's not about me, right, Susan?"

The older gal nodded. "Tonight we want the scoop about you and that Daniel Evans."

"There's nothing to say. Have either of you heard from Samantha?"

Tara munched a chip, then nodded. "Her grandmother thought Samantha would be back this summer. She's trying to land an internship at Mount Vernon."

"That would be wonderful." Ciara could see the young mother thriving in that environment.

Susan used a chip to point at Ciara. "You still haven't told us about Daniel, missy."

Ciara tried to distract the two by starting *Arsenic and Old Lace* right away, but they simply peppered her with questions over the top of the movie. If the antics of the two older sisters and Cary Grant couldn't deter them, Ciara knew she might as well spill the tale.

"There's nothing to say really."

Tara began to sputter a protest.

Ciara raised a hand. "Wait a minute. I have to decide whether I care more for Daniel or our differences. Lately, I've begun to think I've created the differences to keep us apart."

"That's ridiculous." Susan ran a chip through the dip, then popped it in her mouth. "Tara, this is delicious. Want to make some for the shop?"

"Honestly, no. Too much chopping. For you, it's worth it.

For half of the town, there isn't enough money in the world." Tara turned to Ciara. "So? What are you going to do?"

As Cary Grant discovered the body, Ciara realized that was the question she had to answer.

What was she going to do?

Chapter 8

The phone rang and rang as Daniel tried to connect with Detective Howard a couple of days after their dinner. Finally, voice mail picked up and he left a message. Would the man even call him back? In the light of another day, it seemed crazy to consider Alexander a suspect in his father's murder. But he wouldn't walk away from the strong conviction he'd had at the restaurant.

The day soon erupted out of control with client after potential client calling. It felt like the phone had attached to his shoulder.

"You've got to get out of here." His assistant stood in the doorway, a file in hand. "The hearing is in fifteen minutes."

Daniel groaned. "Are you sure the detective hasn't called back?"

"Not yet. What's the rush?"

"Not positive. Gut feeling, I guess."

Clive waved the file. "For now, you have to run."

Daniel pulled his court ID from the desk and stood. "All right."

He hurried to the court and tried not to be annoyed by opposing counsel. Right now, having Ciara stare at him from the other table would be preferable to the full can of air pontificating with wild gestures. One of the old school, this attorney thought everybody loved to listen to his "wisdom." It took all Daniel's self-control not to roll his eyes every other moment at something the man said.

In the end, the judge finally cut him off. "I understand your position. Thank you. I'll have my ruling in a week."

As Daniel collected his materials, his phone buzzed on his hip. He hustled from the courtroom and pulled it out. "Evans here."

"You called?" Detective Howard sounded bored.

"Thanks for calling back." Daniel stood in a quiet corner and filled the detective in on what he'd seen and heard the prior night. "I don't know if it matters, but I thought you should know."

"I'll check into it."

"Any reason to think Alexander might be involved?" Daniel pressed the phone closer to his ear.

"I'll check into it."

"Okay." Daniel closed his phone. He'd done everything he could. Maybe he'd call Ciara and fill her in on his walk back to the office. Two nights ago she'd been too nice to tell him he was insane. Did she still feel the same way?

"Daniel Evans on line one for you."

Ciara glanced at the phone, then back to the legal memo she needed to proof before the close of the business day. "Guess I'll take it."

She took a quick breath, then picked up the phone. "Ciara Turner."

"Hi, this is Daniel."

She smiled at the question in his voice. "Hello."

"I wanted to let you know, I talked to the detective on Judge Banter's case. He said he'd look into the other night." He paused, and Ciara wondered what had him considering his words. "Just thought I'd fill you in."

"Thanks. Here's hoping he can solve the case soon."

"Yeah."

As the silence lengthened, she glanced back to the memo. "Anything else?"

"No. Well, yes." There was another pause. "Have dinner with me Friday."

Ciara stared at her desk, her eyes not really seeing the papers and files covering it. Did she dare? She wanted to, since she'd seen far enough into Daniel in the last weeks not to want to keep exploring.

"Yes, I'd like that."

"I'll pick you up a few minutes before seven if that works."

"Perfect." After their conversation ended, she hung up and looked down. While they'd talked, she'd doodled across one of the legal pads. Heat climbed her neck and cheeks as she glanced at the words. *Ciara* woven into the letters *Evans*. Such a junior-high gesture. She ripped the sheet from the pad, then the next as she saw the imprint. She groaned and slammed them into the trash can under her desk.

Maybe she should have said no.

She stood and hurried to the break room for a cup of tea. She needed to clear her thoughts and make room for her clients. Focus on their needs and how she could help them. Somehow she worked for hours, churned out pleading after pleading. Then she threw a few files in her briefcase and headed to her car. The drive down King Street flowed smoothly, the bulk of rush hour ahead of her.

As Ciara turned into the cul-de-sac, it looked like a block party had broken out spontaneously. Her neighbors sat on their porch stoops. A few had pulled grills around from their backyards and smaller ones from patios. The sidewalks had been transformed with chairs and coolers.

"You got here just in time." Tara grabbed Ciara's hand and led her to Tara's doorstep. "I just brought out some fruit slushes. One's even got your favorite—watermelon."

Ciara grinned as she tugged lightly free from Tara's grasp. "I'll be back in a moment. Let me plop this down first." She wiggled her keys in front of her. "Drop off my briefcase."

"Well, hurry back. I'm not sure how long I can protect the slushes."

"Okay." Ciara wove through her neighbors, a tilt to her lips as she watched the fun. She wanted to jump in, but something held her back. Still, there was no better way to welcome spring than to celebrate a warm day with her neighbors. Ciara unlocked her front door, then threw the briefcase on the love seat. She clattered up the wood stairs and into her bedroom. After yanking on a pair of jeans and a purple cardigan set, she slipped on a pair of flats and hurried back down the stairs.

Her phone rang as she hit the door. She sighed and turned to the kitchen. Ciara grabbed the phone. "Hello?"

"Hey." Daniel's lazy voice made her smile.

"Yes?"

"Just wondering when you're coming out."

"Coming out?"

"Is there an echo around here?"

Background sounds, music from a radio, the scrape of a can

being pulled from ice, the small laugh of a child. Ciara took a step toward the door.

"Where exactly are you?"

"Open the door."

Ciara's steps quickened, and she flung open the door. Daniel stood there grinning, holding a clear plastic glass filled with a pink frothy concoction with a curvy straw stuck in it.

"That must be Tara's touch." She pointed at the pink straw.

Daniel handed it to her. "Ready to join the party?"

There seemed to be more than the surface question in the words. Ciara considered him a moment, then thrust her thought to the side. "Yes."

And now that Daniel was there, she was.

There was a special magic in Ciara's neighborhood. A group of people who enjoyed each other in their non-work hours that Daniel hadn't seen replicated. In a way, it matched Ciara, one who cautiously considered others. But once she accepted you, that was it. She would do anything for you.

Daniel wanted to land back in that place. One where she expected the best rather than anticipated the worst. They'd eased their way that direction, but he was ready to mark the new column firmly and never deviate from it.

Ciara Turner was entirely too special to let her slip through his grasp. Again.

She stepped in front of him to interact with one of the neighbor's children, an adorable little boy with blond curls and large green eyes. He looked up at her with absolute adoration, the kind that said she'd proven herself to him over and over.

And probably through kicking balls around the tennis court.

The little boy scuffed his tennis shoe in the dirt and dropped cherry blossoms along the sidewalk. The kid was enough to make him think about someday. That someday when there'd be a little Daniel and a little Ciara.

Whoa!

He shook his head. Time to dislodge that thought before he got waaaayyyy ahead of himself. She'd barely accept dinner out without studying him as if certain he hid an ulterior motive in his invitation.

He had to stick it out longer than she planned to. Good thing *stubborn* was his middle name.

The vibration of his phone against his hip pulled his gaze from her. He glanced at the caller ID. Alexandria Sheriff? He touched Ciara's elbow, waited for her gaze to meet his. He flashed her the screen. "I've got to take this."

"Sure." She nodded, and he felt her gaze follow him as he stepped around the corner, searching for a quieter spot. "Evans."

"Mr. Evans, this is Detective Morgan."

"Yes, sir." Daniel turned his back on the festivities and focused on the abandoned pool.

"We've got Alexander Banter in custody. He's requested an attorney."

Daniel held his breath as he waited for the detective to go on. "Yes?"

"He's requested you."

The words slammed into Daniel. Could he defend the kid? "Why do you have him?"

"Followed up your call with a few of our own. Mr. Banter is now a person of interest, intense interest, in the death of his father."

Daniel felt the tension cord his shoulders. "I can't represent him since I may be a witness against him. He'll have to try someone else. I wouldn't represent him even if I weren't a possible witness."

"Thought you'd say that. Surprised the kid didn't figure it out. Must really think he's fooled everyone." The detective sighed, and Daniel could imagine him sitting at a battered desk, rubbing exhausted eyes. "Back at it then."

"You'll keep me posted?"

"As much as I can. Seems you care more about wrapping up this case than the son. Weird business sometimes."

After the man hung up, Daniel stared at his phone. Alexander had really asked for him? The kid was a fool. Even if Daniel weren't a potential witness, he couldn't stomach the thought of defending the man in a potential criminal action for the murder of his father.

A hand touched his shoulder, and he tried to quiet the inner war.

"Everything all right?" Ciara stepped next to him. "You look upset."

That word couldn't begin to describe the fire pouring through him, demanding an outlet.

"What did the detective know?"

Daniel tried to couch his words to be light. "Just that Alexander wants me to represent him during his questioning."

"You can't do that." The shock ricocheted in her voice.

"I know. Can you imagine he asked?" He ran his fingers through his hair, wishing instead for something to throw against the tennis court's fence. The resounding clatter would sound so good.

"So what now?" She leaned against his arm as if to lend her

support as he struggled to find footing.

"I guess we let the detectives do their thing. Trust they'll figure out if Alexander was involved. If not. . .I guess we leave it to them anyway." He looked at the woman beside him. "I guess it's time to let them figure it out." He tipped her chin. "There are other things I'd like to figure out."

A sly grin tipped her lips. "Like what?"

He studied her eyes, soaking in the way she had stripped the barriers that used to exist. The ones that separated them from each other like the deepest cavern. If she could do that, then he could bare his soul. Let her know what he wanted. What he was ready to fight for. He leaned down until their foreheads touched.

"What I want is to learn how to encourage a woman like you to fall in love with a man like me."

Chapter 9

The next days confirmed what Ciara had dreaded. Alexander Banter had killed his father. All to receive his small inheritance from his mother's death. He was tired of waiting for his dad to let him make the decisions on the money. That dreadful morning weeks earlier, he'd arrived at his father's chambers ready to argue with Judge Banter. He left a murderer.

The days sped up after that, each one feeling a bit more like spring. Even on the days she met Daniel in court, they didn't feel like adversaries anymore. They couldn't be colleagues. But she now understood he wasn't the enemy she'd created in her mind.

Still, she couldn't decide how far she wanted their growing relationship to evolve. Friendship felt. . .safe. . .if a tad dull. But anything else required risk. She thought she could offer that to him, but each time he pulled back, she exhaled.

Maybe she wasn't as ready as she thought for more than friendship.

Either way, she had to settle the matter in her mind and clue her heart in on the decision. Because right now, anytime her gaze collided with Daniel's, she lost her place. Her thoughts popped like so many bubbles in the spring air. Then her emotions would begin soaring like a kite. Next thing she knew, she'd take up writing poetry. And that would be too much. Way too much.

Daniel's calls dried up. She tried to tell herself it wasn't because the police had resolved the mystery. He simply had a case that consumed him. Probably a stack of clients who all demanded his attention at the same time.

If anyone should know how client crises erupted at inconvenient times, she should. That was the life of a family law attorney.

Yet another reason she'd lectured herself not to fall for Daniel.

Her heart had ignored her advice. Quite good advice. The kind that could protect her.

Ciara swiveled her chair to the credenza, placing the phone behind her. Out of sheer determination, she quit listening for the phone to ring. She had too much to do, too many people depending on her, to let one man distract her focus and energy.

By the end of the day, she felt good about what she'd accomplished, but her phone still hadn't rung with the right voice on the other end of the call.

As soon as she got home, she hurried upstairs and changed into exercise clothes. She tied on her tennis shoes and bolted out the door. Her thoughts roamed over the past weeks. All that had happened to turn her world on odd angles. She prayed she'd never have to find another person she respected and admired facedown and hours away from death. She prayed that somehow she could forgive Alexander for killing his father. And she prayed that she could come to grips with what she felt for Daniel—whatever it was.

She took the bridge across 395 and continued power walking into the neighboring community. Her thoughts churned to the tempo of her pumping arms.

Somewhere she could find peace.

She had to. The alternative of letting a man control how she felt about the rest of her day couldn't be more wrong. *God, help me figure this out. I just want to honor You, especially in my relationships.*

Could there be a more crucial area in which to put God first? She couldn't imagine one.

Her relationships with other people touched every area of her life. From clients to colleagues to people in her neighborhood and at church, her life was a tightly woven web of connections.

Ciara shivered and picked up her pace again. The vibrant beauty of yellow and red tulips, pastel crocuses, frothy cherry blossoms, and other flowering trees couldn't pull her mind from the sense she was holding on to something. Something she needed to relinquish if she wanted to see what was possible in this area of her life.

What did she want?

Her dreams had always envisioned a husband and one or two kids who looked a lot like them completing a family picture that morphed into older images each Christmas. She'd imagined loose teeth and braces. Dolls and LEGOs. Trucks and crafts.

Instead, her life existed in her job and town house, without even room for a dog or cat. As she examined it, it felt pathetic. Empty. Not at all matching the dream.

Her steps slowed as she reached the playground on the back side of the neighborhood. Wasn't it time to chase her dreams? Dreams that involved more than serving her clients? Dreams that would fill her life and her home?

She longed to, but even as she examined the idea, she knew it wasn't entirely true. If it were, she would call Daniel. She wouldn't cling to some old-fashioned notion that he had to call her first.

Ciara sank onto a swing and pushed her feet against the mulch. Slowly the swing rose higher and higher as she pumped. Her hair blew off the back of her neck and she stretched out, letting the swing lift her higher and higher. She closed her eyes and listened to the breeze as she swooshed back and forth.

God, I want to live like this. Abandoned to You and trusting You with my future. She paused. *With Daniel.*

The words released a weight in her chest. Could she trust God? To know her best interests? To protect her heart? Even as she thought the questions, she laughed. If she couldn't trust Him, who could she trust?

Friday evening, Daniel hurried from the office. The days stayed light longer, but if he didn't hurry, he wouldn't have enough time to implement his plan. And if there was anything he was good at, it was building a plan and executing it.

It was what attorneys did every day.

Now he just had to get this one to work out. With a certain girl. Who just might outthink him if he wasn't careful.

He flew through his town house, grabbing the fresh clothes he'd set out the night before. In less than fifteen minutes, he was back out the door and in his car. He turned to a classical station to set a soothing mood as he zipped up King Street toward Cherry Blossom Estates. Toward Ciara.

One chance. He had one chance to get this right.

He shook his head and turned up the music. If he kept telling himself things like that, he'd lose his focus before he even arrived at Ciara's doorstep.

"It's just one night, man." The pep talk didn't help. At all.

At the stoplight, he looked in the rearview mirror, then tried to rub the stress from his face. It wasn't Ciara's fault his day had deepened the circles under his eyes. He really needed to evaluate how he selected clients. Some of them simply weren't worth the added headaches, like today's no-shows. Not showing for a child support hearing stood as the all-time no-no, and these guys didn't get it. Even if you felt persecuted, you had to show up, tell the judge why. Today's yahoos had ignored his advice and now one had an arrest warrant outstanding and the other was one small step away from the same thing.

Tonight would be a great night to avoid work conversations in total.

Like that could happen when two attorneys went to dinner. He'd just have to try hard to come up with ways to steer the conversation in any of a million other directions. All of them far from that courthouse sitting near downtown Old Town.

He pulled his sedan into a vacant slot in front of Ciara's end unit, then hurried to her door. Almost before he knocked, the door opened and Ciara stood there. His breath disappeared as he soaked in the vision of her. At her throat, she wore a frothy pink scarf the same color as the cherry blossoms, setting off her cream dress and adding warm color to her cheeks. Heels elevated her closer to his level, and she wore her hair down in soft waves just below her shoulders. Her eyes sparkled as she smiled.

"Let me grab a coat, and I'll be ready." She turned toward the corner where her coat tree hid and slid into her beige trench coat before he could reach her side. Ciara tugged her hair free of the collar, then quirked her head to the side. "What?"

Daniel gathered his thoughts. "You're the most beautiful woman I've ever seen."

The color in her cheeks heightened, and she glanced to the side. "You say that to all the girls."

He cleared his throat. "Not at all." He offered her his arm. "Ready for an evening out?"

"Absolutely. I am glad to put this week behind me and relax." She took a step on her heels and teetered just a moment when one seemed to slip into a crack on the brick.

Should he reconsider his plans? He studied her a moment, then decided he couldn't. It was time to let her know.

Ciara brushed back a creeping wave of uncertainty. Had she overdressed? Daniel kept looking at her with something in his gaze, something she couldn't read. He opened her car door, and she slid onto the leather seat. After placing her hands in her lap, she took a steadying breath as he hurried around the car.

Daniel started the car and eased out of the neighborhood. "Are you hungry?"

"Not yet."

"Good. I thought we could make a quick stop before heading to the restaurant."

The strains of violins wrapped around her. Usually she found classical music soothing, but today an edge of discord seemed to creep in with the tones. She shook off the thought, one that surely came from her overactive imagination. She eased against the cushion and forced herself to relax. Work had ended and she had time to relax.

In moments, Daniel motored his car through light traffic into the city on 395. They veered off onto the Fourteenth Street Bridge, and soon he twisted through the maze back toward the Jefferson Memorial. Its neoclassical marble dome poked over the Japanese flowering cherry trees that ringed it.

Ciara stayed quiet as he pulled into a parking slot. He turned off the car and looked at her.

"Up for a stroll?" There was a playful glint hiding something deeper—maybe a challenge—in his gaze.

"Always." Though if she'd known, she would have worn different shoes. A pair that wouldn't leave mismatched blisters all over her feet.

Daniel led her to the sidewalk that circled the Tidal Basin and kept a slow pace. For a Friday night, tourists and pedestrians hadn't overrun the area, though several runners zipped around them. The cherry trees stretched branches overhead, each still decorated with the dainty pink and white blossoms that exploded with the advent of spring. Without crazy storms, the blossoms had lasted longer than Ciara could remember seeing them.

Daniel kept up a steady stream of small talk. Anytime a topic showed a hint of petering to an end, he'd turn to something new, almost as if he wanted to make sure one topic didn't show up. Ciara let him lead wherever he wanted. She'd enjoy the moment regardless of the topic, as long as it wasn't a case they shared.

As they reached the end of the circle, he stopped and looked into her face. "Want to sit on the steps for a minute?"

Ciara nodded, even though she didn't want to imagine what might happen to her cream dress. The dry cleaners could try to sort out any mess later. Right now she wanted to enjoy the easy camaraderie between them. Even if it meant cold legs and possible stains.

After he helped her ease to the stone, she couldn't hide a quick shiver.

"Guess I should have grabbed a blanket."

"I'll be fine for a bit."

He slipped his sports jacket off, then slid it over her trench coat. He shoved his hands in his pockets and studied the skyline.

This was what Ciara loved about living in Washington, DC. Moments like this when the reality that she lived in the nation's capital confronted her from all sides. Planes roared into and out of flight patterns for Reagan National Airport, while cars streamed in and out of the city on 395. The monuments and Capitol Building stood in contrast to the sky, while government buildings lined the spaces in between. Throw in the mix of tourists, and she couldn't imagine living anywhere else.

Daniel bumped her shoulder, and she turned toward him.

"I'm glad we've started spending time together again, Ciara." The words seemed almost forced, not the natural delivery she'd expect.

"I am, too." She shifted, feeling the cold penetrate her dress.

Daniel studied his hands, then looked up at her, his eyes piercing her. "I don't have many regrets in my life, but one is letting us drift apart after our clerkship. You are an amazing woman, and when I'm with you, I want to be so much more than the man I am now."

She started to speak, needing to stop wherever he was headed, but he placed a finger on her lips. The contact sizzled into the space between them, and her breath hitched.

"Hear me out."

He must not understand that at the moment she could

hardly form a thought, let alone a sentence. Instead, she almost moaned when he pulled back slightly.

"I know we'll probably never see our cases the same way. . . and frankly, life would get boring if we did." A rakish air hit his eyes, and she caught a hint of Humphrey Bogart. "But I don't want to let us drift apart again. I want you in my life, deeply in my life. I can't imagine it without you now."

He stroked her cheek, and Ciara leaned into the touch.

"I want you, no, need you in my life, Ciara. These last weeks have shown me what a shell I've lived without you."

She nodded. "My life's the same. Full, but not rich. It's missing something crucial without you."

"It's more than that." Daniel took a moment as if weighing what he intended to say next. Counting the cost before saying the words. "I can't imagine my life without you beside me. . . forever."

Ciara kept nodding, even as she searched his gaze for any hint that he didn't mean what he'd said. "I can't go back either."

"I love you, Ciara." He tipped her chin up, then slowly, hesitatingly eased toward her. He stopped, hovering above her lips, giving her the opportunity to back away. . .create space between them. Instead, she leaned into him, met his kiss. The moments evaporated as he held her, a touch as light as if she were a cherry blossom he could crush. Instead, she felt treasured and honored.

After a minute, he eased back, and she hid her face in his chest. Daniel wrapped his arms around her, and she knew she'd found what her heart had searched so long for. . .a place to be loved.

CARA C. PUTMAN lives in Indiana with her husband and four children. She's an attorney and a ministry leader and teacher at her church. She has loved reading and writing from a young age and now realizes it was all training for writing books. An honors graduate of the University of Nebraska and George Mason University School of Law, Cara loves bringing history to life. She is a regular guest blogger at *Generation Next Parenting* and *Writer Interrupted*, as well as writing at her blog, *The Law, Books & Life*. Learn more about Cara and her books at www.caraputman.com. She loves to hear from her readers.

BURIED
DECEPTION

by Gina Conroy

Dedication

So many people have had their hands on this novella that I was afraid there might be no one left to read it! Many thanks to WIN, ACFW, and my ACA family who have tirelessly critiqued and encouraged me with this debut novella. Special thanks to my *Cherry Blossom Capers* partners, Cara, Lynette, and Frances, who believed in me enough to include me in this collection. Special thanks to Amelia Chrisholm and the staff at Mount Vernon who never grew tried of my questions and provided me with behind scenes information about the archaeology program. To my family, who might not "get" this writing thing, but who let me do it anyway. And to my daughter, who prayed every night for mommy to sell a book. Last, but never least, to the One who's brought me this far on my writing journey by teaching me how to surrender.

Chapter 1

"Alex, come back!" Samantha Steele's heart jolted, and she darted after her seven-year-old son. The little renegade ignored her pleas and ran full-throttle toward the dig site behind the slave quarters at Mount Vernon Estates. She glanced at Callie, her nine-year-old, who huffed after her. Why'd her sitter get sick the first day of her archaeology internship?

Samantha pursued Alex through the upper garden toward the archaeology pit where tourists gathered. Her chest tightened. Squatting in the dirt, her boss seemed oblivious to the runaway locomotive about to cause a train wreck.

Samantha prayed that her first encounter with her boss wouldn't be her last, but two years earlier, God didn't intervene.

Why would He now?

"Watch out!" Her warning came late as Alex crashed into a dark-headed man in a navy uniform. God's answer to prayer wasn't a surprise. The God she knew remained distant, often turning up the heat when all she wanted was to escape the fire.

Something thumped against Nick Porter's hip. His drink blew

169

its top, spilling Coke on his security uniform as he dropped his sack. His double cheeseburger and fries tumbled out. "Hey, watch it!"

The kid who'd plowed into him jumped back.

Two weeks on the job and he'd made a mess of things.

A petite brunette in khaki shorts scurried to his mangled meal. She stuffed it back in the sack, hunching as she offered it. "So sorry."

Nick's stomach growled. Just what he wanted. A side of dirt with his burger.

She nudged the freckle-faced kid forward.

The boy resisted. Nick's frown softened. So much like—

She sighed. "My son is sorry, Officer."

"It's Nick Porter, and I'm just security." Security. He hated the sound of it.

"What happened to the Mount Vernon police?"

"One of many cutbacks."

She wrote on a business card and handed it to him. Samantha Steele.

"Send me the dry-cleaning bill."

"Don't worry about it."

The blond girl waved her brochure. "This says there's no food allowed except in the designated eating areas."

"This one yours, too?" He pointed to the cherub-faced girl. "Charming kids, Mrs. Steele." He couldn't hide his sarcasm, the one emotion that remained.

"It's Ms. Steele. My husband died two years ago."

Nick spotted Samantha's naked ring finger. Stupid. As a cop, he never missed a detail. "Sorry." He paused. "I lost my wife, too." Why was he confessing to a stranger?

Her eyes sympathized as if she understood his pain.

Impossible.

The kid dug into his pocket. "Here." Tiny fingers tickled Nick's palm as the boy released the coins. "I'm really sorry, mister." The boy's hazel eyes pierced Nick's soul.

Nick fought the stirring as memories surfaced. A heaviness descended as they walked away. He should've thanked the kid, or at least refused his money. If he could rewind the last few moments, he would. But God didn't give second chances.

If He did, they certainly weren't free.

Gripping Alex's hand, Samantha plodded toward the mansion to catch the tour before her orientation. She inhaled the magnolia breeze, her nerves calming. Something about that security guard unsettled her. Sure, he had Cary Grant looks, but minus the cleft chin and charm he was nothing to swoon over. Besides, she wouldn't play anyone's leading lady again. Oh boy. Classic-movie night with her town house neighbors at Cherry Blossom Estates was getting to her.

The three of them followed the tour into the large mint-green dining room. Samantha admired the intricate white agricultural moldings and crystal dinnerware as the African-American docent dressed in period attire shared the history.

Alex looked up. "This ceiling is huge."

"They're double the size of ceilings at the time." Samantha studied the detailed carving. "Washington was a great innovator."

"They had elevators?" Alex whipped his head around. "Can I ride?"

Callie rolled her eyes. "An *innovator*, not elevator."

"May I have your attention?" The guide adjusted her head scarf. "*Please* don't touch anything." Her plump figure squeezed through the crowd.

"When my younguns misbehave, I take a switch to them." The woman's words grew thick as biscuit gravy. "Can't have them disrespecting the president now, could I?"

Samantha withdrew from the woman. But Alex pointed to her name tag. Althea Washington. "Are you related to George Washington?"

"She can't be related; she's a slave, bozo." Callie elbowed Alex.

Samantha's face flushed. "She's only *playing* a slave."

"Next time I sees Masta Washington, I'll introduce you so you can ask him yourself." Althea returned to the front. "We'll pass through the little parlor with the harpsichord President Washington bought for his stepdaughter, Nelly Custis." Her Southern accent morphed to normal. She glared at Alex. "Please, keep your hands to yourself."

Something seemed off about Ms. Washington's role playing. "Stay close and *act* civilized." Wouldn't want to upset her if she had some screws loose underneath that head scarf.

Walking through the little parlor, Samantha squeezed Alex's hand. Once inside the central passage, her grip relaxed. Marveling at the beautiful mahogany-grained walls, she imagined Washington entertaining guests with doors open as a summer breeze cooled the house.

Callie walked into the front parlor. Samantha followed, her arms swinging, carefree and—empty. Alex?

When did she let go? She spun. Surveyed the entryway. No Alex.

"Where's your brother?"

Callie shrugged.

"Stay with the group." Samantha hurried across the hall into the small dining room. Footsteps echoed. She peeked out, her heart beating a warning.

Just her luck Nick Porter'd be patrolling the mansion while Alex went AWOL.

Samantha waited until Nick disappeared; then she jogged up the staircase and surveyed the second floor. The sign on the first door said CLOSED FOR RENOVATIONS. She checked the other rooms. All empty.

A door slammed. She turned. Alex scurried from the first room.

"Alex!" she whispered, following him downstairs and through the bedchamber. The study door closed. She raced in and gasped.

Perched on Washington's chair, Alex reached toward the terrestrial globe.

"Stop!" She reached for him, holding her breath as if a tiny wind would send him falling onto the antique.

He froze.

She lowered her voice. "I'm not mad." Yet. "Climb down."

Alex eyed the globe, then jumped off and shuffled toward her like Sylvester with a mouthful of Tweety.

Heat exploded inside her. "Do I need to buy a leash?"

For the past two years she'd dealt with Alex's unpredictable behavior. She understood he missed his father, so she'd been patient. "Let's find Callie."

Swinging around for the door, she slammed into a human wall. Her purse fell. Nick Porter retrieved it as she scrambled after her lipstick.

"Ma'am, you shouldn't be in here." He reached to help her up.

Their eyes met. "You?"

"Sorry, we're leaving." But before Samantha grabbed Alex's hand, he raced toward the presidential chair.

Climbed.

Reached.

Touched.

"Don't!" Nick ran to him.

The globe went whirling.

Samantha gasped as the globe's stand wobbled, her world teetering on the edge of destruction. She fought to breathe as she reached for the antique. It was too late. Like dominoes the globe toppled, knocking against the table by the window, which sent the brass telescope on top catapulting to the ground.

Nick snatched the telescope pieces from Samantha's hands. It didn't take a brain surgeon to see the antique was beyond repair.

He set the globe upright, examining it and the table that broke the globe's fall. No scratches or nicks. Now he got his miracle?

"Sorry, Mommy. Are they still gonna let you work here?"

Nick stared at Samantha. "What'd he say?"

"I—I'm doing an archaeology internship. This summer."

This wasn't the last he'd see of her and Captain Chaos? "I'll have to report this."

"Wait. Maybe it can be fixed."

As the kid crawled under the desk, remnants of Nick's paternal heart wanted to comfort the boy. "You'd better come out." Had he remembered to soften his tone?

The kid scooted from under the desk. Samantha stroked

his hair. "I'll make everything okay." She took the eyepiece and barrel from him, tried to fit them together.

"What am I thinking? This isn't a flea market item I can fix with glue. It's Washington's original brass telescope. It survived over two hundred years and millions of tourists, but it couldn't survive *my* son." Tears welled.

Nick shifted his weight, wishing she'd dam that river. He wasn't heartless; he just never knew how to handle women's emotions. "I'm calling this in now."

"Isn't there something we can do?" Her eyes locked on his like a deer caught in his headlights. He rushed to close the doors on either end of the room. He was insane to risk his job to help this stranger, no matter how much she needed rescuing.

There was something about her. . .needing him. Voices echoed outside the door. "Stay here."

"My daughter—I need to get her."

"She'll be fine." Nick stepped out. "Room's closed." He shut the door.

"Did you see Callie?"

"She's fine." His gut knotted. "She won't try a stunt like young Knievel here or turn George's bed into a trampoline, right?"

Color pinched Samantha's cheeks. "Callie would never—just because Alex is curious and clumsy doesn't make me a terrible mom."

"I never said that."

"You didn't have to." She crossed her arms.

He shook his head. "We'll stay put until the tour is finished. Then you'll find Callie, and we'll figure this out together." Together? He definitely needed his head examined. "They have insurance. I'm sure they'll understand when we explain." He took the eyepiece and barrel from her.

Samantha gripped Nick's arm. "There has to be another way."

An unexpected longing panged. He couldn't abandon her now.

With a sigh, he worked the eyepiece into the barrel and sighted toward the Potomac. What? He looked again, his pulse accelerating. A hearty laugh erupted.

"My life's falling apart, and you're laughing?" Samantha's nostrils flared.

"It's not what you think."

"Then what's so funny?"

"The telescope is a fake."

Chapter 2

Afake? You're kidding!" Samantha's face lit as she stumbled backward. Nick reached out, pulling her close. The green flecks in her eyes danced to the erratic rhythm in his heart. He released his grip. "I'm not positive until it's examined." He handed Samantha the pieces. "I think the telescope is designed for longer distances like gazing across the solar system, not the Potomac."

Samantha stared through it. "That's odd. The website said it was original." She shrugged. "Doesn't matter. There's no reason to worry."

Nick should've been elated, but his cop-gut churned. "What if someone lifted the original?"

"What?"

Nick tensed. She didn't have to say it. Samantha thought he was one bullet short of a magazine. He paced. Maybe he was paranoid, but what if smuggling had crept onto Mount Vernon? "We know the telescope isn't original. That means it's either a replica or forgery, and I discovered it."

Samantha stared, hands on her hips. "*My* son broke the telescope."

"Okay, *we* discovered it. Now let me take care of things."

Buried insecurities resurrected from a lifetime of letting others take care of things. Hadn't she proven her independence by now? Obviously not if she was begging this stranger for help.

"You okay?" The pity-filled look on Nick's face ate her confidence.

How could she convince the male-dominated archaeology community that she deserved their respect?

She needed the telescope to be a forgery to save her internship and earn a position at Mount Vernon, but she needed to find the forger to prove herself.

"I'm fine, and I'm going to help you catch the forger."

Nick glared. "Art forgery is dangerous. The guys involved aren't pulling a prank. They're in it for big money."

"How do you know?"

Nick shifted. "I served twelve years as a detective."

Then why play security guard?

Nick shook his head at the kid who'd unlaced his sneakers and was tying the shoelaces in knots. At least he sat quietly. No telling how long the poster child for ADHD would stay occupied. "Shouldn't you take your kids home?"

Samantha sighed. "My orientation's today."

"You brought your kids?"

"My babysitter got sick. And after this, I can't let Alex near the dig."

"Smart girl."

"You're not helping." She glanced at her son. "I can't jeopardize this internship."

"Wish I had the answer. I'm still working on the telescope fiasco."

Her mouth twisted, then slowly curved into a grin. "You could watch my children while I talk to my boss."

Nick retreated, hands high. "I'm not good with kids." Couldn't even protect his own.

"It'd only take a few minutes. I'll be close by."

Darn, those doe eyes! "Fine. First I'll take the telescope to the lab; then I'll babysit."

Why was he attracted to such a fireball? He had no business dreaming about what could never be. He had one shot at love.

Had a scar in his gut to prove it.

Confusion flooded Nick as he walked past the employee parking lot and loading dock to the metal warehouse. What possessed him to agree to babysit Samantha's kids? Insanity. That was what he'd plead. After he made good on his promise to watch her kids, he'd figure a way to avoid Samantha.

Nick entered the archaeology lab, holding the sack with the telescope that could either end his job or promote him to head of security. Carole Huntington emerged from her office clutching a Pepcid AC bottle.

"Don't ever get old." Her voice rasped from a four-decade, two-pack-a-day habit. She kissed Nick on the cheek. "To what do I owe this visit?"

Carole set down the bottle and leaned against the worktable. "I need information, and a favor."

"Anything."

"Is the telescope in Washington's study original?"

"Absolutely. Washington owned at least a dozen spyglasses. That one's the only original tripod we have. It's priceless."

"You're positive it's not a replica?"

"I hope you're asking because you're a dedicated employee, but something tells me that's not the case."

"Can't fool the police chief's woman." He winked.

"Ex-chief. Stop flirting and show me what's in the bag."

Nick slipped on latex gloves and removed the pieces.

The wrinkles in her face deepened. "Tell me this isn't the telescope."

"Wish I could." Nick handed her gloves, then the telescope. "Tell me what you see."

She examined every inch. "If this isn't the original, where is it?"

Nick watched Carole's pursed lips tighten as he explained the accident. "You can't report this until I investigate."

"They're bound to notice it's missing."

"I'll file a report today, omitting the suspected forgery."

"And the lady and her boy?"

"How'd you—"

"Always the protector."

"They'll eventually learn the truth, but if I break this case, I hope they'll credit Samantha with doing them a favor."

"I don't feel right about this." Carole folded her arms. "The last time I kept your secret—"

"That was different." Nick's gut ignited. "You don't think I can handle it. That I'm still using."

"No, I believe you."

"Then what?"

She hesitated. "You shouldn't get involved. Leave it to the police."

How could she say that? Did she forget he had worked beside her husband, Dale, for over a decade? That she saw him through the darkest days of his life?

Of course she didn't forget. That was why she didn't want him to interfere. Nick retreated. "You're right. I should stay out of this. Someone could get hurt."

"I didn't say that."

"I'll stop in later to lift prints." He shook his head. "It'd be a miracle if there were any decent ones left."

"Once you believed in miracles."

Memories squeezed the air from Nick's lungs.

"It wasn't your fault." Carole grasped his hands. "Stop punishing yourself."

Maybe he didn't kill his wife and son, but his attempt to protect them failed. Probably caused their death.

The room shrank as he gasped for breath. He needed out— fast. Nick whipped around and bumped into a lanky man in a dark suit.

"Pardon me." The guy pushed his glasses up the bridge of his nose.

"Nicky, wait." Carole coughed.

He didn't turn back. Carole Huntington was great at restoring relics. Too bad she couldn't fix his broken soul.

Samantha drank in the floral canvas of the upper garden, her apprehension easing as she walked toward the dig. Alex had begged to stay at the Museum and Education Center, and

Nick didn't object. Worrying was silly. They were safe with a security guard. Besides, how much trouble could they get into at a hands-on museum?

Now she could focus on the telescope. If there was a forger, and if she found him, Alex's mayhem at the mansion might be her good fortune. Before she could savor the thought, Alex charged past her toward the archaeology pit. Samantha's heart lurched. She scanned the area. Callie charged after Alex. Where was Nick?

Samantha ran after them. Why'd she think God would give her a break? The testing of her faith produced perseverance, right? God obviously wasn't finished with her, though she felt way past well done. More like extra-crispy with all life's joy burned off.

Alex's arms flailed. Samantha braced for his crash landing, but the archaeologist in a cowboy hat grabbed Alex before he dove into the pit.

"Whoa." The cowboy gripped Alex's shoulder, his drawl dripping molasses. His rugged looks and wild blond hair reminded her of Brad Pitt in *Legends of the Fall*.

"What's got you chomping at the bit?"

Alex wiggled free and scurried to Samantha. "Buried treasure."

Cowboy gazed from Alex to Callie. "This your little mustang and pretty filly, ma'am?"

"Yes, this is Allie. . .Callie and Alex." Her cheeks warmed as his cobalt eyes locked on hers. It'd been too long since a man looked at her that way.

"I'm Samantha Steele. The new intern."

"You don't say! I expected someone taller with whiskers." He smiled, and Samantha reminded herself she was a twenty-eight-year-old mother of two. "I'm your boss, but call me Cody."

He extended his hand.

Alex shook it, but Callie scrunched her nose. "You're filthy."

Cody winked. "Where there's muck, there's brass, darlin'."

Samantha cringed. Time for damage control. "I know it's unprofessional to bring the children. Their sitter canceled last-minute, and they don't start Camp Summerwood until Monday. The security guard said he'd watch them while I explained my situation to you, but. . ."

"No harm done." Cody handed Alex a brush. "How about searching for treasure?"

"Sure!" Alex jumped in the pit.

"Aren't you compromising the site?"

"We've cataloged that section. He can't hurt anything."

If Cody only knew. "I wondered if we could reschedule my orientation."

"Sure, we can start Monday."

"Thanks for understanding." Samantha turned to Alex sifting dirt through a screen. "We leave in five minutes."

He hopped like a frog to the other quadrant. Something fell from his pocket.

"What've you got there?" A skinny guy in a suit snatched it. When had he arrived?

"This is Professor Timmons." Cody slapped his back, knocking his glasses out of place. Timmons turned the dirty penknife in his hand, ignoring the introduction. "He works at the Smithsonian and moonlights here."

Samantha glanced at the knife. "Alex, where'd you get that?"

"Found it."

"Let me see." Cody revealed a rusty blade.

"They sell these in the gift shop. Some kid probably lost it awhile ago." Professor Timmons stared at Samantha.

"Where are my manners? This is Samantha Steele. My new intern."

"You seem familiar. Have we met?"

"No, we moved to Arlington recently."

"Nice place. Whereabout?" Professor Timmons's cheek twitched.

"Cherry Blossom Estates."

"That's quite a commute," Cody said.

"My grandmother owns a condo there. We only pay utilities since she moved to assisted living."

Timmons stepped away to answer his cell.

"May I see it?" Samantha asked.

"It's pretty dull." Cody handed it to her. "Won't hurt him."

"It's a wonderful replica of Washington's mother-of-pearl penknife. Legend says this knife saved our nation."

"How could a knife save a nation?" Callie questioned.

Cody squatted. "George Washington wanted to resign as commander-in-chief during the winter at Valley Forge. Then he remembered his mother's words when she'd given him the knife."

"She said, 'Always obey your superiors,'" Samantha added. "It was given to young George as a reward when he honored his mother's wishes to give up his commission in the English Navy and return to mathematics and surveying."

Cody stood. "Aha. Beauty *and* brains."

"Can I have my knife?"

Samantha slipped it into her purse. "I'll keep this for now."

"But—"

Cody patted Alex's head. "Better do as George did and obey your superiors."

Callie tugged on Samantha's shirt. "Mom, can we go to Pizza Town?"

"But I haven't found any treasure."

Professor Timmons ended his call. "I must skedaddle. Pleasure meeting you, Ms. Steele." He glared at Cody then fled, peering back several times.

Samantha's anxiety eased as he disappeared.

"I'm starved. I want pizza! Now!" Callie whined.

"They have pizza at the food court. My treat." Cody dusted off Alex's shirt. "We could start orientation over lunch."

Samantha sighed. "Okay."

"Then it's a date." Cody smiled.

Was that what it was? Correcting her boss on her first day might not be smart.

Nick's heart ricocheted as he searched the museum galleries. One minute they were there, the next gone. How could he face Samantha after he lost her kids?

Where to look next? Perps sometimes returned to the crime scene. Maybe little boys did, too. Nick scrambled up the bowling green toward the mansion, then slipped through the back door and into the study. No kids, but Althea Washington hovered near the bookshelf.

"Excuse me. This room is closed to tourists *and* guides."

Althea hid something behind her. "Masta, please don't whip me." She trembled, her eyes glassy.

Adrenaline spiked. "Show me what's behind your back."

"Masta Washington lets me come in. Says it'll be mine when he's dead and gone."

Either this lady played her part really well, or she was higher than the Goodyear Blimp. "Ma'am, slowly bring your hands in front and drop whatever you have."

She set a worn black book on the floor. Nick's pulse settled, disappointed she wasn't smuggling an antique. Or maybe she was.

"I did it no harm." She inched toward the door.

"Stay out of here until I say this room's open." Something was squirrelly about Althea. "I have some questions before—" His walkie squawked. When he reached for it, she disappeared.

"Porter." Nick grabbed the Bible by the edges.

"Cody Sparks at the dig behind the slave quarters. I've uncovered some artifacts you'll want to see."

"Why would I care—"

"You'll be interested in this pair. One has pretty brown eyes, the other hazel. They're accompanied by the cutest specimen who's fit to be tied. If you don't get here quick, I might supply the rope."

Chapter 3

Nick hustled from the mansion toward the archaeology pit. How would he explain losing Samantha's kids? Too bad he'd put the Bible in his locker. Angie always said it was a sword. He might need a weapon against Samantha or a visual aid, distracting her with suspicions of Althea.

Laughter echoed through the garden as he neared the site. Little Houdini picked at the grass while some cowboy, too big for his boots, nestled way too close to Samantha. Nick's stomach knotted. He jogged toward them, wearing his apology on his sleeve. Though Samantha wouldn't see it with the way she stared at that overgrown cowpoke.

"One minute they were near; the next they disappeared."

"Nice of you to arrive." She smiled, but her tone stung.

"It's not easy keeping up with your kids." Nick pointed to Alex. "That one needs a tracking device."

She crossed her arms. "Maybe you shouldn't have taken your eyes off him."

"Even with both eyes on him, he's slippery." Nick's hand gesture mimicked a telescope. "And dangerous."

"You two need to sort this out." Cody stepped between

Nick and Samantha. "I'll run the kids to lunch."

She glanced at Alex. "That's probably not a good idea."

"I've got seven younger siblings." Cody winked, then met Nick's glare. "I promise not to lose them."

Nick inched toward Samantha. "How about *we* sort this out at lunch?"

"Cody already invited us." Samantha turned to Cody. "I won't be long."

Cody moseyed between the kids, placing a hand on their shoulders. He shot Nick a triumphant look.

Callie shrugged off Cody's hand as they walked away. Nick chuckled. Cherub-face was a good judge of character. Tension eased until Nick noticed Samantha smiling at the trio. "Sparky has no idea what he's in for."

Samantha spun around. "I'm sorry my kids burdened you. I'm sorry I asked you to watch them. I assumed they'd be safe with a police officer."

Samantha regretted the remark the moment the fire in Nick's eyes faded. Her throat tightened. "Forgive me."

"I should've been more careful."

"Let's forget it. What'd you learn about the telescope?"

"Carole confirmed it should be the original. And I found the mansion guide handling a Bible in the study."

"Althea Washington's our forger?"

"Not until I match her prints on the book with those on the telescope."

"How? You're not in law enforcement anymore."

Nick shifted his weight. "I've got connections."

"What if they don't match?"

"Security has access to employee prints."

"This is like *CSI*."

Nick's trademark scowl returned. "This is nothing like that voodoo science."

"Sorry." Guess she touched a nerve. Way too easy to do with Nick Porter. "Does Carole know how it was broken?"

"Yes. She'll keep it quiet for now."

"How do you know?"

"We go way back."

"How much time do we have?"

"A few days." Nick hesitated. "I promised to file a report this afternoon."

"You didn't!"

"I'll keep your name out of it."

She couldn't depend on Nick to watch her children, so how could she trust him with this? But she needed him. "What's the plan?"

"Leave the detective work to me."

"But—"

"I assure you I'm a better investigator than babysitter. When something develops, I'll tell you. Fair enough?"

No, it wasn't fair. She needed to ride shotgun on this investigation, not be shoved in the backseat. Still, she had no clue where to begin. "What choice do I have?"

"None. You'd better catch Sparky. Enjoy your lunch." Sarcasm tainted Nick's words. "I've got work to do."

Guilt overcame her. "Care to join us? My treat, since Alex destroyed your lunch."

He shook his head, his frown softening. "Another time. Three-wheeling's not my style."

"I thought you weren't in law enforcement anymore. . . ."

Samantha's words rattled in Nick's head as he followed the path to the mansion. Why'd she keep bringing that up? It was obvious she didn't trust him. Why should she? He *had* lost her kids.

Like he'd lost his.

The ache inside deepened. No matter how hard he tried, he'd never wiggle free from the noose hanging around his neck. The one with his wife and kids' blood on it.

Nick's thoughts froze at the sight of Cody Sparks jogging from the mansion down the bowling green. Where were the kids? Obviously not by his side, and Samantha couldn't have reached the food court. Nick snickered. Alex give Cowboy Sparky the slip?

Nick followed, hoping to catch the cowpoke falling off his horse in front of Samantha. But instead of cutting through the grass to the food court patio door, Sparky headed toward the parking lot. Nick's inner radar blipped. Something was off.

With pulse quickening, Nick ducked behind cars, cutting the cowpoke off at the pass. His adrenaline surged. The thrill of the chase. That was what he missed. Sparky answered his cell. That was when Nick dashed behind the warehouse outside of Carole's open window.

He overheard Carole's raspy one-sided conversation about the telescope. The bell on the front door jingled. Sparky called to Carole, something about checking on an artifact. Nick detected deception in his tone. Classic. Get her talking about one thing while you assess the scene for another.

Was he looking for the missing telescope?

Samantha paced outside the food court restrooms. From the moment she begged Nick for help, her independence had slipped. Then she accepted Cody's lunch invitation and lost all grip.

"Alex, hurry," Samantha called through the men's door.

Alex emerged.

"What took you so long?"

"A man's business is a man's business."

Samantha giggled. As much as he drove her nuts, the laughter he brought made forgiveness easy.

Callie and Alex scrambled to the table as Cody ambled from the cash register, breathing heavily. "That took longer than expected." He set down the tray and held out Samantha's chair. "Wasn't sure what dressing you fancied so I grabbed them all."

"How thoughtful."

Cody sat. "Alex mentioned you toured the mansion. Anything exciting happen?"

Samantha dislodged the lettuce from her throat with a sip of water. "A typical day at Mount Vernon, I suppose."

Cody fingered the cross around her neck. "You churchgoing folks?"

Samantha nodded, her face flushed.

"Maybe you'd join me at Christ Church on Sunday. The architecture is exquisite." Cody lingered on the last word.

"I've wanted to visit since we moved here."

"I'll collect you at nine, then treat you to lunch."

"Again?"

"What good's money if it can't be spent?" He winked.

So not fair. "Okay, on two conditions. We'll meet at Christ

Church, and I'm buying."

"Perfect!" Nick scooted a chair next to Samantha. "I decided to accept your lunch offer."

Nick wouldn't normally barge in on someone's lunch, but he couldn't watch Samantha be devoured by that snake. He folded his hands on the table.

Samantha stared at him. "Don't you have rounds to make or something?"

"A guy's gotta eat. I'll take a cheeseburger and fries."

Cowpoke stood, eyed Nick. "You'd let a lady pay for your meal?"

Nick matched his stance. "I didn't hear you refuse her offer to buy *you* lunch."

"Didn't hear me agree."

"Sit, you two." Samantha's neck turned red, but they didn't budge.

Cody pulled out a twenty. "I'll be right back."

"Coke, no ice," Nick called after Cody.

Samantha glared at Nick.

"I didn't come to ruin your lunch." Nick leaned in. "I saw Cody leave the mansion and head to the archaeology building."

"You followed him? There's nothing suspicious about an archaeologist visiting the lab."

"There is when there is a forger on the loose and he's supposedly buying you lunch. Besides, he asked Carole about an artifact."

"The telescope?"

"Not exactly."

"What forger takes along two kids?"

"They weren't with him."

Samantha stopped mid-chew. "There could be a million explanations why—"

"I'm looking for one credible reason. Here he comes."

"That was quick," Samantha said in the skeptical tone she usually reserved for Nick.

"Sure was." Cody slid the tray to Nick, who caught the cup before it toppled. "Lunch crowd must be thinning."

Like his hair? Maybe that was why he wore a cowboy hat.

"Thanks for the grub." Nick whispered to Samantha, "Everyone's a suspect." He sat at the table behind her in direct view of Cody. Nothing covert about his position. He wanted Cody to know he was being watched.

Samantha tried to tune out the noise behind her, but Nick emphasized every bite and chew like those mouth-drooling burger commercials, only grosser. Cody, the forger? The only threat he held was to her neglected heart.

Why would Nick lie about seeing Cody without the children? Jealousy topped *her* suspicions.

"Cody, did the kids give you any trouble?"

"Nope. Had my eyes on them the whole time." Cody swallowed his bite.

"Excuse me." Samantha grabbed her children's hands. "Forgot to wash up."

She let Alex dart ahead. "Callie, did Cody leave you alone?"

"Not really."

"What do you mean?"

"We stayed at the table while he ordered; then you took us to the bathroom." Callie hesitated.

"And?"

"Before that, I went to tell him I wanted sausage instead of pepperoni. He wasn't in line."

The food court was crowded. If Callie couldn't find Cody, did that mean he wasn't watching them? She hadn't checked the lines for Cody before she whisked the children to the bathroom. Had he run to the mansion and lab like Nick said?

When they caught up to Alex, he stood in front of the men's room. A yellow CLEANING IN PROGRESS marker blocked his entry.

"Go with Callie."

Callie pulled Alex into the restroom.

If Cody had an errand to run, why not take the kids?

"Don't mess up." A gruff voice boomed behind the men's door.

"I need more time."

Samantha froze as the door flew open. A gorilla of a man in a suit ogled her, then plodded away. Seconds later, the janitor exited, his fingers shaking as he pushed a bucket to the women's restroom.

He fumbled for his ringing cell. "You'll have it by Thursday." He wiped blood from his lip and glanced around.

Samantha dropped her stare, searched her purse.

"Something's in the works, I promise." He lowered his voice.

If this janitor had access to the mansion, maybe he had something to do with the telescope. She smirked. Nick wasn't the only one who could play detective.

After hanging up, the janitor pushed open the women's restroom door.

Samantha rushed to block his entry. "My kids are in there."

He shook his head. "I make sure it's clear before I go in."

Younger than Samantha first thought, the janitor looked college age. Samantha gazed into his troubled eyes, her compassion overriding her doubts. "Having a tough day?"

"More like a tough year."

"Oh. I understand."

"Really? Your mom has cancer, and you blew your college savings to pay medical bills?" He pounded the mop into the bucket, impaling Samantha's heart.

"I didn't mean to imply—" She wet her lips. "I lost my husband in a car accident."

He stopped sloshing the mop, his posture softening. "That's gotta be tough on your kids."

"I'm Samantha Steele." She stuck out her hand. "Archaeology intern."

"Johnny Newberg. Janitor."

Samantha startled at the hand on her shoulder. "Everything okay, darlin'?" Cody peered at Johnny, who broke eye contact.

Samantha nodded.

"I bought the children cake. Hope you don't mind."

Alex barreled from the restroom and slipped his hand in Cody's. "Cake?"

Callie emerged seconds later. Cody scooped Alex up on his broad shoulders as Nick rounded the corner, glowering.

Nick had to be wrong about Cody.

Chapter 4

Nick approached Cody outside the restrooms. He had Alex perched on his shoulders like a trophy. It took all Nick's restraint not to coldcock the guy. Weaseling up to the kids to get to their mother. Not too original.

"I'd like a word, Sparks, alone." Nick glanced at Samantha, who glared with arms crossed.

Sparky grinned as he slid Alex off, then puffed his chest.

"It's okay, darlin'. I'll catch up." Cody put his hand on her back.

Nick balled his fists, fighting off images of Rocky Balboa in the meat house. How he wished he had Sparks in an abandoned warehouse so he could use his face as a punching bag.

As Samantha ushered her kids away, she glanced from Cody to Nick, where her gaze lingered. Warmth flowed through him, and it wasn't driven by anger. Confusion pounded. Why this need to protect Samantha?

Sparks spread his arms. "What's so important you interrupt my date?"

Despite the lack of evidence against Sparks, he couldn't retreat. "I can see through you."

"All's fair in love and war."

Love? He shook his head. With or without *forger* on his rap sheet, Sparks was a slimeball. There was no way Nick would let another woman be victimized. Not on his watch. Nick jabbed a finger in Sparky's chest. "What's so important at the mansion and lab you had to leave Samantha's kids alone?"

He crossed his arms. "I had my reasons."

"It's only a matter of time before she realizes you're a liar."

"What happens when she finds out about you?"

Nick stretched out his arms. "I got nothing to hide."

"We'll see about that."

Samantha released her fork as Nick charged her, Cody not far behind. The way they acted reminded her of junior high.

Nick pulled her from the table where the children devoured their chocolate cake. "We need to talk."

"What's wrong with you?" She yanked from his grip.

"Nothing. I'm watching out for you."

"I don't need watching."

"Cody's lying about something."

"Sure you're not looking through *green*-colored glasses?"

"What's that supposed to mean?"

"Forget it. Listen. I overheard the janitor talking with a man in an expensive suit. I think he's involved."

"Shaggy? I don't think he could see past the end of his schnoz."

"You're not using that idiom right."

Nick's temple throbbed. "That kid couldn't lift a pack of gum, let alone forge a telescope."

"The man looked like Mafia."

Cody swaggered to the other side of Samantha, putting her in the middle of an ego sandwich. "I think that's enough, Porter."

Heat climbed her neck. "I'll decide when it's enough. I don't need to be taken care of by either of you."

Nick exited Capitol Cleaners, his face warm from the setting sun and tight with a scowl. With the amount they charged for a rush order on his uniform, he felt he'd been. . .well. . .taken to the cleaners. He glanced at Samantha's business card and crumpled it. Stubborn woman. Did she expect him to send her the bill?

She had no business snooping up suspects like Junior the janitor. And to think Cody was innocent and Nick was. . .he couldn't say the word. Jealous? Ridiculous.

Once he compared the prints on the telescope with the ones he lifted from Cody's lunch cup and Junior's broom handle using hot chocolate powder, tape, and ingenuity, he'd prove Cody was hiding something, and Nick's favorite color wasn't green.

A scream pierced the air. There. In front of Pizza Town by the parking meter. A woman down. Nick ran to her. Samantha!

She remained frozen, eyes begging for help.

"You okay?" He lifted her, searched for the kids. Safe in the car. "Samantha?"

"A man—stole my purse." She pointed to the alley.

Something kick-started inside. Nick scanned the perimeter ready to bolt after the guy, but hesitated. "Sure you're okay?"

"I'm fine." Her voice was edgy. "He has my purse. My money."

"Go inside. Call the police."

She grabbed his arm. "My cell's in my purse."

"Take mine." He handed her his phone, then gave chase. Ten minutes later he returned with a yellow purse minus her wallet and his pride. He sat opposite her. "Sorry, no wallet, but your cell phone's there."

"He has my bank cards."

"You'll need to cancel them. I'll wait for the police."

Samantha's stomach growled.

"Hungry?"

"I'm finc." Emotion choked her voice.

Nick pulled a twenty from his wallet.

"I can't let you."

"You have to eat."

"I owe you lunch and dry—"

"You don't owe me anything."

Samantha straightened. "I'll bring you the full amount on Monday. How much?"

Why didn't she just say thank you? His evening plans had included a microwave dinner and vegging out in front of the TV; instead he was playing Rock 'Em, Sock 'Em with Princess Impossible. He spotted the kids at the video machines. "You can starve, but the kids have to eat. I'm feeding them. So deal with it."

The aroma of pizza weakened Samantha's resolve but didn't quiet her hunger. Maybe swallowing her pride would. First, the broken telescope, then the near-disaster at the dig, now her stolen purse. Each time rescued by a handsome stranger. What next? Fabio riding in on a stallion with her wallet?

Maybe the independence she craved was a fairy tale with no chance on her bookshelf. Maybe she needed a prince to rescue her. Or at least a knight. Was she destined to fall into the role of helpless damsel?

Nick approached, looking relaxed in his jeans and white T-shirt, a pizza balanced on one palm, a tray of drinks in the other. By the silly, crooked grin on his face, it could've been the Holy Grail. She took the pie and set it on the table, but before she grabbed the drinks, Alex charged.

Terror froze Nick's face. Samantha gasped, watching the knight topple off his horse, doused in Sprite.

T.R.O.U.B.L.E.

That was what Samantha and her kids spelled. Trouble with a capital *T*. That rhymed with *P*, which stood for. . .peeved. Nick shook his head. Why was he chanting show tunes? Sitting through *The Music Man* was worse than being on the other end of an interrogation. Nick peeled off his wet clothes, squelching his emotions. Must be the Sprite. It made him go soft and fruity.

He slam-dunked his clothes in the washer, letting the lid fall with a bang. Good riddance, Samantha Steele. At least for the weekend. Come Monday he'd dodge her rapid-fire questions. Right now, he'd relax with mindless television.

The phone rang as he sank into his worn leather recliner. The machine answered.

"Nick? It's Nick, right?"

Samantha? Nick clicked on the television.

"I found this number in your phone. I figured you'd need it this weekend. . . ."

Hurry, woman. I can't hear the TV above your babbling.

"...Or maybe you're screening this call. I don't blame you...."

Silence, then "Someone broke into my condo."

Nick scrambled to the kitchen for the receiver.

"Never mind. The police are—"

"Is everyone okay?" This was no coincidence.

"We're fine. I'm at my neighbor's. She had a spare key to my car and condo."

"Anyone go inside?"

"No, I locked up and went to my neighbor Susan's. I shouldn't have bothered you. I can return your phone tomorrow."

"I'll be right there."

Samantha shook in the doorway of her ransacked home while the officer snapped pictures. Books in jumbled heaps on the floor. Couch cushions overturned. Kitchen drawers dumped out. Why was she robbed again?

Nick rounded the corner. "Everything looks secure. No open windows or evidence of forced entry. Maybe you forgot to lock your door."

"I'm OCD about locking up." Tears pooled. "How could this happen?"

"The purse snatcher may have gotten your address from your license and used your key."

"I still have my Missouri license."

Concern crossed Nick's face. "You'll need to call a locksmith." The officer gave Nick a thumbs-up. He put on booties and stepped over debris. "Ready to walk through?"

Samantha followed. Dragging from room to room, she

stopped every few minutes. Nothing appeared missing. In her bedroom, she examined each jewelry box compartment, then started again. Tears wet her face. Her wedding ring was gone.

"Anything else missing?" Nick asked.

She shook her head and followed him to the living room.

The officer zipped his equipment case. "I'm done. I'll have information on the prints tomorrow."

Nick shook his hand. "Thanks for letting me help, Mike."

"Get yourself back to the precinct, okay?"

Nick showed him out, then returned to Samantha. "I'll wait until the locksmith is finished."

He touched her arm, his warmth comforting as her home lay in shambles.

"You don't have to."

"I know."

Chapter 5

Screaming jolted Samantha awake. It took a few seconds to remember she'd slept at her neighbor's. Then another second to remember why. Heart pounding, she rushed to find her children watching television. Her breath released. Only Saturday morning cartoons.

The note Susan Holland left on the refrigerator gave Samantha free rein of the house and invited them to stay tonight, but Samantha needed to regain control of her life now. She inhaled the aroma of amaretto Vienna. Her favorite from Susan's coffee shop, Coffee, Tea, and Sweets.

After two cups, Samantha hesitated before entering her condo, then pushed the debris away. She turned on the television and handed the kids a box of Trix. Not the best parenting move, but she needed to think without interruptions.

Samantha dialed the investigating officer. No news on her wallet or who had broken in. He assured her the crimes were random and the burglar had moved on. She sat at the table, smiling as she remembered the concern on Nick's face last night when he walked her to Susan's and his disappointment when she declined his help to clean this morning. Nick's feelings for her were transparent, even if he wouldn't admit them. Last night, she'd felt something as well, stronger than she had before. But she couldn't deny Cody tickled her fancy.

Enough daydreaming. How could someone steal the telescope and switch it with a replica? Years ago, the study underwent renovations to replicate Washington's last year of life. Many antiques were conserved. It would've been easy to replace the artifacts with forgeries if they went as far as the renovations. Where were they renovated?

Samantha pushed the mail from her laptop and paused. Maybe the burglar hadn't seen it underneath the clutter? After accessing the Internet, she found the information she needed.

"Kids, get dressed. We're going to see the dinosaurs."

Good thing the Museum of American History was next door.

Nick sat at the kitchen bar, gulping his java straight-up, hoping to chase away the lingering up-all-night haze. He hadn't been this foggy since his surveillance days, and all because he'd spent half the night worrying about Samantha and the other half calling in favors with Tony at Dispatch for criminal history on staff who had access to the study.

Unfortunately, no hits on Althea, and the history on Sparks returned Clorox white. His prints weren't on the telescope, but that didn't alleviate Nick's suspicions.

Nick read his notes. *Forged telescope.* According to Carole who called late last night, the Smithsonian's preliminary findings confirmed forgery. *Suspects.* Though circumstantial, Sparks topped his list. As an archaeologist who handled the artifacts, he wouldn't draw attention if he removed an antique.

Nick wanted to write cozying up to Samantha as suspicious activity, but he'd keep this professional.

Althea. Caught with an artifact? His buddy at Forensics would test the Bible, but if it was legit, no need to alert Mount Vernon. Even if it was authentic, Althea might've been about to swipe it. Even with no Bible, her strange behavior warranted suspicion. Plus, Nick's homemade fingerprint kit lifted her prints from the telescope and four others. Nick's, Samantha's, Alex's, and one unidentified.

Nick almost eliminated the janitor, but forgery involved heavy hitters. Samantha mentioned mob ties. Nick hadn't paid attention to her claim, but if Johnny had organized crime connections, he couldn't exclude him. He'd run a criminal history and hope the janitor was old enough for a record.

Despite his lack of sleep, Nick ached to get moving. Since Samantha rejected his help to straighten her apartment, his day was wide open. Carole mentioned she sent the telescope to the Smithsonian for testing. Nick downed his java.

Perfect day for sightseeing.

Guzzling water from the fountain outside the bathroom at the Smithsonian, Nick got bumped by some guy gabbing on his cell. Cold water splashed his face.

"Hey, watch it." Nick studied the guy adjusting his glasses. The klutz looked familiar. Something nagged at Nick. He waited until the guy rounded the corner, then tailed him.

The man climbed the stairs, then checked his watch halfway down a deserted corridor. Seconds later, footsteps clomped behind Nick. He retrieved his phone and faked a conversation.

When the clomping stopped, Nick studied the men.

A long-haired dude in boots towered above the skinny guy who would've been hidden by Bigfoot's hulking frame, if he hadn't been twitching like a snitch dropping off a high. Before they entered the room, Nick snapped a photo with his cell and caught the big guy's profile.

Sparky? Nick crept toward the door. It was ajar. Voices grew louder from within.

"I don't have time," the skinny man whined.

"I appreciate you fitting this in," Sparky said.

"I can't possibly—"

"You *will* get it done before it's too late. Now about the telescope."

Footsteps faded, then minutes later approached the door. Nick hurried away. Would Carole send Sparky to follow up on the telescope, or was he involved in the forgery?

Samantha's open-toed heels echoed on the Museum of Natural History floor, her floral skirt flitting as Tara Whitley, her neighbor and confidante, ran ahead with Alex and Callie. Last night Tara apologized for getting sick and today insisted on watching the children while Samantha investigated at the American History Museum next door. Samantha hurried to join them at the elephant rotunda, but the kids disappeared inside the dinosaur exhibit. Her lips pursed.

Tara touched Samantha's shoulder. "Relax, it's a hands-on exhibit."

"My kids have a heavier hand than most."

"Last night you admitted if Alex hadn't destroyed the

telescope, you wouldn't have discovered the forgery."

"Or be indebted to Nick Porter."

"The security guard?"

Samantha nodded. "He rescued me from the purse snatcher and came to my condo last night."

"Sure *he's* not stalking you?"

"That undercover operation at the White House has gone to your head. Nick's not a threat. He used to be a detective."

"Why's he working security?"

Samantha wondered the same thing.

"Whether he left the department or was fired, life must've roughed him up." Tara's eyes lit. "What if he's the forger?"

"Stop before I become paranoid like Audrey Hepburn in *Charades*."

They laughed as they headed toward the colossal T. rex and found the children. Maybe now was a good time to see which artifacts had been renovated at the Museum of American History.

"Samantha?" Her belly fluttered at the masculine voice.

Samantha gazed into Nick's bright eyes. "What are you doing here?" Was Tara's stalker theory true?

"Following up on the telescope. Carole confirmed the forgery."

"The Museum of *American* History next door authenticates the historical artifacts."

Nick's jaw clenched. "How would you know? You're not checking—"

"Simply spending Saturday at the museum." Samantha pointed to her children. "If I was checking on the telescope, I'd be at the museum next door."

Nick's self-assured grin straightened. "I have work to do."

"I'll go with you."

"I'm doing the investigating, and you're spending the day with your kids."

"Why are you fighting me on this? Are you the forger?" No, she didn't say that. Nick's mouth gaped. Yes, she did.

"You're kidding?"

She faux-punched his arm. "You said everyone's a suspect."

His scowl deepened. He wasn't buying her act. "Every time something bad happens, you're there."

"Your kid plowed into me. He broke the telescope. Your purse was stolen and house ransacked. Each time I was minding my business and there you were, Tsunami Sam. Did you think maybe I have better things to do than rescue you?"

Samantha's chest ached. "You're right. You never should've gotten involved."

"I didn't say that. Just stay away from Sparks."

"He's a suspect?"

"At the top of my list with his name flashing in neon lights."

"Where's the evidence?"

"He ducked inside a lab with some guy to discuss a special project. Their conversation sounded suspicious."

Maybe Nick's machismo-flexing yesterday wasn't about her. Maybe Cody was guilty.

"I've said too much. I need to check things out."

"If I talk to Cody, maybe he'll explain."

"If Cody's clean, I'll be first to apologize, but if he's not, if you keep snooping, you're gonna get hurt."

"Fine. I'll keep away from the investigation for now, but I can't stay away from Cody. He's my boss."

"Then be careful."

Samantha nodded. How dangerous could attending a church service be?

Nick hurried to the staff parking lot where the guard allowed him to park his Jeep. One minute Samantha played the damsel in distress. The next, she morphed into the Iron Giant, obliterating anyone in her path. He slipped in the driver's seat and pulled his laptop from underneath. After searching the Smithsonian's paleobiology staff, he found his guy. Kyle Timmons, department head. The perfect cover for an artifact smuggler.

He dialed Dispatch. "Tony, anything on Newberg?"

"The kid's clean. Whatcha working on?"

"Can't say."

"We're gonna get involved sooner or later. Spill it."

"No can do. I need concrete evidence. Then it'll go to Courtland."

"FBI?"

"I've got another name."

"Not sure I can run it through without drawing attention."

"Sure you can. I need addresses and a criminal check ASAP on Kyle Timmons."

"When ya coming back?"

"Didn't say I was."

"Face it. It's in your blood."

In his blood. He'd heard crusty old cops spout the mantra, but never understood until now. Maybe it took time away to see it. To feel it. To realize not even a transfusion could get the cop out of his blood.

He convinced himself he took a leave of absence to kick his addiction, but the reason he quit wasn't because of painkillers. It was because of the pain.

Timmons exited the building and entered his Duster.

Adrenaline swooshed through Nick's veins. How could he pretend he was anything but a cop? Until he met Samantha, he'd been walking out his death sentence. Now he ached to be on the other side of the bars. He couldn't bring his family back, and he'd forever welcome the guilt, but police work pulsed through his veins.

Timmons drove off.

If Nick stood a chance at being a respected cop again, he had to find the forger.

Samantha hesitated outside paleobiology at the Museum of Natural History and listened. Reaching for the knob, her heart quickened. She eased the door open and tiptoed inside. Fluorescent lights stung her eyes as she stared at casts and fossils littering worktables. She sighed. Empty. With sweaty palms she closed the door, switched off the overhead lighting, and turned on a table lamp. Where should she search for evidence of Cody's innocence?

A bang sounded from the rear of the lab. Samantha's heart thundered.

Someone else was in the room.

Chapter 6

Samantha crouched below a table in the paleobiology lab and listened. Silence. Had she imagined the noise? She peeked toward where she heard the bang. A dimly lit object caught her eye. Washington's telescope?

With pulse throbbing, she grabbed a chisel from the table and waddled toward the telescope, the tool poised in her shaking hand.

A strong hand clamped her forehead; another snatched the chisel. She screamed.

"Sam?"

"Nick?" Fear left, but Samantha's heart raced. "You scared the life out of me."

"Good!" Nick examined the chisel. "What do you think you'd do with this? Anyone could use it on you like a letter opener."

"Thanks for the nightmares."

"Serves you right. I told you to stay out of it."

"Obviously I didn't listen."

"Like mother, like son," Nick mumbled.

"What?"

"Nothing. Since you're here, you might as well help."

Samantha headed for the telescope.

"That's mine." Nick pointed to the desk near the door. "Look for invoices. Appraisal quotes. Anything related to the sale of an artifact."

Samantha slumped away. Why was Nick keeping her from the telescope? She flipped on the lights. Nick had the time and resources to steal it. Maybe he hired someone to replicate the original. She peeked at him searching through some drawers and quieted her suspicions. He said he'd worked at Mount Vernon less than a month. Not enough time to orchestrate the forgery. Samantha searched the cluttered desk, then moved aside books on wood restoration and gasped.

Nick rushed over. "Everything okay?" His hand on her arm gave her unexpected chills.

She shoved a paper at him. "Proof Cody's not involved."

"An invoice for a refurbished rocking chair? Keep searching and don't scare me again."

"Why are you stuck on Cody's guilt?"

"You said the artifact should be at the Museum of American History. Why is it here? Why was Cody here talking to Timmons?"

"Professor Timmons?"

Nick's eyebrows raised. "You know him?"

"Cody introduced us yesterday."

"See, something's not right."

"All I see are two professionals in a working relationship."

Nick shook his head. "I know the ladies drool over the cowboy type, but I thought you were smarter than that."

Samantha's face flushed. She turned away, huffing and puffing, ready to blow the desk down as she riffled through papers.

She'd prove she was nobody's fool.

Nick returned to the telescope as Samantha attacked the desk, throwing papers around like grenades. How could Cody blind this intelligent woman?

True, Nick had no evidence against Sparks. Carole might've asked him to follow up on the telescope, and Nick might've been fueled by jealousy. There, he admitted it, but that didn't mean he'd pardoned the cowpoke. Though it did move him one spot lower, bumping up suspect number two.

"Let's go." Nick nudged Samantha toward the door.

"Where?"

"To find your kids so you can take them home while I continue the investigation."

"Tara drove them home." Samantha smirked. "Guess you're stuck with me."

The twenty-three-mile drive to Fort Belvoir took over an hour on a Saturday afternoon filled with DC traffic. Nick didn't mind the drive or Samantha's silence. It allowed him to strategize.

After exiting Route 1, he entered a well-to-do neighborhood and parked in front of a two-story colonial way beyond a tour guide's price range. Samantha reached for the handle.

"Before you charge off, let's cover the rules."

"Rules?" Samantha's neck turned pink.

"First, let me do the talking."

Samantha's mouth opened.

Nick held up his hand. "Second. Don't say a word."

"That's the same rule."

"Third, keep your mouth shut."

Less than ten seconds later, Samantha broke the rules.

Nick stopped. "What part of 'Don't say a word' didn't you understand?"

Samantha stomped up the steps and stood behind Nick as he rang the bell. Nick Porter was infuriating. Althea answered the door in black slacks and a red blouse. A modern contrast to her eighteenth-century costume.

Nick introduced himself and Samantha, but when she didn't recognize them, he continued. "We work at Mount Vernon."

A polite smile creased Althea's expression. "Come in. Would you like some lemonade?"

"Yes, please." Nick held the door open, then stepped into the entryway.

"Make yourselves comfortable in the library." Althea pointed to the right, then disappeared to her left.

Samantha lingered, mesmerized by the great room. Grand piano. Marble tables. An ornate mantel over the fireplace. How could a docent afford this home? Samantha elbowed Nick and pointed to the family photo above the fireplace.

Althea didn't own the home.

Samantha entered the library lined with three walls of books while Nick dawdled in the hall. A book on the table in the center of the room drew her attention. *The Knave of Hearts* by Louise Saunders. She opened it. First edition, signed. Her palms perspired as she held the book, remembering the story from college.

Carefully, she flipped through illustrated pages and recalled a line she'd memorized. "We are distracted by violence, we are deceived by hypocrisy, until only too often villains receive the rewards of nobility and the truly great-hearted are suspected, distrusted, and maligned."

She remembered how the seemingly low knave wasn't a thief and became the hero who rescued Lady Violetta by supplying her with the tarts that won her the crown.

"Nick?"

Standing by the picture window, he turned to her.

"I want to apologize for interfering." She wet her lips. "It won't happen again."

"Why the change of heart?"

She showed him the book. "Something I read reminded me I should trust more."

Nick took the tray from Althea and placed it on the table between the two leather chairs. "Please sit, Ms. Washington."

Samantha settled in one chair, Althea in the other.

Nick rested on the arm of Samantha's chair and whispered, "Watch and learn."

He gulped his drink. "Fresh squeezed?" Time to establish a baseline of truth, but Althea nodded instead of answering.

"Let's get to the point." Althea's crossed leg bobbed. "You're here because I touched that book."

Nick set his glass on the coaster. "I'm here on a matter of security."

"I'd never take anything. My ancestors were slaves on Washington's estate. I volunteer every summer to be near my heritage."

Nick braced for wild eyes. Nothing. "I'm not accusing you. We need your assistance to prevent that from happening."

Althea leaned forward. "How can I help?"

"Could an employee steal from the mansion?"

"People working there want to preserve history, not steal it."

"Not everyone is there for noble reasons."

"Several students from NOVA take summer jobs. I can't imagine them stealing."

"Any vulnerable spots?"

"Due to cutbacks, there's less staff in the mansion and security patrols the rooms. Security and janitorial staff have keys to the mansion. Employees go through background checks, but you know all that."

Althea's nonverbals showed she was nervous, but about what? "Mind if I use your restroom?"

Nick followed Althea's directions to the bathroom, then hurried past to where he guessed she roomed. Bingo. Bed made. Room neat. Laptop on table. Nick booted it up. Not much on desktop. Games. Document folder. He clicked it open. Recipes. Althea's memoirs? Nothing suspicious.

Nick powered off the computer and searched the nightstand. A worn black Bible. A newer book, *An Imperfect God: George Washington, His Slaves and the Creation of America*. A tattered book with an illegible inscription and date. 1775. The year before the revolution? Did Althea take it from the study? Could Althea be the Mount Vernon thief?

Nick snapped a photo of the books with his cell. Samantha's voice rose in the hall. "I'm sure he's fine."

Then Althea. "I'd better see if he's lost."

Footsteps pounded. Althea's humming got louder. He returned the books and slipped behind the door. It creaked open. No way he'd talk himself out of this.

"Nick?"

"Sam!" Nick exhaled. "Where's Althea?"

"In the laundry room."

Nick peeked out. "All clear." They tiptoed through the hall. Samantha stopped at the bathroom. "I'll catch up."

"No rush." After realizing Althea's affinity for old literature, he needed to poke around the library. The perfect place to hide stolen books.

Lavender permeated the air as Samantha dried her hands on the embroidered towel. Reapplying her lipstick, she noticed a magazine in the basket on the floor.

Archaeology Today with Mount Vernon on the cover. She turned to the showcased story. The article detailed more than sixty thousand artifacts excavated from the brick-lined root cellar below the slave quarters from 1984 to 1991. Beautiful photographs brought this dig to life. The array of domestic artifacts and food remains provided information about slaves who lived on the estate.

Their current excavation site wasn't far from this one. Uncovering one significant artifact could propel her career forward.

So could finding the forger.

Though a bit quirky, Althea seemed a devoted employee curious about her ancestry. Nothing more. She returned the magazine and noticed a prescription bottle in the trash.

Althea Washington, *haloperidol*. If Althea took this medication and had run out, that might explain her bizarre behavior. Samantha jotted the prescription information on a receipt from her purse. Maybe Althea warranted further investigation.

After Althea apologized to Samantha for not showing them out and disappeared in the kitchen, Samantha found Nick slumped in a chair in the library.

"Interesting spin on a nursery rhyme." He waved at *The Knave of Hearts*.

"There's always more than one side to a story." Samantha sat.

"Reminds me of *Hoodwinked*, the cartoon about Little Red Riding Hood told in different points of view. Turns out the big bad wolf wasn't the villain."

"It was the bunny."

"I pegged him early."

"Fairfax police training at its best?"

"Doesn't take a detective to recognize a suspicious character."

"What about daredevil granny?" Samantha laughed. "I think I enjoyed the movie more than my kids."

"Me, too." Nick's levity broke.

"You have children?"

"Had."

Samantha froze. She never thought. . . Why did she ask? "I'm sorry, I shouldn't—"

"Their death was my fault." Nick's voice held no emotion. "He'd be six this summer."

"On our tenth anniversary, we learned Angie was expecting again after trying for years." Nick sucked in air, barely able to breathe, but compelled to spew. Confession wouldn't purge his soul, but it might clear his head. "We stopped at a convenience store. It was snowing. Angie asked me to leave the motor running. I knew better. Walked in on a robbery. I blocked the door. Shouldn't have intervened. Thought I could protect them. Didn't think about the rear exit. He shot me. I fired. Hit him, but he escaped—in my car." Nick swallowed, holding back tears. "He killed my family."

Samantha's gasp drew him from the scene, winded and numb as if he'd experienced the horror for the first time. After a year and a half, he couldn't shake the emotions. Or the guilt.

The warmth from Samantha's hand resting on his arm resuscitated his soul.

"Oh Nick. I'm so sorry. I blamed myself for my husband's death. If I hadn't asked him to get a movie on the way home, he'd be alive." Tears brimmed.

She understood.

Nick didn't know how much time passed, but in the quiet moment in a suspect's home, something shifted.

Maybe confession was good for the soul.

After Nick learned about Althea's empty prescription from Samantha, they drove in silence. An hour later, Nick searched the house numbers of Alexandria's most crime-ridden neighborhood. Each neglected shack spawned a jungle of bushes separated by chain-link fences. A visual reminder of the mess in his soul.

What had made him spew? Ever since he met Samantha, ever since her son nicked open his heart. Ever since he started helping her, his soul began to itch like a scab, healing from the inside out. He wasn't sure whether to pick it or leave it alone.

He banished the psychobabble.

The old book found in Althea's room with the haloperidol fueled his suspicions of her. Later, he'd dig into Althea's medical condition, but first he'd fry another suspect.

Nick parked in front of a gray house with broken shingles. Johnny Newberg needed money in a bad way.

As they walked the cracked sidewalk, Samantha's silence surprised Nick. She stumbled, and he caught her. Her unassuming smile soothed like Neosporin on his soul. For a brief moment he allowed himself to visualize the healing.

Samantha waited next to him as he knocked. A salt-and-pepper-headed lady peeked through the curtain.

"Hello, ma'am. Is Johnny available?"

"What do you want?"

"We work with Johnny."

"Then you'd know he's not here." She let the curtain fall.

Nick knocked again. She returned.

"Sorry to bother you." He flashed his security badge. "We need to ask him about an incident at work."

"You can't be too careful in this neighborhood." The woman unlocked the door and spoke through the screen. Her pale face looked as if the sun hadn't kissed it in years. "I'm Johnny's aunt Trudy. He's due home from that law office of yours any minute."

Samantha's expression mirrored his surprise.

"Do you mind if we wait?"

She hesitated, then opened the door. "Forgive the mess. I've cared for his mama ever since she got the cancer."

A musty odor hit Nick as he entered the dimly lit room. Dark spots covered the walls, the stench of mold overpowering.

"She's finally resting." Trudy put her finger to her lips and looked at the skeleton-thin woman in the hospital bed in the living room. She motioned to the couch, but before they sat, Johnny barreled through the door, halting when he saw Nick. "What do you want?"

"Hi, Johnny." Nick glanced at Johnny's mom who didn't stir, then eyed him. "Had a couple of questions about work."

Trudy wrung her hands. "Johnny'd never do anything wrong."

"Never said he did."

Trudy brightened. "He works hard. He gets medication from the clinic."

"Mom'd get better if I could get us out of this dump. I'll get money for more chemo, you'll see."

Nick didn't doubt that. "I just need a minute."

Johnny checked his text. "I've got a meeting." Johnny glanced at his aunt and exited.

"Like I said. Johnny's a hard worker."

"I'm sure he is." Nick handed Samantha his keys. "I'm following Johnny. Drive my Jeep to your house. I'll pick it up later."

His suspects were multiplying like cockroaches.

Chapter 7

Nick tailed Johnny from the Metro to an Italian neighborhood Nick hadn't visited in years. Memories flooded. Stuffing his face with cannolis as a kid with Uncle Vince, romantic dinners with Angie, and his last run-in with the Marascano family.

Johnny ducked into Bellina Cucina, home and operation of the Capolinis. Years earlier, Nick worked the scene of a mass hit. Marascanos' retaliation on the Capolinis for stepping into their territory.

Now he was stepping into the Capolinis' territory. When Johnny shot past the hostess, it confirmed Nick's suspicions. Johnny wasn't craving their ravioli. Nick followed, his stomach growling at the nostalgic aromas. Johnny slipped through a door marked La Famiglia.

Nick entered the bathroom next door. "Luck Be a Lady Tonight" played through the speakers as he climbed on the toilet. *Here's hoping, Blue Eyes!* He put his ear to the vent.

"I'm good for it." Johnny came through shaky and clear.

"Oh, I believe you." Sarcasm laced the Italian-American voice. "But people are worried. They need assurance."

"I gave you it all."

"An acquaintance is in the market for really old silverware."

"I almost got caught last time."

"Then I guess we're done." A chair squeaked. "The terms of our agreement are simple. If you don't pay, we're gonna collect. It's up to you, Johnny."

A door closed. Nick stepped down and answered his vibrating phone.

"Carole, slow down," he whispered.

"Washington's penknife is missing. It's not in the boxes in the mansion." Carole coughed. "I can't keep this quiet any longer. My shoulders are killing me from the stress. And I really need a smoke."

Nick's chest tightened. "Take a couple of aspirin, but let me follow a lead. One more day."

Silence. "Monday morning I'm telling Dale, and you're paying for a massage."

"Deal."

A door closed. Nick exited the restroom. So Johnny stole antiques for the Capolinis. He probably swiped the knife, but why not leave a replica?

Garlic bread tempted his taste buds as he hustled after Johnny, but he'd lost his appetite. Johnny was playing stickball with the big kids. And Nick hoped the Capolinis didn't use his head as the ball.

The fragrance from the cherry blossoms in the courtyard called Samantha home as she walked toward her condo, clutching Nick's car keys. Though Cherry Blossom Estates didn't compare to her Missouri farm, it was a safe place where she could watch the kids play from her window.

At least it used to be.

Samantha found Tara and the children under the tree in the middle of the garden. Callie read, while Alex whittled. Her heart tripped. That knife? He must've taken it before her purse was stolen.

Her cell rang. Cody. "Hello."

"Mom!" Alex ran, knife pointed.

"Alex, stop." To Samantha's surprise, he listened. She covered the phone. "Give me that knife—you'll hurt yourself."

Alex obeyed. "Dad'd let me keep it."

Alex's words stung as he bolted.

"Sorry, Cody."

"Can't wait to show you Christ Church tomorrow." Cody's Southern twang dulled the ache Alex had left.

"Me, either." They chatted until the pink tree blossoms blended into the sunset, reminding her of the late hour. Samantha said good-bye, her gut swirling like a tornado kicking up emotional debris. How could she be attracted to two very different men at the same time?

After visiting suspects' homes and learning they had more motive for stealing than Cody, she felt certain he wasn't involved. Maybe spending time with him tomorrow would help her sort her feelings. So would a good night's sleep, but sleep would wait until Nick picked up his Jeep.

Maybe she should make dinner for four.

Darkness delayed morning as Nick stumbled to the kitchen for java to chase away the regrets. Last night, he'd intended to head toward Samantha's and share the latest on Johnny until she invited him for dinner. Then he remembered *The Knave of Hearts* and lost his appetite. After ditching Samantha, he tossed all night, reviewing the case, but always came full circle to Samantha, his attraction to her, and facing her Monday.

Waiting for his coffee, he flipped on the television. A beautiful brunette lounged on a couch, enticing viewers to call the singles' line. *You're killing me.*

Nick switched the station. A church service aired. Though the robed man wasn't his style, Nick listened. It was Sunday after all.

"Power is perfected in weakness."

Yeah, right!

"Most times God chooses not to take you out of the trial, but to give you strength to endure it." The man spoke as if he'd lived the words. As if he'd wrestled with his weakness and won. Nick retrieved his brew and sat.

"Therefore I am well content with weakness, with insults, with distresses, with persecutions, with difficulties, for Christ's sake; for when I am weak, then I am strong."

What? Nick rewound the last few seconds, thankful for DVR. Didn't the scripture say, "When I am weak, *he* is strong"? That made sense. God takes over when we can't. He got that, but Nick had never been weak before. He listened again. "When I am weak, *I am* strong." Impossible. He switched it off. Psychoanalysis wasn't on his to-do list.

Samantha soaked in the tranquility of Christ Church as Cody's musky scent competed with the blossoming flowers for her attention. He looked dashing in his tan Dockers and oxford shirt. A contrast to his rugged cowboy look, but equally pleasing. Seeing him this morning almost made her forget about Nick.

But it was the old brick archway with *1773* on top that transported her from her troubles. The ones that kept her awake with nightmares about an escaped mobster with Nick's face, who stole a telescope and was apprehended by falling into a pot of mac and cheese. She chuckled at the absurdity. But Nick had better have a good excuse for standing her up last night.

"Let's walk through the churchyard before services." Cody inched closer. They strolled the brick walkway past the parish house while the children skipped ahead.

The churchyard, scattered with graves that were centuries old, sobered her mood. Samantha paused before a gravestone and read. "In memory of Sarah, the wife of John Wrenn, August 13, 1792, aged 28 years." Her age. "All you who come my grave to see, as I am now you soon will be. Prepare and turn to God in time, for I was taken in my prime." She paused. "I read in 1986, Alexandria Archaeology excavated here and found more graves than headstones."

"You don't say." Cody tugged her sleeve. "Come see where they're excavating now."

They viewed the site, then rested on a stone bench while the children picked dandelions.

Her body relaxed.

"Since we're at church, I should confess." Cody took her hand. "My motives weren't entirely pure."

Samantha's heart stuttered. "Oh."

"I wanted to spend time with you before I become your boss."

Warmth climbed Samantha's cheeks despite the shade of the tree.

Cody scooted closer. "I hope you don't mind me pulling the wool over your eyes?"

Samantha stood. "We should go. Service is starting soon." Maybe the sermon would quiet her romantic thoughts, or she could review suspects. "Come on, kids." They headed toward the church.

Something about Althea bothered her. According to the pharmacy, the prescription hadn't been filled in a year. An online search showed haloperidol was prescribed for delusional disorder. How could she act normal without her meds? Maybe Nick would know.

"Everything okay?" Cody halted and faced her. "Whatever it is, I'm here for you." He stroked her cheek.

Her face tingled, the humidity growing thicker by the second.

"I realize we just met, but I feel this connection between us." He caressed her hands, gazed deep. "I think you feel it, too." He moved closer, his breath on her nose.

"Someone forged the telescope in Washington's study."

Cody stepped back. Obviously, he hadn't expected that. Her pulse settled. For the next few minutes, she relayed the entire story except Nick suspecting Cody.

His eyes narrowed. "Who else knows?"

"Carole Huntington, a few neighbors—and Professor Timmons."

"Don't tell anyone else."

"I'll be discreet in my investigation."

"Whoa there. That's not a good idea."

"How else will I catch the thief?"

"You could get your pretty head in a heap of trouble."

"I need to prove I'm good enough."

Cody cupped Samantha's chin, his eyes burning through hers. "You don't need to prove anything. Promise you'll quit snooping." Passion stirred in his expression.

She pulled away. "I can't, but I'll be careful."

The children scampered over. Cody grabbed Alex and twirled him like a helicopter. When Cody set Alex down, he stumbled to Samantha's side. Maybe it was too soon for another man in his life.

"Excuse me, my phone's buzzing." He walked off and soon returned. "I've got to go. That was Graceful Living Nursing Home. They couldn't rouse my grandmother to take her meds."

"Go. Don't worry about us."

As Cody jogged off, Samantha hoped his grandmother was okay, but she couldn't help her smile. The invoice on Timmons's desk proved Cody wasn't guilty.

Samantha thought her Sunday afternoon jaunt through downtown DC would work off lunch, but it only left her exhausted. She pushed open her door and tripped over a toy.

"Alex, Callie, pick up your toys."

"But my show is on," Alex whined.

"Not until you clean. I'm taking a nap. Keep the TV low."

Halting at the toppled plant in the hall, she set it up, too exhausted to clean or ask who made the mess. Right now her inner child begged for a nap. After changing into shorts and a T-shirt, she slipped into bed.

Noises from the children's room startled her before sleep took hold. She held the pillow over her head and drifted. Several more bangs, then a scream. Samantha jolted awake and sprinted to the kids' room. Callie blocked the bedroom door. Inside a masked man held Alex. Samantha screamed. "Callie, run!"

A phone rang.

Callie bolted. Alex kicked the man and ran to Samantha. The intruder gave chase. Samantha pulled Alex into her bedroom, locked the door. With each bang, the door rattled. She ran to the window, unlatched the lock, pushed. It wouldn't budge. She tried again. The pounding grew louder, more desperate. She glanced at Alex, then the window. No use. It was stuck. The man grunted, his blows more forceful.

"Alex, under the bed. Stay." She grabbed her cell. Dialed 911. It rang once. Twice. "Answer." A call beeped in.

"Where is it?" the man outside her door growled. "All I want is the knife."

Nick exited the bus and dialed again. "Where are you?" Samantha hadn't answered her home phone or cell. He should've confirmed she was home before he bought a pizza, but if she was out, he could leave it on the porch with an apology note and get his Jeep with his spare key. His apprehension faded. Sounded like a plan, until Samantha answered.

Locked room. . . Alex. . . "Slow down. I can't understand you."

"He's back. I'm locked in my bedroom." Samantha sucked in a breath. "Alex is with me. I'm scared."

Adrenaline spiked. "I'm on my way." Nick jogged toward Samantha's complex. Something thudded over the phone. Samantha screamed.

"Call nine-one-one."

"Nick, don't hang up." Her voice, desperate.

"I'm almost there."

"Wait, it's quiet. Maybe he left. I should che—"

"Don't open the door. Call nine-one-one."

Darkness shrouded Nick as he ended the call and uttered an awkward plea to God. The last time he prayed, his family was murdered. Nick chucked the pizza and sprinted. Samantha's door, wide open. Nick grabbed his Glock and slinked into the house. Living room, kitchen, empty. More banging. He approached the bedrooms slowly, senses heightened.

Back hugging the wall, he rounded the corner. Perp in a ski mask kicked the bedroom door. "Stop! Police!" He aimed.

The guy spun, caught Nick's stare, then bolted for the room across the hall. Exactly what he hoped wouldn't happen.

Nick secured his firearm and gave chase, grabbing the dude's foot as he dove through the window. The shoe released as the perp slipped out. Nick hurried outside and sprinted. The skinny dude glanced behind, then scaled the chain-link fence like a monkey and landed, twisting his shoeless ankle. Nick pursued over the fence, not as nimble as in his rookie days. He tapped his reserves and dove for the punk. They tumbled to the ground.

Nick dropped his knees on the perp's back and shoulder, torqued his arm up, applying pressure. No cuffs or backup. Guess he'd improvise until the police arrived, but first he'd see the guy's face.

Chapter 8

Nick removed the ski mask. Johnny? "What were you doing in Samantha's apartment?" Johnny remained silent, sprawled on the ground.

"I know about your debt with the Capolinis. The stuff you stole from the mansion. Breaking and entering is nothing compared to the other felonies." Knees digging into Johnny's back, Nick leaned in. "Right now I don't care about that, but messing with Samantha and her kids *bothers* me. Cooperate and maybe I won't call the police. Lie and I'll make sure you rot."

Johnny's eyes shifted.

Nick yanked him up, slammed him into the brick wall. "Hands over your head." Johnny shuddered as Nick kicked his legs spread-eagle. Patted him down.

A pocketknife. Nick's chest tightened. "Why were you at Samantha's?"

The kid remained silent, but trembling.

"We can do this the easy way"—Nick pulled him into a shoulder lock—"or my way." He applied pressure to Johnny's wrist.

Johnny winced. "Looking for the knife."

"The one you lifted from the mansion?"

"I didn't take it."

"Then who?"

"Her kid."

"Who wants it?"

Johnny stiffened.

"What about the telescope?" Nick tightened his hold.

"I swiped dishes, that's all."

"Who sent you?" Nick raised his elbow.

Johnny grimaced. No one would stay quiet unless avoiding a bigger threat.

"We'll protect you. Put you in a safe house."

Nothing.

Nick's temperature rose. "Fine, we'll do it my way." Nick applied pressure to his wrist and led him toward Samantha's apartment. "It's too bad your mom doesn't have much time left. A few weeks, maybe."

Johnny cringed.

"It's a shame she's going to die knowing her son's rotting in jail."

"Leave her out of this." Johnny struggled.

More pressure. Johnny yelled. Stumbled over his feet.

"I can't leave her out of this." Nick shoved him forward. "Too bad you won't attend her funeral."

"All right! Just keep me out of jail."

Officer Mike Daniels plodded between the apartments. "We'll take it from here."

Nick handed over Johnny. Great! Right when the kid was ready to spew. Now he would lawyer up.

When Nick reached the apartment, Samantha's arms enveloped him. He held her trembling body, his anxiety melting. With her in his arms, things felt right.

She sniffled. "You took too long. I thought—"

"I'm fine." He gazed into her moist eyes. No longer doelike and desperate. Instead, wide with longing, anticipation. Her lips quivered, begging to be comforted. His yearned for the same.

Nick inched closer and stroked Samantha's cheek as emotions swelled. Fear. Elation. Confusion. Longing. Her heart raced, anticipated. Then he grunted, lurched forward, and knocked his forehead against hers.

"Ow." Samantha eased from Nick's arms, head stinging, stifling a laugh.

Alex hugged Nick's waist. "You saved us."

Nick scooped him up. "I wouldn't let anything happen to you or your mom."

Samantha willed her pulse to slow, but couldn't control the thrill coursing through her veins. She wasn't certain if it was because of the anticipated kiss or Alex in Nick's arms.

Nick set Alex down and tickled him until he cried for mercy.

"Mom." Callie barreled through the door and hugged Samantha, then Nick. "I was so scared."

Warmth soaked into Samantha's bones.

An officer exited the bedroom. "Someone left the window open."

Alex shook his head. "Wasn't me."

Samantha exhaled. "Go watch TV, you two. We'll discuss this later."

After the police left, Samantha boiled water. Nick crouched before Alex. "Hey buddy, can I see the knife you found?"

Alex pulled the knife from Samantha's purse.

Nick held it with his fingertips.

"Is that the one from Mount Vernon's exhibit?"

"Not sure until it's tested, but the original is missing. Do you have a sack?"

Samantha handed him a lunch bag.

"Johnny came for the knife. Probably broke in earlier. When he couldn't find it, he returned to look again."

"Johnny's the forger?"

"Probably not."

Samantha grabbed a box of mac and cheese.

"I brought pizza, but ditched it when you called."

Samantha smiled. "Did Johnny mention the telescope?"

"He claims he doesn't know anything. I think he's telling the truth."

"It doesn't make sense." Samantha dumped the macaroni in the pot.

"It does if Johnny's a pawn in a forgery ring."

"Ring?"

"You were right about mob ties."

"Cody's off your suspect list?"

"I erased his name. I can add it when I find evidence."

"You won't. I have proof, and I'm willing to bet dinner on it."

"Mac and cheese." Nick's brows arched. "Hardly worth it."

"Winner chooses any restaurant in DC." Samantha offered her hand. "Deal?"

Nick shook. "Now convince me."

"Remember the books on wood restoration in the Smithsonian lab? That invoice we found is proof of a legitimate business transaction. Your suspicious project is a rocking chair for Cody's grandmother."

"Who's conveniently dead so we can't question her."

"She's at Graceful Living Nursing Home. Alive. At least she was this morning when we were at Christ Church. Cody left early. They couldn't wake her. I should check on him."

"I should check on him."

What was she, Cody's mother? Actually, that sounded better than the alternative. Nick clamped his teeth. To think he'd spent his entire Sunday searching prints and criminal history, while Samantha and Cody—his stomach roiled.

What was wrong with him? Samantha could do what she wanted. See who she wanted. The fire inside intensified. Who was he fooling? Samantha had weaseled into his heart, and Nick was powerless to evict her.

Samantha hung up the phone. "Melba is stable."

"The toast?"

Samantha shook her head. "Cody's grandmother. He said she's a stubborn old woman and won't go without a fight."

"And I'm Mr. Universe."

"What do you have against Cody?"

"Get a pen. I'll make a list."

Samantha's arms crossed.

"I'm not being petty. Carole'd never involve Timmons and Sparks without telling me."

"Maybe she forgot to mention it."

Samantha's last name fit perfectly. Steele. Tough and unbendable.

"Tell you what. On the way to dinner we'll visit Grandma. If Cody's story checks out, I won't mention him as a suspect again."

"I'll call my neighbor to watch the kids." She dialed. "Who's buying?"

"We'll let Grandma decide."

"I'll start with calamari, then the Trio Classico." Nick handed the waiter the menu.

"Bruschetta, chicken parmigiana, and artichoke dip." Samantha smirked. "Since you're buying."

"Why don't you take that salt and rub it in?"

"Say it again." Samantha rested her elbows on the table.

"I've said it twice. At the nursing home and in the car."

"Third time's the charm."

"You were right. Grandma's alive and rockin'." Though a little forgetful, she confirmed Cody's story. "I won't mention Cody as a suspect again. Now drop it." Nick removed the straw and gulped his Coke. How much of his ego could this woman devour?

"Losing graciously is a side of you I haven't seen."

"Because I don't lose." The waiter returned with the appetizers. Nick dunked his bread in the artichoke dip and took a bite. "This stuff isn't bad."

"Two affirmations in one day? What's gotten into you?" She nibbled her bruschetta.

"I drop my guard when I'm hungry."

Samantha's face glowed from laughter or maybe from gloating. Either way, she looked amazing. This night, the two of them far from everything, was exactly what they needed.

Samantha's eyes clouded. "Monday is twelve hours away. We haven't identified the forger."

So much for a relaxing dinner. "The only evidence is Johnny breaking into your condo."

"He confessed to stealing antique dishes. That proves something."

"That he's a thief. Doesn't mean he forged them."

"If we find the dishes at the Capolinis—"

"They're probably on the black market with the telescope. We should let it go and enjoy dinner."

"We can't give up. Maybe Althea works for the Capolinis."

"Too unstable."

"She seemed normal the other day."

"Probably medicated with street drugs."

"Why, when she has a prescription she could refill?"

"People with delusional disorder sometimes think doctors want to hurt them."

"What about the fifth set of prints?"

"Someone's running a criminal check, but if nothing hits, all leads are dead. There's not enough time anyway." Nick dunked his bread. "I could've cracked this case if I had more time."

Samantha exhaled. "Why's it taking so long?"

The waiter brought the calamari. "I'm sorry, ma'am. Dinner should arrive shortly."

"Want some?" Nick waved a little tentacled squid.

"No, thanks." Samantha watched the waiter hurry off. "You know what I meant."

"Things don't move in TV time. If we have eyewitnesses, plus concrete evidence, it can take days to get evidence lined up. Most times it's months of detective work and then not all cases get a conviction."

"I never realized what it takes to do your job. You should consider returning."

He didn't deserve her respect or a place on the force. He'd botched this case. Maybe if he had his head in the game, instead of chasing Samantha and her kids, he could've solved this case. Samantha sipped her water, seeming lost in thought.

Without Samantha, he wouldn't be in the game. He'd be schlepping from his apartment to work with no chance of returning to the PD.

What chance did he have now? In twelve hours, Carole would spill it all.

The waiter brought their entrées.

Samantha cut a piece of chicken. "The telescope was in Professor Timmons's lab."

"I suspect he's our fifth print. Can't prove it since his criminal history hasn't come back, and I can't access his records at the Smithsonian."

"He must be on file with Mount Vernon Security."

"He works on the estate? Stupid! Why didn't I do a search?"

"You didn't know he worked there."

"That's no excuse, but there still might be time to connect him to the forgery."

Monday morning, Nick hustled toward the archaeology lab to intercept Carole before she reported the telescope. Last night, he'd accessed security records and matched Timmons's fingerprints with the unidentified print on the telescope. He told Samantha, but couldn't reach Carole. No luck this morning, either. Former Chief Huntington probably knew about the forgery, but if Nick could stall Carole and keep them from reporting it, maybe he could break open the case.

Adrenaline started a slow drip when Nick opened the door and saw Timmons hunched over the worktable. He scanned the room. "Where's Carole?"

Timmons adjusted his glasses. "She won't be in all week. I thought my services could be useful with the new exhibit launching soon."

Why didn't Carole tell Nick? Stepping in further, he dialed her number. Voice mail. He tried Dale. No answer.

"What happened to the telescope I dropped off Friday?"

Timmons's eyes shifted. "Carole didn't mention a security guard discovered the forgery."

"Never said I did." Nick circled to the other side of the table. "They arrested the janitor for breaking into Samantha Steele's home to steal an antique pocketknife."

"How is that relevant?" Timmons's mouth twitched. "Is she our forger?"

"No, but I think you know who is."

He broke eye contact. "I resent that insinuation. If there's nothing else, I'm extremely busy."

The dweeb looked ready to crack. If Nick pressed, maybe he'd get a confession. Nick's cell buzzed. Samantha. She'd have to wait.

"You're head of paleobiology at the Museum of Natural History. Working here's beneath you." Last night Nick learned Timmons was a prodigy, gifted not only in science and math, but in art, with PhDs coming out the wazoo.

Timmons's cheeks flushed. "I'm not beneath archaeology."

"A man of your importance has to be extremely busy. Why not send an intern to do the grunt work?"

"If I extracted anyone, the summer program would be disrupted."

"Removing the head of the program isn't a problem? Guess you're not so valuable."

Timmons's jaw clenched. "I've deferred my responsibilities to my assistant to aid a fellow scientist."

"That explains why you're here now. Why volunteer this summer?"

"The field is a nice change."

A big chunk of change. "A guy with your degrees should aspire to something more prestigious than shoveling dirt."

Timmons fiddled with the artifact and turned away. "Excuse me. I have work to do."

"One more question."

Timmons spun around in a huff.

"What was Mount Vernon's telescope doing in your Smithsonian lab?"

Squatting in the dirt, Samantha brushed sweat from her brow. Why hadn't Nick returned her call? Did Mount Vernon know about the forgery? She inhaled the sweet scent of the upper garden, but her angst didn't fade.

Cody handed Samantha another brush. "You look tuckered out."

"I didn't sleep well."

"Still fretting about that telescope?"

Samantha nodded. "I hoped to discover the forger. I need Mount Vernon to notice me."

Cody lifted her chin. "I've noticed you."

Samantha's face flushed. "I need to do this."

"Catching the forger isn't the only way to impress them. Hard work will."

"You're right." Samantha sorted through bits of pottery she'd uncovered. All good finds, but hundreds of the same could be buried in the stratigraphic level. Ten minutes later, she uncovered the edge of an unfamiliar object. With gentle strokes, she brushed the surface. The soil fell away easily, unlike the hard sediment she'd dug millimeters to the left. Her heart quickened.

"What'd you find?" Cody worked the edges with a brush and carefully removed it.

"Well?" Samantha anticipated his answer as he examined the square object.

"Has potential. Let's keep this quiet until Timmons examines it."

Samantha's breath caught. Not Timmons!

Nick stared in the men's room mirror. Dark circles and bloodshot eyes made him look ten years older. Pretty much how he felt. Four hours of sleep. Not much more the entire weekend. He dried his hands with a paper towel and made a three-pointer into the trash.

Too bad he hadn't scored brownie points with Samantha last night. Her distance after dinner made him wonder what he'd done wrong.

He hadn't scored at the precinct, either. Carole and Dale were still AWOL and nothing reported missing or forged at Mount Vernon. He didn't buy Timmons's story that Carole asked him to return the telescope. If so, why didn't Carole mention it? Why wasn't it in her lab now?

Nick's cell buzzed as he entered the food court. "Samantha?"

"I need your help. I can't process an artifact I found with Timmons in the lab."

"He's after the high-end stuff he can sell for quick cash, not broken pottery."

"This could be George Washington's cuff link."

"I'm on my way."

Heat rose off the asphalt parking lot as Samantha paced, waiting for Nick. She'd been so preoccupied with the cuff link she forgot to ask if Carole reported the forgery. What did it matter? With this new discovery, she could still get noticed.

Nick jogged over. "What've you got?"

"See the etchings. *G.W.* I can't process it with Timmons in the lab."

"If Carole were here, we wouldn't have a problem."

Samantha gasped. "What if she's the forger?"

Nick's eyes widened.

"She handles the artifacts. No one would suspect her."

"The same could be said about Sparks."

"Why isn't she here?"

"It's not because she's a thief."

"Then why hasn't she reported the forgery?"

"I don't know, but you need to back off. I'll get Timmons out of the lab."

"How?"

Nick dialed. "Timmons, I've uncovered interesting information about your connection to the forged telescope.

Meet behind the mansion in ten." He turned to Samantha. "I'm all yours."

Samantha looked at Nick like he was *pazzo*, crazy, one fry short of a Happy Meal. "What did you say?"

"The lab's free. It's all yours."

"You said '*I'm* all yours.'"

Nick's cheeks warmed. "Wishful thinking?"

"Freudian slip?"

More like a landslide. This woman not only weaseled under his skin, but was now swimming in his head, wearing a bikini. Nick drowned the image. Okay, a modest one-piece. He took her hands. "I don't want to stop seeing you after the investigation."

"I'm not going anywhere."

He hadn't blown it last night? Nick checked his watch. "But I need to." He back-shuffled. "Let's catch up later. How's pizza sound?"

"Perfect."

Nick jogged off. What in the world had come over him? He'd acted like a lovesick teenager. He forced the bounce in his step to a stride. Porter, back in control.

Who was he fooling? Samantha had him whipped, and honestly, he didn't mind the beating.

Samantha crouched below the open window of the archae-ology lab.

"I owe you nothing."

Professor Timmons? He should've left by now.

"You've put me in a precarious position, Arthur." Timmons's voice trembled. "I won't jeopardize my reputation any longer."

A long pause. *Who's Arthur?*

"No. That's my final answer."

The front door slammed. Samantha stilled, recalling a similar conversation she'd overheard. The goon who'd pestered Johnny near the bathrooms. Could Timmons be indebted to the same thug?

"Sleeping on the job?" Cody's voice startled Samantha. He helped her up.

"What'd Porter want? I saw him hightail it out of here."

Samantha shifted her weight. "He thinks Professor Timmons is involved in the forgery."

Cody laughed. "Timmons? He's a lab geek, not a forger. I'm surprised Porter hasn't fingered me."

"He did, but now everything points to Timmons and Johnny Newberg."

"Seriously? I didn't think he'd stoop this low."

"What do you mean?"

"He's tainted you against me, and I didn't even mention the demons in his squad car. What kind of man gets his wife and son killed?"

Samantha's gut clenched. "It wasn't his fault."

"Getting kicked off the PD for drug abuse wasn't his fault, either? Darlin', he's pulling the wool over your eyes. If you ask me, he's the most likely suspect."

"I don't believe it."

Cody shook his head. "He's worked here two weeks and already uncovered a forgery? You said Nick discovered it was a fake? How'd he know?"

She'd dismissed her concerns about Nick before, but a security guard would be a good cover. If there was any truth to Cody's accusation of drug abuse, she had to know. Had she trusted Nick only to be deceived? Something inside Samantha crumbled.

One more reason she'd never rely on a man again.

Samantha walked to the dig, sorting through her muddled feelings. Cody's allegation against Nick had awakened her from her male-induced stupor.

Men couldn't be trusted.

That was why she'd left the cuff link in her locker. She'd ask her attorney neighbor, Ciara Turner, about legal ramifications before taking it off Mount Vernon property.

Rounding the corner, hundreds of tourists stood by the dig. Samantha gaped at the blond reporter standing by the pit. How'd news leak so fast, and who authorized the crew?

The swarm of activity hushed as the cameraman lifted three fingers, two, one, then pointed at Lydia Taylor, the region's best-known broadcaster.

"This is one of the biggest finds at Mount Vernon since 1991 when over sixty thousand artifacts were excavated in the root cellar below the slave quarters." Taylor peered at the pit. "A cuff link with the initials G.W., thought to belong to our founding father, President George Washington, was unearthed by archaeology intern Samantha Steele. Though it will undergo testing, Mount Vernon has no reason to doubt its authenticity. Which leads to another question. If it is Washington's cuff link, why was it found behind slave quarters? Could it've been stolen by a slave? Or a gift? Could George Washington be more than just the father of our country? More on this as events unfold. Lydia Taylor, Channel Four News."

Samantha cringed. Guess there was no dirt on the current president, so they went after a dead one.

A heaviness landed in Nick's gut as Samantha chatted with the reporter. He should be happy for her, but his heart felt jammed in a vise. He wanted her to need him, and now she didn't.

After the crowd dispersed, Nick approached Samantha.

"Channel Four wants to interview me for the six o'clock news." Samantha avoided his eyes.

"That's great."

"You don't sound thrilled."

"I'm about to break this case. We don't need extra people around." She didn't need to know his meeting with Timmons had bombed.

Cody called Samantha.

Maybe Nick should back down and give Samantha her shot at happiness. His suspicions of Cody had been fueled by jealousy and tainted his judgment. Time to give the guy a break. Give Samantha a break. "Sparky needs you. I've got an investigation to wrap up."

"Wait." Samantha grabbed his wrist, then released. "I overheard Timmons talking on the phone about wanting out."

The warmth from her touch lingered. "Stay away from Timmons. You don't want to be around when cleanup starts."

Nick glanced at Cody, arms crossed. "I hope you find what you're looking for."

Samantha's shoulders slumped, but she didn't argue as she walked away.

Defeat dug its claws in as Nick's heavy heart pulled him down. His grip released as he slipped back into the darkness Samantha had helped him escape.

Chapter 9

Nick paced the orientation center waiting for his buddy Jack Courtland. It'd been awhile since they talked, but with no concrete evidence on any suspect, it was time to relinquish the investigation to the Feds and turn in his badge for good.

Jack sauntered over in his raid jacket and khakis like he was on top of the Washington Monument. With a fiancée and new career at the FBI, he was.

"Hi Jack, it's been awhile." Jack shook Nick's hand. "Too long. But glad you called. You were vague on the phone—mind filling me in?"

Nick divulged everything, including the discovery of the new cuff link.

"Why didn't you call sooner?"

"I screwed up, I know. I should stop playing hero."

"Let it go. Let them go. God doesn't want you living like this."

Pressure built in Nick's head. "What does He want? Nothing I do is ever enough."

"Nothing will be. . .until you surrender."

"It's mine, I tells ya." Althea Washington broke from the crowd as Lydia Taylor finished her interview with Samantha.

Out of nowhere, Nick appeared and restrained her. Agent Jack Courtland, Tara Whitley's fiancé, stood by his side. Guess the forgery wasn't a secret anymore.

"Let me go. It belongs to me." Althea pulled something from her pocket as she struggled with Nick. "Here's proof." She handed over a cuff link.

Samantha examined it. "Looks like the match."

Nick released Althea as Lydia Taylor pointed to her crew.

"Roll it. An identical cuff link to the one excavated at Mount Vernon has been found by. . ." She glanced at Althea's name tag. "Althea Washington. Though this one appears to be in remarkable condition. Ms. Washington, where did you find this?"

"Masta Washington gave it to me. Said one day everything'll be mine"—she spread her arms—" 'cause I'm his blood."

Samantha's mouth gaped.

"You're claiming you're Washington's heir, and he personally gave you this cuff link, when history records President Washington had no biological children?"

"Yes, ma'am."

Lydia Taylor waved for Nick to escort her away, then strolled so the camera didn't catch Nick dragging Althea off.

What could make her delusional today when Saturday she'd acted normal?

"New discoveries. New mysteries. Who exactly is Althea Washington, and why does she have the cuff link marked with President Washington's initials? Is she heir to Washington's estate or a delusional employee?" She eyed Samantha. "Maybe there's more to dig up at Mount Vernon."

Nick closed the passenger door with Althea inside.

"Thanks for calling, Mr. Porter." Custis Washington, Althea's son, shook Nick's hand. "I'm sorry." His husky voice softened. "We've tried to regulate her medication, but Mom's stubborn. Doesn't like doctors."

"How long has she been like this?"

"Years. It's been harmless, until now." Custis rubbed his forehead. "We have a family history of schizophrenia. Doctors diagnosed delusional disorder when her symptoms first appeared." He looked at Althea, rocking. "Time for more tests."

"Does she have a history of stealing?"

"Not that I know of. Why?"

"I'm curious where she got the antique book dated before the Revolutionary War." Nick hoped he wouldn't ask how he knew about it.

"That's a family heirloom detailing life with the Washingtons. Mama's proud of her heritage."

"Is there any truth to her claim about being related to Washington?"

"None. If our ancestors had his children, it'd be in there."

Nick recalled the research he found on the other book in Althea's room, documenting West Ford's claim he was a descendant of Washington from an affair with a slave girl. It was never proven, but that book probably fueled Althea's delusions of being Washington's heir.

"Thanks for your time." Nick handed him a card with his

cell number. "If she mentions anything, please call."

No chance she pulled off the theft and forgery. That left Timmons, Sparks, and Newberg.

"He said no harm would come to me," Althea chanted.

"Who, Mama?" Custis leaned in the window.

She squinted at Nick. "Masta?"

"I'm Nick Porter. The security guard."

"Where's Masta Washington? He gave me a gift. Said no harm would come to me."

Could the answers to the forgery be buried in Althea's mind? Nick looked at Custis. "Can I ask her a few questions?"

"Sure."

"You're talking about the cuff link?"

Althea nodded.

"Who gave it to you?"

"Found it in my apron. I know it was from him."

Nick flipped through the photos in his cell. "Recognize anyone?" She didn't flinch at the first two. Her face lit at the third. "There you are, Masta."

Samantha hurried to her car. She'd told Jack Courtland everything she knew about the telescope and her suspicions that more items in the study could be forged. Now things would return to normal. All she wanted to do was get the children, go for ice cream, and call an impromptu movie night with her girlfriends. Something light like *The Bachelor and the Bobby-Soxer*.

Searching for her keys, Samantha noticed a paper under her wiper. She'd forgotten about Nick. Probably best if he canceled tonight. She opened the note, her heart crumbling.

You should've stayed away. Now your children will pay.

With shaky hands, she fumbled the door open and the key into the ignition. She found her phone and hesitated. Who should she call? She didn't have Jack Courtland's number. She scrolled her recent calls. Nick?

Jack had assured her Nick wasn't involved in the forgery and had kicked his addiction. She believed him. Nick could've hurt her or the children anytime. He hadn't. She needed to trust him.

Again.

She dialed. The phone died. *Dear God, let them be okay.* Of course they'd be okay. Camp Summerwood wouldn't release them without her consent. Whoever wrote the note only meant to scare her. She breathed deep and pulled onto Route 1.

God, I beg You, don't take my kids from me. I can't go through this again.

Running to the dig site, Nick tried Samantha's cell again. Voice mail. The site, deserted. He hustled to the lab. Banged on the door, then peered through the windows. Dark. Empty.

Where are you?

He raced to the parking lot. Her vehicle, gone.

He climbed in his Jeep, found his laptop, and Googled Kyle Timmons and Cody Sparks. On his initial search, he couldn't find their connection. What was he missing? He scrolled the links, stopping on an article.

BU Student Killed in Car Accident. Nick clicked and searched. *Kyle Timmons, graduate student at BU, came upon the burning vehicle of Arthur Bundrum, BU undergraduate.* He almost clicked the next link, but the following paragraph caught his attention. *Arthur Bundrum was charged with forging paintings and selling them as originals. He was set for trial until his death.*

Could Timmons have been involved in art forgery in college with Arthur Bundrum? He tried Samantha's phone again. Voice mail.

Nick's cell buzzed. Tony. "Whatcha got for me?"

"Timmons is clean, but I dug deeper into Sparks's past like you asked."

Nick mentally pistol-whipped himself for not doing it sooner. "Tell me."

"Still no record, but Cody Sparks goes back thirty-five years to Washington State. Same address for a year, then no record until fifteen years ago when he reappears."

Nick's gut churned. Identity theft. The only explanation. "One more favor. Run Arthur Bundrum, and quick." Though Nick didn't need a report to know Arthur'd stolen some dead kid's identity fifteen years ago and was working at Mount Vernon now. He had to find Samantha. He couldn't let another woman he loved die because of his mistakes. "Get ahold of Courtland. Tell him what you found and get me a safe house. The thing I was working on just blew up in my face."

"I'm sorry, Mrs. Steele. They've been collected."

Samantha's breath choked. "By who?"

Mr. Kingsley, the camp director, pointed to the name on the list. "I'm sorry. The kids knew him."

Samantha's hands shook as she read the name. Kyle Timmons? The same handwriting as the note.

Chapter 10

Samantha leapt from her car to make a call at a gas station pay phone. With shaking hands, she deposited coins, misdialed twice. *Please.* Her chest loosened when Nick answered.

"Samantha, are you okay?"

"Timmons took Callie and Alex." Sobs erupted.

"I'll find them. Where are you?"

"A gas station." Samantha located a street sign.

"I'll be there in ten minutes."

Samantha's hands shook. "I can't sit here. What can I do?"

Silence. "Pray. You can pray."

Had Nick told Samantha to pray? Where'd that come from? Desperation? Definitely. A dormant seed of faith waiting for the right moment to sprout? He hoped so. He'd spent too long in the pit he dug. He was ready to climb out for good and ask God for help.

Those kids. . .if anything happened to them. . . He choked back emotion. Swiped tears. *When you're weak, you're strong.*

He couldn't find them on his own. He needed to surrender.

Telling Samantha he'd find her children had been easy on the phone; seeing her glassy-eyed in his passenger seat nearly destroyed him.

"Where are we going?" Samantha's voice sounded robotic.

"To a safe house. It's not far."

"What about Callie? Alex?"

Thunder boomed in the distance, storm clouds stealing daylight. He needed to move fast.

"They put an APB on Timmons. We'll find them." And Arthur, but now wasn't the time to tell her.

She grabbed Nick's arm. "They're all I have."

Dread rose. He punched it down. He couldn't lose another child. Nick prayed. Another grain of pressure lifted. Two prayers in one day.

Two more than he'd prayed in a long time.

Approaching the safe house, Samantha wanted to scream at God. Bang her fists on His holy chest and holler, "Why, God, why again?" Why was *she* safe? What had her children done to deserve this fate? Yet only a pathetic, whispered prayer escaped.

The door opened. Someone helped her to the couch.

"Keep the shades closed."

Nick. He went to the kitchen, then returned. "See if one of these phone chargers works."

She clutched them, letting the numbness shroud her.

"I'll find them." His lips brushed hers.

She didn't feel a thing.

"Lock the dead bolt. Don't answer for anyone but me."

She stared past him and didn't hear him leave.

When she couldn't sit any longer, Samantha rose to use the restroom. Nick? She searched the house. When did he leave? She filled a glass with water, guzzled it. Setting it in the sink, she noticed a small box on the counter. She opened it.

A gold rose pin? From Nick? If her children weren't in the hands of a madman, if she wasn't drowning in despair, she might've allowed her excitement at the gift to rise. But she couldn't. She squelched thoughts of Nick, of Cody, of everyone but her children, and wished she had died instead of Jim.

Then her children would be safe.

Samantha wept until her tears dried up, then removed the pin and attached it to her shirt. She was ready to swallow her stubbornness and admit she needed Nick and the hope he brought to her life. Standing alone, she finally admitted she needed God.

Samantha moved to the couch and waited for her cell to charge.

Waited for Nick to call.

Waited for her kids to come home.

The waiting gnawed a hole in her gut.

She switched on the television. "Breaking news from the Smithsonian, where a murder. . ."

Samantha's mind jolted. She raised the volume.

Next to a green car stood a reporter. Flashing lights in the background. "Kyle Timmons found dead in his car with a single gunshot wound to the head. Police say a suicide note has been found with a signed confession to a forgery at Mount Vernon and the murder of two children."

Life drained from Samantha's body. *No, God. Not my babies.* Air whooshed in and out, but she couldn't breathe. She ran to the kitchen, splashed water on her face, sucked in air, choking, choking, choking.

Hunched over the sink, she vomited. Wiped her mouth, then spewed again. Screaming in her head. Ringing in her ears.

Ringing.

Ringing.

Ringing. . . Her cell phone? She answered.

"Did you see the news?" The voice unnerved her.

"Who is this?"

"You should've stayed away."

Her body shook with rage. "What've you done to my babies?"

"Nothing. . .yet."

"The news said—"

"Reporters are so unreliable."

"Mom!" Alex's cry ripped through her heart.

"I'm coming, baby."

"Come alone or your kids'll drop like flies."

Nick drove toward Camp Summerwood, his knuckles white as he gripped the wheel. How'd Timmons's name get on the list? Why'd the kids go with him?

He clicked on the GPS transponder website. Stupid! He forgot to pin the tracker—that darn rose pin—on Samantha. He grabbed the phone, but didn't know the safe house number. Idiot! Maybe Samantha had charged her phone. He dialed.

Voice mail. His fists slammed the steering wheel.

"God, if it's true I'm strong when I'm weak, then I'm Hercules, 'cause I got nothing left."

Nick's cell buzzed. "Tell me something good, Tony. I'm losing it."

Tony relayed the news about Timmons and the children.

"Are you sure?" Rage and helplessness battled for control inside of Nick. He encouraged the inferno within, so he could finish what some maniac started.

"No bodies yet. So sorry, man."

Nick threw the phone on the seat. Timmons killed the kids, then himself? Something smelled fishy. Like the Capolinis. If Timmons's death wasn't suicide, the kids might be alive. But where did Arthur Bundrum fit into all this? Was he another pawn in this twisted game of Italian roulette?

Chapter 11

Samantha entered the Metro, beating the downpour. Almost six o'clock, yet the sky darkened like midnight. Thunder clapped. Her mind cleared.

Her children were alive.

She slid into a seat and swallowed her pride. Instead of prayers of desperation, she cried prayers of defeat.

Nothing felt better.

Hope she hadn't experienced in years brightened before her. She replayed the man's words in her mind.

"Dropping like flies."

Understanding illuminated in a flash of lightning. She found her phone, praying it had enough charge. Nick needed to know where her children were. He needed to know she trusted him. She dialed Nick's number. The screen went blank. Her spirit sank.

No one to rely on except God.

Nick jammed the horn. "Move it!" If he was a cop, he'd throw up his lights and be through the intersection. He checked the tracking transponder. It had moved from the house, continuing at a steady pace. Had Samantha pinned it on?

Where are you going? He followed her. Thunder clapped. The transponder faded. Ominous clouds rolled in. He floored the pedal, hoping to beat the storm.

A steady drizzle fell as Samantha hurried through Christ Church's arch. The once-busy street was now deserted as people dodged rain, seeking refuge. Quickening her pace, Samantha shivered. The sky had grown black, too quick. The church building and courtyard dark, empty, but she wasn't alone.

The rain pelted. A hand clamped her mouth from behind. Dragged her across the wet lawn. She gagged at garlic breath as he threw her down. Fear strangled. Lightning flashed.

Her children were near. Rags in their mouths, hands bound. Then darkness. She heard whimpering and pulled them close.

Another flash of lightning illuminated eyes. Once attracted to them, now she was repulsed.

"You don't look surprised."

Where was the cowboy lilt that had her swooning? Gone. Never was. His carefully planned deception buried deep beneath lies. "I'm not surprised."

He squatted, gun in hand. "I thought we had a future. I planted that cuff link hoping you'd give up, so we could be together." He stroked her cheek. Samantha jerked away.

He yanked her up, then the kids, and pushed them toward a pit.

Samantha studied Cody's face, searching for some humanity. "Why'd you kill Professor Timmons?"

"You gave me no choice."

Were those tears in his eyes or just the rain?

"Just like I don't have a choice now." He pushed them toward the pit.

"You can disappear. We won't tell anyone."

"How'd I explain that suicide note? No dead kids to confirm the story."

Desperation snaked through her. "How will you explain two dead colleagues?"

"I won't explain anything. I don't *know* anything."

Cody's trigger finger twitched. Rain hammered, the storm building overhead. If he was going to shoot, it would be after the next flash of lightning, during the thunder. Not much time. Nothing more to do but trust God.

No matter what.

Peace settled as if she nestled safely in the eye of the storm. She removed her children's gags, kissed their lips. "I love you. We'll be fine."

One way or another, they'd be fine.

Lightning flashed. Cody raised his gun. "Darn it, Sam! Why'd you spoil everything?" Thunder crashed. Samantha screamed, shoved her children. Fire radiated, then darkness.

Nick tackled Cody as the gun exploded; then Samantha disappeared. Cody's fist contacted Nick's jaw. Pain surged. Where was the gun? Lightning flashed. There. Nick's arm snaked around Cody's neck and pulled as Cody reached for the gun. A knee jab to Cody's kidneys. He screamed, recoiled. Nick grabbed for the weapon. Teeth dug into his forearm. He grunted, squeezed the trigger. Cody hollered. Blood seeped from his hip. Nick handcuffed Cody as he writhed.

Lightning illuminated a mound of dirt. He scrambled toward it and gazed in a pit.

"Lord, don't let me be too late." He pulled Samantha from the grave, laying her gently on the grass, then helped Alex and Callie. Untied their bonds. Both of them weeping, but alive. He wiped their tears, fighting his own. Looked them over and hugged them.

Cody moaned. Alex shivered.

"He can't hurt you anymore. He's going to jail for a long time."

"Is Mommy okay?" Callie asked.

Nick's gaze drifted to Samantha's limp body. Tears crowded, chest burning. How would they handle the loss of another parent? How would he handle the loss of another love?

Alex looked at Nick with big, bloodshot eyes. "You were supposed to save her."

Nick cradled Samantha. *Don't take her from me. From them.* The children clung to each other. He searched Samantha's neck for a pulse, the rain pounding. He couldn't tell if life flowed through her veins in the awkward position he held her. His chest tightened.

He'd have to let her go.

Resting her head against the ground, he noticed her blood-soaked shirt.

"I'm sorry, Samantha." Tears fell. "Lord, don't make her pay for my mistakes. Punish me instead."

God doesn't want you to pay for their deaths. He wants you to trust Him.

Truth echoed through his soul. He embraced it and pressed

his lips against Samantha's, drinking in their warmth.

Warmth?

He felt for a pulse. She was alive. The wound. On her. . . shoulder! He applied pressure. Sirens wailed. She'd be okay. He scooped her in his arms and this time he wouldn't let go.

Samantha's eyes fluttered open.

"Hey, you." Nick brushed rain from her face.

"Callie? Alex?"

"They're fine."

"Cody—you were right."

"Shh, we'll talk later. Rest your eyes."

To Nick's surprise, she did.

Chapter 12

Alex barreled into the hospital room with a dandelion bouquet and ran to Samantha's bedside.

"These are for you. Make a wish."

"They're lovely." She took the bouquet as Callie, then Nick, entered. "But I've got everything I need right here." She caught Nick's smile.

"There you are, squirt." Nick ruffled Alex's hair. "We've already lost him once."

"Alex!" Samantha's chest ached and it wasn't from the gunshot wound in her shoulder.

Alex shrugged. "They disappeared, so I followed my gut."

"Into the cafeteria." Callie grabbed the television remote as everyone laughed.

"Seriously, champ. Don't give your mom a hard time while she's recovering."

"Knock, knock." Carole Huntington walked in dragging an IV.

Nick hurried to her side. "What happened? Where have you been?"

"Had my pipes cleaned after a heart attack early Sunday morning."

"You didn't tell anyone?"

"Been busy fighting for my life." She kissed Nick on the cheek. "You're my hero."

"Why?"

"I took those aspirin like you said. It saved my life."

"He's *my* hero." Samantha grabbed Nick's hand. "I thought we were dead, when Cody—Arthur—shot me."

Jack sauntered in wearing a suit, with Tara beside him carrying a plastic-wrapped plate.

"Cookies While You Sleep?" Samantha craved Tara's melt-in-your-mouth meringue confections. Alex snatched them and settled near Callie by the window.

Tara nodded. "I was up all night worrying, so I didn't sleep."

"Talk about nightmares. I can't believe Professor Timmons is dead." Carole sat down.

"Timmons's mistake was conspiring with Arthur in college." Jack looked at Nick. "After Arthur stole Cody's identity, he blackmailed Timmons into forging his archaeology credentials and replicating the artifacts he stole. Things got complicated when Alex destroyed the telescope and you started investigating. Someone needed to take the fall. Timmons was an easy target. Nice work, Nick. Even if I don't agree with your tactics. The Bureau could use a man like you."

"I need to ease back into Fairfax PD first."

Samantha reached for his hand. "You're returning?"

"Only with your blessing."

"If it's what you want."

"You're what I want." Nick kissed her forehead. "But the PD comes in a close second."

Samantha's cheeks flushed, warmth flowing through her body. She hadn't realized her stubbornness would harden her to love.

She was ready to trust God with her future. Ready to move forward with Nick. Ready to live. Because no matter what happened, she knew she'd never be alone.

Nick stared at Samantha. With bruises and bags under her eyes, she was stunning. Her lips begged to be kissed, but he glanced at the door instead, his heart hammering.

"Hope I'm not late." Nick's uncle, Vince Martinelli, rushed in with a long package.

Next came Samantha's neighbor, Susan Holland, carrying coffee. She stopped and glanced at Vince. "You know Samantha?"

"Nope." Uncle Vince handed the package to Nick. "This is my sister's kid, Nick Porter."

Nick eyed the widower.

Uncle Vince shifted his weight. "This is Susan. We met in the elevator."

Samantha cleared her throat. "Can we pause introductions until I get my coffee?"

"How'd you know?" Susan handed her the cup.

"I have a nose for amaretto." Samantha took a sip. "Continue."

Nick held up his hand. "Introductions can wait. I have an announcement."

"So do I." A blond in a tailored skirt and Jackie O pearls walked in. "I just came from Arthur Bundrum's arraignment. He named the person who bought the original telescope and turned over the real pearl-handled knife in exchange for a lighter sentence."

Samantha's brow wrinkled. "Will he get off easy, Ciara?"

"Don't worry, he's got a tough judge." Nick studied the blond.

So the attorney was Samantha's neighbor Ciara Turner.

"What about Johnny?" Even though he broke into Samantha's home and pawned her wedding ring, the kid was worth saving.

Ciara set down her briefcase. "He pleaded to breaking and entering, and theft of antiques from Mount Vernon, but he rolled on Bundrum, who caught him stealing the plates."

"Arthur Bundrum used the theft as leverage until he got Johnny to steal your purse to find the knife." Jack tugged on his cuffs. "When he couldn't find it, Bundrum forced Johnny to break into your apartment."

"What about the mob?" Samantha asked.

"Johnny's not saying. I don't blame him." Nick shrugged. "I suspect he sold the plates to the Capolinis, who saw a way to make a bigger profit using Johnny." He laid the box on Samantha's lap. "Enough business."

"Long-stemmed roses?" She opened the box. Confusion filled her expression. "A telescope?"

He smiled. "Take a look."

Samantha glanced through the lens and frowned. "There's something wrong."

Nick looked through it. "Something's obstructing the view." He removed the lens and something tumbled out. He knelt.

Someone in the room gasped. Samantha's eyes grew doelike as she peered over the hospital bed at Nick.

"Um, this isn't going to work. I can't see your face." Nick rose, tried to scoot next to her, but got trapped between the pillow rails and lower bars. "As if this wasn't hard enough, I have to make an idiot of myself."

"Love does that to a person." Jack pulled Tara closer.

"You can do this, Nicky," Carole rasped.

Uncle Vince turned to Susan. "Better him than me."

Nick stood close and took Samantha's hand, ready to swallow the bullet and surrender his life to the woman he loved.

Samantha glanced at the diamond ring, then at Nick. Two-day-old stubble, scratches on his chin. Her knave.

Her knight.

Before he asked the question, Samantha knew the answer.

Yes.

She was ready to crack the binding on her fairy tale.

With the ring on her finger and congratulations in the room, Nick reached over, closing the gap. She felt his breath on her lips as he glanced at the children, a tremble as he committed, and the promise of a future together as their kiss deepened.

"Ewww." Alex ran to the other side of Samantha. "You know, you'll have to marry my mom now."

"Really? Then I should do it again, just to make sure." Another kiss. More cheers.

Callie huffed and rolled her eyes. "Get a room, will ya?"

Nick winked at Samantha. "Oh, we plan on it. Right after the wedding."

Writer, speaker, leader, teacher, home-schooler, **GINA CONROY** was born and bred in New York, but now makes her home in the Southwest with her husband and four children. She has had a passion for the written word all her life and has been writing for publication for over twenty-five years. She is an active member of American Christian Fiction Writers and founder of writerinterrupted.com. Gina loves to hear from her readers. You can contact her at gina@ginaconroy.com or find her on Facebook and Twitter @GinaConroy.

COFFEE, TEA, AND DANGER

by Frances Devine

Dedication

For all the coffee, tea, and mystery lovers out there, I hope you enjoy reading this as much as I enjoyed writing it.

And to the memory of Carolyn Keene and Agatha Christie, thanks for all the grand adventures.

Chapter 1

Susan Holland stepped through the massive oak door, clutching the key in her hand, and stopped inside the dark foyer. A musty odor clung to the vast room, conjuring up thoughts of mummies and graveyards. She shivered and ran her fingers through the short waves of her hair, then hurried to open a window, allowing the late September breeze to blow away her childish illusion.

She thought Uncle Albert had sold the old mansion years ago. Apparently, he felt as sentimental about it as she did. And now it was hers. What in the world would she do with an old mansion in Virginia?

"Miss Holland?"

Startled, Susan turned. A short, gray-haired woman stood on the porch with her hand raised to knock on the door frame.

"Yes."

"I'm Mary Turner, ma'am." She smiled, but the worry lines between her eyes spoke volumes.

Oh yes, the woman who lived in the cottage out back. According to Uncle Albert's lawyer, she'd been the caretaker here for twenty years.

"Nice to meet you, Mrs. Turner." Susan stepped back.

"Would you like to come in?"

Mary nodded and took a deep breath as she stepped inside. "I was wondering if you'll be keeping me on or if I'm going to have to find another place to live."

Another decision to make. But not right away. She needed some time to think.

"What exactly are your duties here, Mrs. Turner?"

"Oh mercy, call me Mary." She shifted her slight form from one foot to another. "I mostly just keep the cobwebs out of the place and make sure no one breaks in and vandalizes it. That's all Judge Holland instructed me to do."

Susan glanced around and ran her finger across the small table beside the door. "I think you must have done a little more than knock cobwebs down or there'd be a lot more dust."

A spark of humor filled the woman's eyes and her thin lips curved into a smile. "To tell the truth, ma'am, I sort of like to come to the house and think about what it must have been like in the old days."

A memory washed over Susan like a warm breeze. She stepped to the french doors on the left and pulled them open. Her breath caught. The last time she'd seen the gigantic fireplace with its splendid scrolled mantel, candles stood tall and elegant among a festoon of greenery and red berries that draped from one end to the other.

She inhaled deeply. Her cousin Jo was still here then. They'd been ten years old. She glanced around. Heavy covers hid what surely must be the old familiar sofas and chairs. She swallowed past a sudden lump in her throat and closed the doors against the nostalgia that tried to grip her.

"The house was incredibly beautiful." She forced a smile. The woman was apparently nervous at the thought of being cast out of her home. "I'm not sure at this point what I'll do with the house. It may be awhile before I make a decision. So I guess in the meantime, you should keep doing what you've been doing."

"Do you want me to go upstairs with you?" Mary glanced at the stairway then back to Susan. "It's a little spooky up there, it being empty so long and all."

At the eagerness in the caretaker's voice, Susan almost said yes, but shook her head. She needed to be alone this time. "I'm not afraid of spooks, but thanks anyway."

"Well, if you need me for anything, I'll be at my place." Sadness slid across her face. "Guess it's not really my place, is it?"

"Well, for now, at least, it is most certainly your home."

Mary nodded and headed for the door with a slight limp Susan hadn't noticed before. Sympathy tugged at her heart. What would it be like to know you could be kicked out of your home at any time?

Susan strode to the sweeping staircase, her high heels clicking on the polished wood floor. She placed her hand on the newel post and looked upward. Jo's shrieking laughter as she slid all the way to the bottom echoed in her memories. Susan straightened her shoulders and started up the stairs, running her fingers along the smooth banister. Would everything here always remind her of Jo?

She ambled through the second-floor rooms, lifting the furniture coverings one by one, releasing a faint scent of cedar polish. Apparently, Mary had done much more than Uncle Albert had required of her. Most of the familiar old pieces were antiques, same as the ones downstairs. They appeared to be in good condition.

Shadows fell across the hallway as she strode toward the third-floor stairs. Unease bit at her. Mary was right. It did seem a little spooky. But the only ghosts around were her memories. She paused at the foot of the stairs. She couldn't bear to see the old English-style nursery today. The place she and Jo had played and laughed and shared their secrets.

Besides, it was four o'clock, an hour late for closing up the coffee shop. She knew Tonya would be a trusted employee, given time, but as of now she didn't know how to close the shop and would be anxious for Susan's return.

She turned and headed back toward the stairway. A faint scuffling sound came from behind her. Susan whirled, her heart pounding against her chest. The empty hallway, with its line of closed doors, stared back at her. Her nervous laugh echoed off the high ceilings and she hurried to the stairs.

Sudden pressure on her back forced a gasp from her throat and she lost her balance She lurched forward, the stairs rushing up to meet her as she tumbled down the long staircase. Frantically, she reached for the rail and found only air. Her head bumped against the railing and bounced off and she spiraled downward. She landed hard on the foyer floor.

Pain shot through every part of her body. She moaned and pushed her hands against the floor, lifting herself slightly. The room began to revolve slowly, then faster. Nausea overwhelmed her and she dropped to the floor.

"Miss Holland!" someone shouted.

Gentle hands brushed against her forehead and a distressed voice cried out, "Don't move. I'll get a wet cloth."

The front door slammed. Susan moaned as knifelike pain stabbed through her head. A moment later, footsteps crossed the foyer and cool dampness eased the pain behind her eyes.

She blinked. Mary bent over her, her face tight with fear.

"Thank heaven you're alive. You stay still while I go back home and call the doctor."

Mary started to move away but Susan grabbed her arm. "No, not the doctor. Call the police. My cell phone is in my handbag."

"Why would you want the police? You just fell down the stairs. I think you're confused. I'd better call the doctor."

"No. I didn't fall. I was pushed." She sank onto the floor and blackness claimed her.

"Now, miss, don't you think it's more likely you tripped on the step?" The officer's smile didn't reach his blue eyes as he leaned over Susan's chair. "You've got a good-sized lump on that pretty red head which could account for your confusion."

Susan took a deep breath then gasped at the pain. "Officer Stanton, I know what I felt. Something pressed against my back *before* I fell." And her hair was not red. It was brown with red hightlights. Or else she was changing hair stylists.

A young policeman came down the stairs and stood respectfully by Officer Stanton.

"Yes, Stewart? Find anything?" The older man asked.

"Yes, sir. The second-floor carpet by the stairway has a rip. A good-sized piece of the carpet is sticking up."

With a satisfied look, Officer Stanton faced Susan. "There's your explanation. You most likely tripped over the torn rug, Miss Holland." He looked pointedly at her three-inch heels.

Susan frowned. "The only tear I saw on the second-floor carpet was in the bedroom at the end of the west hall."

Impatience crossed his face. "Miss Holland, Stewart didn't imagine the rip by the stairs." He gave her what was clearly a forced smile. "But if you'd like, I'll go take a look."

She'd like to slap that condescending expression from his face. "But of course you believe I imagined that someone pushed me."

"I suspect you dreamed it when you were unconscious. Now why don't you go to the hospital and get that bump on your head checked out?"

Fine. She wouldn't argue with the man and make herself look crazy. But she knew what she'd felt. And she hadn't dreamed it. "I'm fine, thanks. I have to get back to my shop in Shirlington." She knew Tonya would be worried. She'd call her before she headed back.

"All right, then. I have your statement and will file a report. You take care of that bump, though."

Officer Stanton left, accompanied by the young police officer.

Mary clucked her tongue. "Honestly, I wish you'd at least let someone take a look at that knot on your head."

"I'm all right, Mary." She stood and limped slowly to the door. Pain stabbed her hip and rib area. But at least the dizziness was letting up. "I'll see you tomorrow."

She slid into her red SUV and grabbed her cell phone, punching in the number of the shop.

"Coffee, Tea, and Sweets." Her employee's voice held a tinge of concern.

"Tonya, I'm sorry to be so late. I'm on my way. Be there shortly."

Before the girl could begin asking questions, Susan said a quick good-bye. She started the car, drove to Highway 50, and headed east, eager to leave Falls Church. Confusion battled in her mind. Was it possible she had imagined the hand on her back? But she remembered it so plainly. No, it happened. She was sure of it. She reached 7 Corners and turned onto King Street. Converging with late afternoon traffic, she drove toward Shirlington.

She slid into her parking space in front of Coffee, Tea, and Sweets and sighed with relief. As she entered her shop, the friendly jingle of the bell above the door greeted her. She kicked off the heels and found her hip didn't hurt quite so much without the worry of trying to maintain balance. Blended aromas of exotic coffees and cinnamon rolls tantalized her nostrils as well as her taste buds. She'd forgotten to eat lunch.

Tonya swept her purple bangs back with one hand and hopped up from the corner table. "Oh, Susan, thank goodness you're here. Until you called, I was afraid you'd been in a wreck or something."

"Sorry. I got tied up Why didn't you just lock up and go home?"

"And leave the register full of cash? Uh-uh, I don't think so. That's an open invitation to a burglar." She shook her head; then her eyes widened. "How'd you get that bump on your head?"

"I took a tumble down a flight of stairs, but I'm okay." She tossed her handbag onto the countertop.

"Are you sure? Did you see a doctor?" Tonya's voice rose several decibels.

Susan sighed. "No, but I'm fine. You run along home now. You've worked long hours today."

"All right. If you're sure." Tonya grabbed her purse from under the counter. "I'm beat. Conrad and I were swamped this afternoon. Standing room only—people were leaving because the place was packed out. You ought to think about a bigger building."

"I know, I know." Susan waved and went to lock the door behind Tonya, then stepped behind the counter. She opened the register and began counting bills and credit card receipts. Tonya hadn't exaggerated when she said she and the bus boy had been busy. Maybe it *was* time to think about a larger building.

She hurried through closing, wishing she had a bottle of aspirin in the shop. She'd been looking forward to Friday movie night with some of her friends at Cherry Blossom Estates, the town house complex where she lived. If she didn't feel so rotten, she'd like to run the incident at the mansion by them, but all she wanted to do now was to soak in a hot bath and go to bed with an ice pack on her head. Chances were, they wouldn't have all been there anyway. Now that they all had men in their lives, it was getting more difficult to find time together. All except her, that is. She sighed. At forty, she'd begun to wonder if she'd ever meet the right guy.

The ruggedly handsome face of Vince Martinelli filled her mind, but she quickly shoved it away. He'd made it clear when they'd met that day in her neighbor Samantha Steele's hospital room that he had no intention of getting serious about anyone. Still, he'd come into the shop for coffee several times since then. Just this morning, in fact. He'd told some humorous story then winked at her. Butterflies darted around in her stomach at the memory just as they had then. She quickly got them under control. She wasn't about to get foolish ideas. He dropped by because she served the best coffee in town. That was all. And, besides, she was doing just fine on her own.

Chapter 2

Vince Martinelli signed off on the supply list and handed it back to his foreman. "There you go, Carl. I think I'll head on home. Tell the crew to be here on time Monday morning. We've got a busy week ahead of us."

He slid into his truck and sank with relief onto the leather seat. Who'd have thought a truck could be this comfortable? An image of his dad's old International pickup crossed his mind and he grinned. That old clunker was top of the line when Gramps had bought it, but by the time Vince came along and his dad owned it, it looked and drove like a discarded tank. Today it sat on blocks in his brother Frankie's garage.

He glanced in the window of Coffee, Tea, and Sweets as he drove by. Except for the security lights, the place was dark. *Of course, idiot.* He laughed and shook his head. She wouldn't be there four hours past closing. Hunger pangs shot through his stomach and he realized he hadn't eaten since the roll he'd had at the coffee shop midmorning. He grinned at the memory of Susan's cute little laugh when he'd told some stupid story. And those gorgeous brown eyes that crinkled at the corners when she laughed.

He shook his head as he pulled up to the drive-through

menu board and looked it over, shoving aside the memory of Samantha's very attractive friend. Just because his nephew Nick Porter had the good sense to propose to Samantha didn't mean Vince was interested in a relationship. He placed an order for two burgers and a large order of fries, and when the girl at the next window handed him his food, he cast a guilty glance at the warm bag. His cholesterol had been a little high when he'd had his last checkup. Doc told him to go easy on fast food. But the delicious aroma seeping through the bag sent his stomach growling like a junkyard dog. Well, he'd start tomorrow.

He headed home. Home. Yeah. The town house was nice enough. It was the third place he'd lived since he'd sold the house ten years ago. He thought he'd leave the memories and pain of Elena's death behind with the house. He hadn't known pain traveled with you.

After he moved here six years ago, he finally realized only time could erase the hurt of losing his wife. So he'd stopped running and little by little the grief had receded. That's when he discovered he could keep the memories without the pain.

He pulled into his garage and went inside. The first thing his eyes rested on was Elena's photograph on the table in the corner. He ran his finger across the glass and sighed. He'd never marry again. What if history repeated itself? He couldn't go through that pain again. Susan Holland's smile flashed into his mind. He sighed. Maybe he should go back to Joe's Diner for his morning coffee.

Ignoring her aching body, Susan placed three cans of tomato sauce in the cupboard, then opened the refrigerator and plopped a plastic bag with bell peppers into the crisper drawer. She pulled out a chair from the table and sat. It felt good to be off her feet. She probably should eat something, but wasn't in the mood to dine alone. As she'd expected, all three of her friends had begged off for tonight, so she'd laughed off the knot on her head and they assumed it had happened at the shop.

The more she thought about her accident at the mansion, the more certain she was. It was no accident. And she was certain the carpet by the stairs hadn't been torn at all when she fell. But why would anyone want to hurt her? It wasn't like she'd disturbed a burglar. She'd been leaving when it happened.

Susan drummed her fingers on the table. The shrill ringing of the phone startled her. She reached for the cordless on the table, answering on the second ring.

"Hello? This is Susan."

"Susan Holland?" The man's voice was strong and cordial.

"Yes. How can I help you?" Probably a salesman. She really must remember to get on the no-call list.

"My name is Victor Gordon. And I might be able to help you."

At the jovial turn of his voice, Susan sighed. "Mr. Gordon, I'm not interested in whatever you are selling. Perhaps you should try someone else."

He laughed. "I'm not a salesman. To the contrary, I'm a potential buyer."

"Buyer? The only thing I sell is coffee. You've got me confused with someone else." Susan made no attempt to hide the impatience that tinged her words.

"Forgive me. I should have immediately come to the point. I understand you've inherited a three-story house that belonged to the late Judge Albert Holland."

Susan perked up. "You want to buy the mansion?"

He hesitated. "Actually, I have been authorized by a third party to acquire it."

Now, this was getting interesting. "And who might that third party be?"

"I'm not at liberty to say at the moment, but I assure you, I'm authorized to offer a substantial sum for the property even though it is in a state of disrepair." He named a sum that would have sounded like a fortune the day before. Of course, she hadn't any idea what the going rate for old mansions might be.

The doorbell chimed.

"I haven't decided what I want to do with Uncle Albert's old home. So I'm afraid I can't help you at this point." The bell chimed again. "I need to go. Good-bye."

"I'll call back at a more convenient time." His voice sounded tense. "In the meantime, please consider my client's offer. After all, he might decide to lower it."

"Good-bye." Susan slammed down the receiver and hurried to the door. She wasn't about to sell Jo's home to someone who wouldn't reveal his identity.

She opened the door to see a smiling Tara Whitley standing with a pizza box in one hand and three DVD cases in the other.

The tall brunette laughed and came inside. "Don't look so surprised."

"What happened to the dinner date with that handsome FBI agent of yours?"

"Jack got called away and I was left all alone and hungry. I figured you were, too, so I picked us up some dinner." She held out the DVDs to Susan. "Here, I'll even let you choose the movie."

Susan took the DVDs and grinned. "I have movies."

Tara laughed. "Yes, I know. But I'm not in the mood for *Casablanca* for the millionth time."

"I don't know why you'd think I'd choose *Casablanca*." Susan got a pitcher of iced tea from the fridge, trying not to grimace as pain shot through her elbow. Tara took plates and glasses from the cupboard.

When everything was spread out on the coffee table, Susan glanced through the movies, hardly seeing them.

"Hey," Tara said. "I was kidding about the movies. We can watch anything you want since you're the invalid tonight."

Susan bit her lip. "Would you mind if we skip the movie and just talk instead? I could use a little input about something."

"Sure. I never turn down a chance to give advice." Tara reached for a slice of pizza. "What's going on? Does this have something to do with your uncle's will? That was today, wasn't it?"

"Yes, Uncle Albert left me everything he owned, including the family mansion that hasn't been lived in for years." She stared as Tara popped a slice of pepperoni into her mouth. "I can't believe a White House chef can sit here and eat pizza as if it's some delicacy."

"Assistant chef," she reminded. "And who says chefs can't like pizza? Did you say mansion?"

"Well, it used to be. I thought it had been sold years ago. The place has been neglected and it shows."

"So are you going to restore it or get rid of it?"

"I don't know." She shrugged. "I haven't had time to think about it. I did get a call from someone a few minutes ago, wanting to buy it."

"Really? That was fast. You only inherited it today." She frowned. "Doesn't that seem a little strange?"

Come to think of it, it was fairly odd. "Yes, and it's not the only strange thing that happened today."

As Susan related her fall down the steps, Tara's face registered horror. Leaning over, she took Susan's hand. "You should have said something. You let Ciara, Samantha, and me all think that knot was from a little bump on the forehead at the coffee shop." Although Ciara Turner, the fourth in their group of friends and neighbors, hadn't looked too convinced. "Are you all right? Did you get checked out?" Tara asked.

Susan wished people would stop asking her that. "Yes, I'm fine. No, I didn't go to the emergency room. I had to get back to the shop and close. I was nearly two hours late when all was said and done, and Tonya was a little worried and straining at the leash to get out of the place." She laughed then grabbed her ribs.

"Susan, you aren't all right. Let me take you to the ER."

"I promise I'm okay. Just a little sore in spots." To prove her point, she got up and touched her toes a couple of times, ignoring the catch in her side. "See? Fit as a fiddle."

"All right." Tara didn't seem too convinced. "But if the pain doesn't ease up in a day or two, please get checked."

"I will. I promise."

"So the police didn't believe you about being pushed?"

Susan took a deep breath and shook her head. "The officer seemed convinced the blow to my head had confused me. For a while he almost had me convinced, but the more I think about it the more convinced I am that I was pushed. And I'm absolutely certain that section of carpet wasn't torn at all when I was upstairs. I would've noticed."

"What are you going to do?" Tara gave her a worried look.

"For one thing, I'm going back tomorrow to take a look at the carpet and then go through the third-floor rooms." She gave a short nod. "And while I'm there I'll keep my eyes open for anything out of the ordinary."

"You're not going through the house alone again, are you?" Consternation crossed her face. "I'd go with you, but Jack and I have appointments all day."

"Don't worry. I'll ask Mary to go upstairs with me. She offered today, but I wanted to be alone."

"But how do you know she wasn't the one who pushed you?"

"Mary? No, of course it wasn't her." Susan paused and bit her lip. "Although she did get there right after I fell, so I guess it is a possibility." And that look on her face. Susan had forgotten about that. Was it fear? Susan had thought the woman had been afraid that Susan's injuries might be fatal. But what if that wasn't it at all? What if she was afraid she'd be found out?

"Maybe she thought if you were out of the way, she wouldn't lose her home."

Susan laughed. "She wouldn't try to kill me so she wouldn't have to move. She'd have to be insane." She shook her head. "Of course, I don't know her, but she seems nice."

"Psychos often seem quite nice. Didn't you ever hear of the Boston strangler?" Tara pursed her lips and frowned as though in deep thought. "And then there was. . ."

"All right, all right. I get your point." Who else could she take with her? Ciara had said something about an appointment. And Nick was taking Samantha and her children to the zoo.

Tara put the slice of pizza on a napkin. "Susan, promise me you won't go there alone."

Susan sighed. "You're right. Maybe I'll spend the day searching for a new location for Coffee, Tea, and Sweets."

Tara grinned. "Maybe you should keep the old mansion and

turn it into a B and B. You could have your coffee and tea shop there."

"And advertise a resident ghost, I suppose." Susan laughed and went to get more iced tea.

Chapter 3

Susan's gaze roamed over the three-story redbrick building. Was it as warm and welcoming as it appeared? Or had her memories of family togetherness tinged her judgment? Someone must have agreed with her. This morning she'd received her third offer for the property. And it wasn't even on the market yet.

Her heels clicked on the brick walkway, scattering a few newly fallen leaves, as she made her way to the door, a bag filled with pastries and flavored coffee packets in her left arm and her hand fumbling in her pocket for the house key. She stepped onto the white columned porch.

"Good morning, Miss Holland." A slim man with buzzed hair and light blue eyes stood on the sidewalk that wound around the house.

Susan's heart pounded and her hand reached for the pepper spray she'd forgotten to stick in her pocket. Who was he and how did he know her name?

Mary came into view and stopped beside him. "Miss Holland, this is my nephew Tim. I'm sorry if he startled you." She frowned at Tim. He shrugged and walked toward the cab that was pulling into the driveway.

"Is your nephew visiting?" Susan flung the words over her shoulder as she inserted the key.

"He's staying with me for a while, until he can find a job. I thought I told you about him." She shook her head. "Goodness, that boy goes through more jobs than anyone I've ever known."

"Has he been with you for long?" He'd made Susan uneasy, even after she knew he was Mary's nephew.

"About three weeks. He moved in a few days before you inherited the house." She sighed. "He's my little sister's boy. She passed away last year, and I didn't have the heart to turn him away when he needed a place to stay."

The *boy* must have been at least thirty. Susan set the bag on the table. On second thought she turned and locked the bolt on the door.

Mary flashed a grin at Susan. "Something sure smells good."

With a laugh, Susan motioned to the bag. "I brought your favorite, apple fritters, and a mix of others."

"You're spoiling me, Miss Holland, but thank you."

Susan sighed, waving aside Mary's thanks. She'd tried to get the older woman to call her Susan, but to no avail. "Did they ever get the water pipes fixed?"

"Yes, ma'am, and the water is turned on." Her eyes danced. "And this time, I didn't get soaked."

Susan laughed. She'd called to have the utilities turned on last week, but when Mary turned on the kitchen faucet, water sprayed everywhere. They called the plumber who found leaking pipes all over the house as well as a few burst ones. Probably due to last winter's freeze.

"I'm not going to stay very long today. I think we've covered most of the house and I have my list of repairs." She glanced at Mary, who was nibbling on a roll. "I think the third-floor bathroom needs to be looked at again. But for now, I'm concentrating mainly on the first two floors."

Mary touched a paper napkin from the bag to her lips. "I'll go up with you."

"Good. I know it's silly, but I'm still a little uncomfortable going upstairs alone, even though my fall was more than likely an accident." Over the last couple of weeks, she'd begun to think she must have imagined the hand on her back. Maybe she had dreamed it as the police officer had suggested.

Mary's eyes darted away for a moment; then she smiled. "I don't like going up there alone myself."

Now, what was that furtive look all about? Did Mary know something she wasn't telling her?

They reached the top of the stairs and Susan paused to look at the torn section of carpet. Would she have missed that when she was looking around that first day? Uncertainty bit at her. Could Mary's nephew have pushed her? That might explain why she hadn't told her about him. *Oh stop it, Susan.* What possible reason could he have for wanting to hurt her?

She headed down the long hallway, glancing in each room. Once they finished the repairs, perhaps she'd do a little renovating before she put it on the market. She climbed the stairs to the third floor, Mary following behind.

She'd intended to go directly to the bathroom, but the nursery drew her. She'd already removed the covers and done some cleaning in here. Except for some faded wallpaper, it looked the same as it did thirty years ago. The last time she saw JoJo.

Mary gave her a curious look. "Memories?"

"Uh-huh. Some good ones and some very sad. My parents and I came here often when I was a child. My cousin JoAnne and I used to play for hours." She sighed. How could a memory be so sweet and painful at the same time? "JoJo and her mother died in a car accident when we were ten. Uncle Albert moved out of the house a month later."

They checked the bathroom, Susan deciding the old linoleum definitely must be replaced.

Susan followed Mary down the stairs, pausing on the second floor to glance at the master suite. It had been her grandparents' bedroom at one time. She continued down, deep in thought. She hated to sell the house away from the family. If Dad hadn't sold his half to Uncle Albert years ago, Susan's family might have lived here once her uncle had moved. But she certainly didn't want to live here alone. The vastness would swallow her up.

When they reached the first floor, she glanced around the foyer, then strolled through the other rooms again.

"Mary?" she said with sudden resolve. "How would you like to help me run a bed-and-breakfast?"

Vince walked through the door of Coffee, Tea, and Sweets and headed for his usual stool at the counter. The tantalizing aromas of vanilla, cinnamon, and coffee welcomed him, and he was glad he'd broken his three-week avoidance of the place. As he'd told himself this morning when he was shaving, why should he deprive himself of the best rolls and donuts in town? What was he afraid of? Did he think Susan Holland would hog-tie him and drag him to the preacher?

"Hi, what would you like this morning?" The waitress with the purple streak in her hair wasn't who he was expecting. The disappointment in his gut surprised him a little.

"Hi yourself. How about a couple of glazed donuts and a cup of black coffee?" While she went to get his order, he looked around; then, realizing he was craning his neck, he turned and focused on the menu board.

"Here you go. Enjoy." The young woman placed the donuts and coffee in front of him and grinned. "If you were looking for Susan, she's not here."

Disappointment tugged at him. Guess it wasn't just the coffee and donuts he missed. "I only came in for the best coffee in town."

"Okay, then you won't be interested in the fact that she just pulled into her parking spot." She grinned and walked away as he jerked around. He watched through the window as Susan walked toward the door carrying a large box.

Vince shoved up from his seat and opened the door for her. He tried to take the box, but she held on.

"Vince." She pushed past him and stepped through the door, her face beaming. "Just the man I wanted to see."

He caught his breath. "Oh yeah? Then I guess it's my lucky day. Can I buy you a cup of coffee?"

"Sure. Stick around for a sec. I'll be right back." She grinned and took the box through to the kitchen. Vince went back to the counter and stared into his cup. A moment later she stood behind the counter in front of him.

"So why are you looking for me?" Vince asked.

"I'm looking for a contractor. Do you do remodeling?"

Not sure whether to be relieved or disappointed, Vince nodded. "Depends on what needs remodeling."

"A really old three-story home in Falls Church. I'd like to turn it into a bed-and-breakfast, but it might take a lot of work."

Those beautiful brown eyes he'd tried so hard not to think about gazed straight into his.

He blinked and exhaled slowly. "I'll have to check my appointment calendar and see when I can look at it. Or we could go after work tonight." Now why the blazes had he said that?

Surprise crossed her face; then she smiled. "I have a movie date with friends tonight, but I'm free tomorrow if you are."

"Sounds good. What time?"

"How about ten o'clock? Do you want directions, or would you rather follow me?" she asked.

"Why don't we ride over there together?"

She hesitated and he hastened to add, "I have a car. You won't have to ride in the truck."

"Riding in a truck doesn't bother me." Her lips tilted slightly. "But that's fine. I'll meet you here at ten." She picked up the coffeepot and refilled his cup.

"Did you know you have the best coffee in town?" He saluted with his mug.

"So they tell me, but you really should try some of the flavors." She smiled and waved her hand toward the syrups.

Vince wrinkled his nose. "No offense, but I'll keep mine straight. I like my coffee to taste like coffee."

She laughed. "To each his own." She lowered her voice. "To be honest, first thing in the morning, I like black coffee, too."

Halfway home, Vince realized he was still grinning. He pressed his lips together. What was that woman doing to him? He'd dated casually a number of times over the years, but he hadn't felt this way about a woman since— He groaned and turned into his parking space.

He went inside and his gaze fell on Elena's waiting photograph. He paused, waiting for guilt to hit him. To his surprise, it was only a faint nudge. He breathed a sigh of relief. Not that he planned on any deep relationship with Susan. But she was mighty pretty. Maybe they could become good friends.

Susan crawled between smooth, cool sheets. The evening with the girls had been fun. It was nice to have them all together. Tara wouldn't be with them much longer. Susan chuckled. Who'd want to spend an evening watching movies with a bunch of females when she could stay at home with a great, handsome guy like Jack? Ciara and Samantha would probably follow suit before long.

Susan loved the way they could all laugh and cry together while they lost themselves in their movies. Tonight had been mostly tears as they watched *An Affair to Remember* again.

Samantha teased her a little when she found out about Susan and Vince's plans for the next day.

"You know, Susan, the Martinelli men are all extremely romantic. You could do worse."

Susan gave a choked laugh. "Samantha. It's strictly business."

"Okay. Sure." Samantha nodded and grinned.

It was all in fun, but Susan's stomach quivered now as she thought of the handsome man. Those eyes that crinkled when he laughed. Where did he get those deep blue eyes? And his short black curls that made her want to run her fingers through them just to see if they were as soft and springy as they looked.

She gave herself an inward reality check. All she needed was to make a fool of herself over a man who'd made it plain he wasn't available. Of course, he'd seemed interested today. But that was more than likely her wishful thinking. She had to get these silly ideas out of her head before she ended up acting like a lovesick girl. No sense scaring the man off before she even got an estimate on the remodel.

Chapter 4

Even in disrepair, the interior of the mansion brought a whistle to Vince's lips. He'd known Susan's coffee shop did well, but he had no idea she was in this class.

Susan flashed a grin in his direction. "I know. It's pretty daunting, isn't it?" She sailed across to the french doors on the right and slid them open, revealing an enormous dining room.

He followed her and glanced inside, running a practiced eye over the ornate room. "It is, and I've worked on a lot of houses."

"My uncle left it to me. At first, I planned to put it on the market. But the more I think about a B and B, the more I like the idea." She gestured toward the room. "I thought my shop could go here. There's a short hallway leading to the kitchen, so it should be perfect."

After touring the rooms on the first floor, they went upstairs. The master suite took one end of the hallway to the right of the stairs, with two other bedrooms directly across and a bath on the end. On the left side of the stairs, they looked into a sitting room and three bedrooms with another bath on that end. Vince refrained from whistling again as they came to a set of carpeted stairs going up to the third floor.

He followed Susan up. They paused in the doorway of a

charming children's apartment. The main room was a sitting room on one end and a playroom on the other. An enormous teddy bear overlooked a conglomeration of stuffed animals. Some kid was really lucky.

Vince chuckled. "They had their own zoo."

"Pretty much." Susan glanced around, a nostalgic smile on her face. "My cousin and I had a lot of fun here on holidays, and I spent a couple of summers here, too."

She motioned to a closed door. "The bedroom is through there with a connecting door to a bathroom, then the nanny's room. Two rooms across the hall and one bathroom. I'd like to convert this for my own private apartment. The rooms across the hall would be for live-in employees." She stepped into the hallway.

He nodded as he followed her down the stairs. "Sounds like you've thought things through pretty well."

"I suppose I've had the idea simmering in the back of my mind since I inherited the house." She paused as they reached the stairway leading to the first floor. She bit her lip and glanced at him. "Vince, before you decide to take on the job, there's something I need to tell you. . . ."

Her voice trembled, and something almost like fear crossed her face. He frowned. "Is something wrong?"

"I'm not sure." She took a deep breath. A tap on the front door interrupted her, and a gray-haired woman walked into the foyer.

"Oh, there's Mary, the caretaker. Let me introduce her." She hurried down the stairs, a welcoming smile for the little woman on her face. Vince followed and stood beside her.

"Mary, this is Vince Martinelli. I'm hoping he'll undertake the renovations for us. Vince, this is Mary Turner. She lives in the caretaker's cottage behind the house. She has a key to the house and all the rooms and can let you in when I'm not here."

With a few instructions from Susan to the caretaker, they left and headed back to Shirlington.

Vince waited for Susan to get back to their former conversation. Instead she began to point out the changing colors of the trees. A little impatient, he gave her a sideways glance. Her hands were clenched around her handbag, and worry lines furrowed her brow. Something besides autumn scenery was on her mind to create this much tension, but apparently she'd decided not to talk about it.

Should he bring it up? If something would cause problems during the renovations, he needed to know before he brought in his crew.

She continued to make small talk until they pulled up next to her car. "Thanks, Vince. We'll talk tomorrow?" She reached for the door handle.

Vince wasn't about to let her go without at least trying to find out what was wrong. The expression on her face as she stood by the staircase had been almost frightened.

"Before you go, how about telling me about the mystery that might prevent me from taking on such an interesting renovation project?"

She shrugged. "It's probably nothing, but—" She took a deep breath. "All right, let's go inside and I'll make coffee. I think there might be a couple of those bear claws you like so well."

Vince grinned. "I'm flattered you remember what I like."

Her cheeks darkened into a pretty blush. "Hazard of the trade. I tend to remember people by the pastries they like."

Feeling slightly deflated, he followed her inside and sat at the counter while she went to get their coffee.

When she set the mugs on the counter, his was strong and black, and hers had a hint of cinnamon wafting up from the cup. The bear claw was warm and buttered, just as he liked it. He suppressed the grin this time, unwilling to get shot down.

"Now," he said. "What's bugging you about that house?"

"You'll probably think it's much ado about nothing."

"How about letting me be the judge of that?"

She sipped her coffee and lifted a slender shoulder. "The day I went to the mansion, I fell down the stairs. All the way from the second floor to the foyer. My head hit the stair rail and the hard foyer floor. I blacked out for a sec."

His heart thudded in his ears. "That could have killed you." That was an understatement, but he couldn't think of anything else that might be more appropriate. The thought of her bleeding at the bottom of those long stairs made him shudder.

"I was definitely in divine hands that day." She stirred her coffee. "When I came to enough to think, I told Mary to call the police."

"What for?" He imagined her calling an ambulance, but the police?

"I felt a hand on my back right before I fell."

Vince started. "What? Someone pushed you?"

"The police didn't think so. They think I imagined or dreamed it while I was unconscious."

"But they investigated. Right?"

She sighed. "Well, that's the thing. They found a portion of ripped carpet at the top of the stairs and assumed I tripped over that."

"Is it possible you did?"

"No." Frustration filled her voice. "If it was simply my

memory of the hand on my back, I might wonder. But I had examined the floors and there was no tear in that location."

Vince frowned. "Then you think someone tore the carpet to make it look like an accident."

"Yes, that's exactly what I think. Although I have no idea why anyone would try to hurt me." She paused. "There is one possibility. Mary's nephew, Tim Weiss, lives with her, apparently freeloading. It occurred to me, he may have been in the process of looking for something he could sell, and thought I saw him."

"But you didn't?"

"No," she sighed. "I didn't see anything. There was only that pressure on my back before I went careening down the stairs."

Susan reduced the speed of her treadmill and took a swig of water, thoughts of Vince rambling through her mind. Had he really believed her? He seemed sincere, but he could have just been humoring her. She stepped off the treadmill. The short jog had calmed her nerves and burned off a few calories. She kicked her running shoes off and dug her feet into her thick bedroom carpet as she headed to the bathroom. Halfway there, the phone rang. She hurried to answer, intending to get rid of whoever it was so she could shower.

"Susan?" A familiar, jovial voice rang out from the receiver.

"Uncle Ollie? Is that you?" Lionel Oliver, an old friend of Uncle Albert's, had always been a favorite of Susan's, and it was good to hear a voice that reminded her of her uncle.

"It's me, honey. I'm near your neighborhood and thought if it's not inconvenient, I'd drop in for a few minutes. I haven't seen you since Albert's funeral."

"I'd love to see you. Give me fifteen minutes, will you?"

"That's perfect. I'll see you shortly."

Susan hurried through her shower and donned a pair of jeans and a T-shirt. She dried her hair, raking her fingers through the brown curls and admiring her new red highlights. She should have had that done years ago. She quickly added lip gloss and went to the kitchen to make iced tea.

The doorbell chimed and she threw the door open. Peace washed over her at the sight of the tall, white-haired man who radiated dignity. "Uncle Ollie, I'm so happy to see you."

"And you're a sight for sore eyes. I should have stopped by sooner." Then she was enfolded in his arms.

A few minutes later, they were seated in the living room with frosted glasses of iced tea.

Susan smiled at her old friend. "I miss Uncle Albert. I know you do, too."

"More than you could possibly know," he said. "Do you know how far we go back?"

"Law school?"

"Further than that. I moved to Falls Church when I was seventeen, going into my senior year of high school. As I was walking to school, a gang of three boys jumped me. They pummeled me good. But the worst part was that I couldn't get my breath. I thought I was going to die right then and there."

"What happened?"

He chuckled. "The next thing I knew the weight was gone and I could breathe. When I could finally sit up, the boys were scattering every which away." He shook his head. "Albert had a bat in his hand and had threatened to knock their brains out if they didn't leave me alone. He stood there laughing as they ran helter-skelter down the street. Then he turned and held out a hand. From that day on, we were best friends."

Susan laughed. "Yes, I remember I always felt safe when Uncle Albert was around. I think he was a natural protector. So you went to high school together?"

"Oh no." He smiled. "Albert and your father attended a very exclusive private school. My family couldn't afford that. Not that we were poor, just not private-school wealthy."

"What a great story. Please tell me more. I know so little of their childhood. Father wasn't one to talk much about the past."

"Of course, Howard was a couple of years younger. I do remember we used to make his life miserable." He gave her a commiserating look. "Albert and Howard drew closer as they got older, but back then, Albert was the typical big brother."

So much for the protector theory. That must have come later.

He managed to pull out a few more humorous stories, most from college days; then he sighed and gazed at Susan. "But the main reason I stopped by was to see if you'd take pity on me. Jan is out of town for two weeks, and I'm beginning to get very lonely without her. How about going to a concert and dinner with me next Friday night? We'll go someplace fancy and I'll tell you more stories."

"You've talked me into it. I'd love to." The girls would have to get along without her for movie night. They'd be so busy talking about their guys, they probably wouldn't notice much anyway. "Speaking of dinner, how about if I make us some supper? It's nearly six."

"I'd love to, but I'm attending a benefit with some friends tonight." He stood. "I'd better get home and get ready. It's formal."

Laughing at his exaggerated grimace, she walked him to

the door. Uncle Ollie loved rubbing elbows with Washington's political elite, just as Uncle Albert had.

After they said good-bye, she dead-bolted the door and walked into the kitchen. She grabbed a bottle of water from the refrigerator and settled in front of the TV, surfing channels until she came to a romantic comedy she hadn't seen for a while.

Vince's quirky grin popped into her mind and she smiled. He was one handsome guy, although usually he acted nervous around her. He hadn't seemed quite as fidgety today. And unless she was imagining things, he'd even flirted a little. She wondered if it could go anywhere. She sighed. Probably not. According to Samantha, he'd pretty much kept women at arm's length since the death of his wife.

How sad. To lose someone you loved that much. Well, there was no denying she was attracted to him, but not enough to try to compete with a woman who'd been gone for ten years.

Still, he'd seemed so concerned about her accident. As if he really cared. Susan chuckled. Just because he was sorry she'd fallen down the stairs didn't mean he was romantically interested.

Maybe she should accept a date with Paul from church. He'd asked her enough times. But his smile didn't make her stomach do flip-flops. And he'd never given her a wink that turned her knees to gelatin.

Chapter 5

Susan walked past the garage and stepped onto the porch of Mary's cottage. As she lifted her hand to knock, a loud voice raged from inside.

"It's not gonna kill you to loan me a couple of hundred bucks to get my car fixed."

A thud sounded as though a solid object had hit the floor and Mary's voice cried out. The door flew open and Tim shoved past, nearly knocking Susan off the porch. "Get outta my way, you nosy broad."

Stunned and indignant, Susan stood, her heart pounding as Tim disappeared through the hedges.

"Mary, are you all right?" At the sound of sobs, Susan stepped through the open door.

Mary sat on the sofa, an empty metal box standing open in her hand, tears rolling down her cheeks. She bit her lip as she saw Susan. "He took my money. Broke the lock and took every cent. Nearly five hundred dollars I had in here."

Susan sat next to the distraught woman and put an arm around her shoulders. "Do you want me to call the police?"

"No, I can't do that. I know it would serve him right, but I just can't." She sighed and closed the box. "It's not the money

I care about. I have savings. But I never thought he'd do anything like this."

Susan bit her lip. The man shouldn't be allowed to get by with this, but that was Mary's decision. It must be difficult to go against someone you loved, no matter what they did.

"Are you sure this doesn't put you in a bind financially?" She peered at Mary. "I could call the lawyer and get you an advance."

"No. Thank you, but I have plenty in my checking, and if I had to I could withdraw from savings." She looked at Susan through watery eyes. "You have no idea what my salary is, do you?"

Susan blushed. Uncle Albert's attorney took care of that and she hadn't bothered to check into it. "No, honestly I don't, but if Uncle Albert wasn't paying you enough, we'll certainly take care of that."

Mary patted her eyes and smiled. "My salary is more than sufficient. Your uncle was a generous man."

"I'm glad to hear it." She grinned. "I'd hate to think of back pay for the last twenty years."

Mary smiled. "Was there something you needed, Miss Holland?"

Susan stood. "I need to start packing some things before the renovations begin and decide what to do with the furniture, but you don't need to help. I'm sure you're too upset for that."

"No, I'm not. It'll help get my mind off things." Mary stood, leaving the metal box on the sofa cushion.

"If you're sure. I can't stay long. I have a concert and dinner engagement tonight. The lunch run lasted longer than usual today or I'd have been here sooner." She'd been looking forward to her evening with Uncle Ollie all week. He'd hinted at someplace special for dinner.

"Did the packing boxes arrive?" she asked as they walked to the house.

"Yes, they got here yesterday."

They went inside and Susan headed for the dining room. She glanced around.

"I suppose I need to call a storage company to come get the furniture. It can't be left here during renovations." Susan frowned. "But we'll need to get the covers off. Whoever I call will have protective wrappings for the pieces."

Most of the bedding and accessories in the house had been stored away or disposed of when Uncle Albert moved out, leaving only the furniture with its massive covers.

"You could store them in the attic." Mary said. "I just did some cleaning up there last month. I'd just need to dust a little."

Surprised, Susan looked at her. "Is there room?"

Mary chuckled. "Miss, the attic is as huge as the rest of the house, only not divided into rooms. There were old broken pieces piled up there, but Mr. Albert told me to have them hauled off. Some boxes in the corners are all that's left. Plenty of room for the furniture."

"I don't know, Mary. I don't think I want to store these antiques in the attic. There could be mice." Most of the pieces were worth a lot, not only in sentiment, but in money as well.

"Do you think they'll be safe?"

"Yes, there are companies that handle mostly antique furniture. They're more expensive, but also more trustworthy." She thought for a minute. "Yes, I'm putting them in storage."

"I guess they'd better be sturdy workers to get all these heavy pieces moved," Mary said.

"I'm sure they'll know what they're doing. I'll see if I can get them here next week. No sense in waiting." She turned toward the door. "We'd better go to the third floor."

As she stepped onto the second floor, she stared at the rip then moved on. After the incident with Tim, she thought again of the possibility of him being the one who'd pushed her. If he was capable of treating Mary the way he had, he probably wouldn't think twice about shoving a stranger down the stairs. But for what purpose? That was what she couldn't wrap her head around. There didn't seem to be a point.

She led the way up the stairs and into the nursery. She tapped one foot as she glanced around. Uncle Albert had left the nursery untouched. She sighed. Maybe by leaving it this way, he'd been able to hang on to some illusion of Jo's presence.

She turned to Mary. "Did Uncle Albert come here often after he moved?"

Mary nodded. "He didn't at first. But after about three years, he showed up one day and came up here. After that, he'd drop by every now and then. I don't think he ever got over that little girl's death."

How sad. Yet he'd never once, in all those years, mentioned Jo to Susan.

She took a deep breath. Well, it was time to put the old memories to rest. Her gaze went to the mountain of stuffed toys. She'd have all the toys cleaned and donate them to children's organizations. Standing against the wall were three upright bears of varying sizes, each with a tin drum around its neck.

"These were my favorites." She grinned and bent over to lift the smallest one. "JoJo called this one Tailend." She sighed. "Wish I could keep him, but I guess I'd better pack him away with the rest."

By the time they had everything packed neatly into boxes, it was after five o'clock. Tonya would probably be fidgeting, although Susan had told her she'd be late.

She stood in the doorway, looking at the room. Already, it appeared different. But that was the way things were. You couldn't hang on to the past.

Before she left, she picked up the little drummer bear she hadn't been able to pack. After all, it was hers to do with as she liked. It wouldn't hurt to keep this small memento of the past, would it?

"Uncle Ollie, thanks so much. How did you know I love Josh Groban?" They stepped out onto the sidewalk and waited for the car to be brought around.

"Well now, let's see. First clue, you're a woman. Second clue, you're a woman." He grinned. "Actually, I called your shop and talked to Tonya. She was quite sure that talented young man would be a winner."

"Well, I might have to give that girl a raise." She scooted into the passenger seat and buckled her seat belt.

He threw his head back and laughed. "You might at that."

Susan leaned back and listened to Uncle Ollie's humor as she enjoyed the night lights of the city. They pulled up in front of a swank hotel, which didn't surprise her. Uncle Ollie always did things up big. She smiled at the doorman as they went through the ornate doors, then turned left toward the dining room. At a tug on her arm, she glanced up to see a mischievous smile on his face.

"No, no, not there." He led her to the elevators where they rode to the top.

She caught her breath when they stepped out onto the

elaborate open-air rooftop dining room where a smattering of diners sat. Apparently the chill in the air had deterred most people.

"Uncle Ollie!"

"I said I had a surprise for you. Well, this is it." He led her to a small table near the corner of the rooftop. The table was set with fine china and sparkling crystal, and soft music played. Susan was accustomed to upscale restaurants, but this was over the top.

Uncle Ollie regaled her with more humorous stories about him and Uncle Albert while they dined on French cuisine from the bouillabaisse to a tarte tatin, the caramelized apple tart Susan loved so well.

After the table was cleared, they watched the stars and listened to the soothing light classical music.

"Mmm. This has been a perfect evening, Uncle Ollie."

"I'm so happy you've enjoyed it, my dear. And so have I."

Susan leaned forward to pat his hand. Something whizzed by her ear.

She gasped and stood, her eyes darting around in panic. "Uncle Ollie. Someone just shot at me!"

He jumped up and grabbed her to him. "What? Where? I don't see anyone. Are you all right?"

"Yes. It missed me, but only because I leaned forward when I did."

"But did you see someone shoot? Where are they?" He scanned the rooftop.

"No. I only felt it whiz by my ear and cheek."

"Get your wrap. Let's go." He ushered her toward the door, signaling their waiter. "Get everyone off this roof and get the manager. Someone needs to call the police."

"Sir, what is wrong?" The young waiter looked frantic.

"This young lady barely missed being hit by a bullet." He scowled. "Don't just stand there. Get the people off here." He gripped Susan's elbow, guiding her into the elevator that stood waiting.

"But sir, there is no one else. You were the last ones." He scurried onto the elevator and pushed the button for the lobby.

As soon as they stopped, Uncle Ollie, his hand still gripping Susan's arm, headed toward the desk. "I need to see the manager at once. And call the police. Someone fired a shot."

A moment later the manager, with ashen face, appeared. "Mr. Oliver, I'm Jason Flack. I've called the authorities. Please come into my office until they arrive."

They followed the man down a corridor and into the office. With relief, Susan dropped into the deep cushions of an overstuffed chair while the manager ordered coffee.

The door opened and Susan glanced up. She groaned as she saw the tall, sturdily built policeman. Officer Stanton. And by his side the young policeman who'd discovered the tear in the carpet. Or his clone.

Officer Stanton looked at Susan and stopped short. "Miss Holland, isn't it?"

"Yes." She gave a short nod.

Uncle Ollie stepped forward. "Lionel Oliver. I hope you can get to the bottom of this affair, Officer. My young friend just missed being hit by a bullet."

"Did anyone see the shooter?" He fired the question at Uncle Ollie, but his eyes were on Susan.

"No. He must have been on the roof of one of the surrounding buildings."

"But you did see the bullet." He stared from one to the other.

"No, neither of us saw anything. Miss Holland felt it as it passed her." He stepped over and stood by Susan's chair, his hand on her shoulder.

The officer glanced at Stewart. "You getting this all down, boy?"

"Yes, sir." Stewart scribbled a few more lines on his notepad.

"Let's go up so you can show me." Officer Stanton motioned to the door and they all filed out.

Susan's heart sped up as they stepped out onto the rooftop. The music still played and candles flickered, reflecting on the crystal and silver. But the scene didn't appear so elegant to her now. Uncle Ollie stayed close to her side.

They showed the officers where they'd sat. Stewart checked the rooftop for a bullet, and when he returned, shaking his head, Susan told them once more exactly what she'd heard and felt.

"And from that, you assumed it was a bullet?" Sarcasm blended with impatience.

"What else could it be?" Susan snapped. Apparently, he'd already decided she was imagining things again.

"Oh, a bee maybe?"

"On a rooftop, in October?" She could be sarcastic, too.

Amusement filled Stanton's eyes and he twisted his mouth as though hiding a smile. "But there's no sign of a bullet."

"Well, there wouldn't be if it kept flying. It's probably embedded in a building somewhere."

"Well, Miss Holland, I'll check out the waiters and the other guests who were up here. Maybe someone saw something. But if I were you, I'd forget about it. It could have been anything. I doubt anyone shot at you."

Chapter 6

Susan stared across the table at Vince as he looked at the menu. His curls, black as midnight, invited her fingers. She quickly looked down at her own menu. She couldn't deny the excitement that had been dancing around inside her since he'd called her that morning and invited her to dinner. This time he'd been straightforward in his invitation, rather than using business as an excuse.

The server brought their iced tea and took their food order.

Vince leaned back, his eyes crinkling as he flashed her a smile. "You look beautiful tonight."

Susan felt the blush and bit her lip. She'd worn a new deep green dress that the girls insisted was her best color. "Thanks, Vince. You're not looking too bad yourself."

"Well, I try." He took a drink of his tea then put the glass down. "How are things going at the house?"

"Everything's packed up and thrown away, given away, or stored."

"No more accidents?"

Susan hesitated. Should she mention the incident on the rooftop? She took a deep breath. "Not at the house, but something

313

happened a few nights ago, when I was at dinner with an old friend."

He straightened, his eyes alert. "What happened?"

"I almost hate to mention it." Once again she hesitated before going on. "We were seated in the rooftop dining room when a bullet barely missed me."

"What?" He reached for her hand, jostling his glass. He steadied it then took her hand. "Were they shooting at you?"

"Well, if I hadn't leaned forward to say something to Uncle Ollie, it would have hit me. It was so close to my ear, I heard and felt it."

"You did call the police?" Concern filled his eyes.

"Yes, they found nothing and it seems no one saw anything, including Uncle Ollie. So. . ." She sighed.

"They didn't believe you." He pressed his lips together.

"They think I 'imagined' it." She tried to smile but couldn't quite manage it. "The police officer was the same one who came to the mansion when I fell, so he just had a field day being condescending to me. Said it was probably a bee. Rotten luck, huh?"

"I think it's time I had a talk with Nick. Now that he's back on the force, maybe he can do something."

She withdrew her hand. "No, I'd rather you didn't. But thanks for the offer."

Frustration passed over his face. "Susan, can't you think of anyone who might hold some sort of grudge against you?"

She shook her head. "Not to the extent of wanting me dead. Besides, I'm not even sure the two incidents are connected."

"Why not?"

"I still suspect Mary's nephew of pushing me. He seems shady. He stole money from Mary a few days ago and then yelled at me as he left. He may have been looking for something to sell when I walked through the mansion that day."

His eyes narrowed. "I'll be starting some preliminary work at the mansion next week. How about I talk to him?"

"Oh, but Vince, I couldn't ask you to do that. It's not your responsibility."

"I'll make it my responsibility." He touched her hand then drew back. "I don't want anything happening to you, Susan."

"All right. Thanks. It would ease my mind to know for sure." She took a relieved breath. "But please be careful. We know little about him."

"I will." He smiled. "I promise."

She nodded. "Good. And now let's talk about something else. You didn't ask me to dinner to hear about my woes."

"Your woes are my woes," he said. His gaze grabbed and held her. "And I'm not kidding."

She wasn't sure what he meant, but suddenly she felt safe. "Thanks again. It's nice to know I'm not alone in this."

Their salads arrived, and Susan broke contact with his mesmerizing eyes. Time to move on to safer territory.

"How many are in your family, Vince? I know Nick is your nephew, but I assume, since you have different last names, that he must be your sister's son. If you don't mind my asking."

"I don't mind at all. I have a great family. And a great big family." He chuckled. "There are six of us kids, four boys and two girls, Anna and Victoria. Anna is the eldest of the bunch and Nick's mother. My grandmother was still alive back then and had a 'fine Italian boy' picked out for her. She was crushed when Anna married someone else." He grinned. "She didn't get over it until little Nicky came along. And then, of course, there's our mama and papa."

"Goodness. That's wonderful," she said with a wistful sigh.

"I'm an only child."

He smiled. "Well, at least you didn't have to share everything. That's one advantage. Do your parents live around here?"

She shook her head. "They've both been gone for several years. Mom of cancer and Dad had a bad heart."

"I'm sorry to hear that, Susan." His voice was kind and sympathetic. "Do you have other family?"

"No, not since Uncle Albert died."

"No cousins or anything?"

"Uncle Albert had one daughter, JoAnne. We called her JoJo. She and I were the same age and very close. When we were ten, she and my aunt were in a car accident. Neither survived. I still miss her." She'd better change the subject. No sense in turning their first real date into something they'd look back on in sadness. What in the world was she thinking? Look back on? As though they had a future together.

"You'll have to meet the family sometime. You'll feel like one of them in no time."

She looked at him in surprise. "You're not teasing me, are you?"

"Of course not. I'm very serious."

Susan blinked back tears. "I don't believe anyone's ever offered to share their family with me before."

"Plenty to go around. They'll love you at first sight." He smiled. "How about splitting a hot fudge cake with ice cream?"

Mentally, Susan began to calculate calories and fat grams. She really needed to lose five pounds. Oh why not? "That sounds delicious."

Vince took Carl through the house and gave him a quick

summary of what they'd be doing for the next few weeks. "I'd like you to double-check the work. I want everything in top shape before we turn it over to Miss Holland. So make sure no one tries to slipshod over something."

Carl rocked back on his heels and looked at him. "What are you talking about, Vince? You know this crew isn't like that. For one thing, they know you wouldn't stand for it."

"I know, but everything has to be perfect on this job."

Carl grinned. "Okay, boss. I think I understand."

Vince stared at Carl through narrowed eyes. "What exactly do you think you understand?"

"Don't squint those eyes at me. I know when I see a man falling for a woman."

"We're not talking about this." Vince stalked off. Carl was getting too all-fired cocky. He thought just because they'd been friends for fifteen years, he could read Vince's mind. He chuckled. Okay, so he came pretty close sometimes. And this time, he'd hit the truth straight-on.

For days he'd replayed the evening he spent with Susan. When he got home that night, he realized he hadn't been so relaxed in years. She was some lady, all right. Too bad about her family. But he could fix that. The Martinelli family would welcome her with open arms. Especially if they got an inkling about his feelings for her. Mama had been after him for years to find himself a good woman and get married. Whoa! Hold on there. Where'd that come from? Was he really thinking in terms of a long-term relationship?

Susan seemed to like him, but she might not be interested in anything but friendship.

The sound of a revving motor drew his attention. He walked to the front window and saw a low-slung car pull into the driveway and head on back toward the guest house. Must be Tim.

Vince walked down the hall and through the sunroom to the back door. He stepped outside just as Tim got out of his car and slammed the door.

"Hi there." Vince walked over and ran his hand along the silver hood. "Nice car."

"Yeah, my pride and joy. Doin' some work on the place, huh?" He looked toward the house.

"That's right. My name's Vince Martinelli." He held out his hand, and Tim gave it a halfhearted shake. "You Mary's nephew?"

A guarded look crossed Tim's face. "Yeah. What's it to you?"

"Oh, I'd like to talk to you for a moment, Tim."

"What about, man?" He took a step backward. "I don't even know you."

"That's right. But I believe you know my friend Miss Holland?" Vince took a step forward.

Something like panic swept across Tim's face. "Oh yeah. Listen, I left in a hurry one day and almost knocked her over. Tell her I'm sorry, okay?"

"You should probably tell her yourself. That wasn't very nice, now was it?"

"Hey, man, I said I'm sorry." He eyed the door of the cottage.

"So you did. But that's not what I wanted to talk to you about. I'm more interested in who pushed Miss Holland down the stairs a few weeks ago."

Tim straightened from his slouch, and fury stormed across his face. "I knew it. I knew I'd get blamed for that. Well, you can't pin it on me because I wasn't anywhere near here. I was at a bar with some friends that day with plenty of witnesses." He whirled, stomped up the stairs, and shoved through the door.

Vince stayed planted where he was until he was sure Tim wasn't roughing up Mary. He didn't hear anything, so he turned and headed back inside.

He leaned against the sunroom door and dialed the number of Susan's shop.

"Coffee, Tea, and Sweets. Susan Holland speaking." Susan's voice rippled with laughter.

Vince grinned at the sound. "Hi there. What's so funny?"

"Vince, hello." Susan laughed. "One of my customers just told a joke as he was leaving. But don't worry. His joke wasn't near as funny as yours are."

"That's good to know. I always want to be able to make you laugh."

"Are you still at the house?" Her voice still held laughter.

"Yes. I've been explaining your plans to my foreman. But that's not why I called. I talked to Tim."

An indrawn breath, then, "What do you think? What did he say?"

Vince related most of the details of his talk with Tim.

"Do you think he did it?" Her voice held anxiety.

"No, I really don't. Not that he's not capable of it. He definitely has character flaws, but he seemed confident about his alibi."

Her sigh tickled his ear. "I'd almost hoped it was him. Because it would have explained things."

"What do you mean?"

"If it wasn't him, then both incidents must be connected. And I can't imagine anyone wanting to get rid of me unless it has something to do with the house." Her voice trembled.

Vince closed his eyes tight against the fear in her voice.

"Listen, Susan. We're going to get to the bottom of this. All right? Just be careful."

"I will," she whispered.

"Say, how about we grab a hamburger or something later?"

"Oh Vince. I'm so tired. I think I'll just go home and take a casserole out of the freezer to heat up." She paused. "But I wouldn't mind sharing my casserole with a friend. How about it?"

"Are you sure?" Vince felt like dancing a jig or something.

"Very sure. Six o'clock too early?"

"Six is perfect. Can I bring dessert?"

"I have fresh fruit for a salad. But if you want something richer, then feel free to bring it."

"Fresh fruit salad sounds great. See you at six, then."

As soon as he disconnected the call, Carl's voice broke into his happy thoughts. "Hey, Vince. Get that silly grin off your face and explain how this coffee shop is going to be set up," Carl said. "That is, if you can come down to earth long enough."

Vince laughed. "You're just jealous because no one will look twice at your ugly mug."

Carl howled and slapped him on the back. "Do you think Miss Holland has an unattached friend?"

Chapter 7

The upbeat new worship song she'd learned in church on Sunday kept running through Susan's head as she polished the furniture and ran the vacuum cleaner over the living room carpet. *All things are possible, believe it, all things are possible, through Jesus Christ, through Jesus Christ our Lord.*

That was the only line she could remember, so she sang the words over and over. She wondered if Vince went to church anywhere. Maybe she'd invite him to go with her next Sunday.

She shook her head and smiled at the way the big, handsome Italian intruded on her every thought.

She glanced at the clock on her mantel and stowed the vacuum in the hall closet. She washed her hands then headed for the kitchen, where she popped a chicken casserole into the oven and began chopping veggies for a salad. The fruit salad was already chilling in the refrigerator with a delicious strawberry cream cheese dressing ready to dab on the individual portions.

Once the salad was made, she changed into a pair of designer jeans and a soft, long-sleeved sweater. The table was set and flames were leaping in the gas fireplace when the doorbell rang.

She opened the door to Vince's grin and a bouquet of long-stemmed red roses.

"Am I too early?" He handed her the roses as he stepped through the door.

"No, just in time." She inhaled the aroma wafting from the flowers. "Thanks, Vince. I love red roses."

"I hoped you did." He sniffed the air. "Something sure smells good."

"Dinner is almost ready. Why don't you sit in the living room while I get a vase for the roses and finish up?"

"Or I could help."

Oh, she loved a man who wasn't afraid of a kitchen. This she could get used to. "Come with me, then. I never turn down offers to help."

They carried the food to the table together; then Susan went back for the frosty pitcher of iced tea.

"Would you like to ask the blessing, Vince?"

"Sure." He bowed his head and spoke a brief prayer of thanks and blessing.

Susan flashed him a smile as she poured the tea. "It's nice to see a man who is comfortable praying. That means a lot to me."

"My mother insisted we take turns asking the blessings, as well as evening prayers." He helped himself to a scoop of the steaming casserole. "Ah. I can already tell you're a great cook."

Susan laughed. "Well, thanks, but maybe you'd better reserve judgment until you taste it."

He winked and took a bite, then held up his fingers in the okay sign.

"I see it passed the taste test." She turned to her own plate.

"It more than passed."

"Okay, stop with the flattery." She grinned and shook her head. "It's only a casserole."

They continued the light banter throughout the meal.

Vince insisted on helping her clear away the dishes and load the dishwasher.

They'd just carried mugs of hot coffee into the living room when the doorbell rang.

Susan excused herself and went to open the door. Samantha stood in the hallway, flanked by her son and daughter. Susan grinned at the children. "Come in. Guess who's here?"

They craned their necks and spotted Vince. "Uncle Vince." The next minute they were all over him, while he laughed and rumpled their hair.

Samantha shook her head and came in. "We can't stay. We're on our way to a birthday party. I got some of your mail by mistake." She thrust two envelopes at Susan. "Hi, Vince. Shove those two back in this direction, please. We have to go."

With laughter and promises to get together soon, Samantha and the kids hurried away.

Susan tossed the mail on a small table by the door and joined Vince on the sofa. She laughed. "They always leave me feeling like a whirlwind went through."

"Yeah, they're active kids." He took a swig of his coffee then set the mug on the coaster.

"But well behaved. They're simply exuberant. Samantha has done a great job raising them."

"Yeah, Anna is crazy about them already. Nick'll be a good dad."

Susan leaned back. "I hadn't been around children much until I met Samantha's two. I had so much fun the few times I watched them for her. Made me wish I had one of my own."

"Yeah, me, too." The minute the words were out of his mouth, surprise crossed his face and he caught his breath and glanced at her.

Heat rose in her cheeks and she sat up, clutching her mug. "So how long do you think the renovations will take?"

"Huh?" He looked confused for a moment, then shook his head and gave a little laugh. "Hard to tell. If everything goes according to plan, it could only take two or three months. But you never know what you're going to run into in these old buildings." He looked thoughtful. "I'll be able to pinpoint it for you better after a few weeks on the job."

"I see." She fumbled around in her head, trying to find something impersonal to say, and found nothing.

Vince stood. "Well, I'd better be going. We both have to get up early."

She walked him to the door where they stood looking at each other.

"Susan." He started to take her hand, but she avoided it, pretending not to see.

"Good night, Vince. Thanks so much for coming."

He nodded and said good night.

Susan closed the door and leaned against it for a moment. What was he going to say? Or maybe he would have kissed her good night. Why had she stopped him?

She sighed and grabbed her mail off the table, then flopped down on the sofa. She glanced at the return address on the top letter. Senator Anthony Noble? Why was she getting mail from him? It couldn't be a campaign letter. He had retired several years ago. Besides, it looked more like an invitation.

She ripped open the envelope and her eyes scanned the card. She frowned and reread it. Why would Senator Noble invite her to an informal dinner? This must be a mistake. Well, it was too late to call now. She'd have to wait until morning.

Susan glanced around the crowded room. She still hadn't formally met her host. But she'd been assured by his secretary that the invitation was real. She'd come more out of curiosity than anything. Dinner had been long and boring, but the food was delicious. She wondered when, if ever, she'd find out what she was doing here. Other than Uncle Albert's infrequent mentions of the senator, Susan knew little about him. Though, by the looks of his house, he was very wealthy. It made the Holland mansion look like a shack.

"Miss Holland." She turned at the sound and found a short man with a trim mustache standing at her elbow. "The senator would like to speak with you privately. Follow me, please."

She did as instructed and a moment later stepped into a room with a magnificent fireplace. Bookshelves lined three walls, and sofas and overstuffed chairs in varying shades of brown stood comfortably around the room. Susan had seen Senator Noble on TV, but it had been years. She wasn't prepared for the sight of the emaciated white-haired man who motioned her over to the high-backed paisley wing chair where he sat next to the blazing fire.

"Forgive me for not standing, my dear. My legs don't work quite as well as I'd like." It was obvious the old gentleman was of a different era. Even his speech spoke of elegance and courtesy. He motioned to a sofa across from him. "Please sit."

She sat. "Senator, I appreciate your invitation, but I'm confused about the reason. We've never even met, have we?"

He gave her a fond smile. "Perhaps a time or two when you visited Albert's daughter. But you were very young. You wouldn't remember."

"Oh. But I still don't understand."

He coughed, holding a white handkerchief to his mouth. When the coughing spell was over, he caught his breath. "I merely wanted to talk about your uncle. I miss him. We were good friends for many years."

Susan looked at him in surprise. As far as she knew, there had been no close friendship between Uncle Albert and the senator. Maybe the old man was senile and imagined a friendship that hadn't existed. Still, she and Uncle Albert had been close but not that close. He probably had friends she knew nothing about.

"I miss Uncle Albert, too, sir."

He nodded. "I'm sure you do. And he must have been very fond of you. After all, you are his only heir. He left everything to you, didn't he?"

His eyes had narrowed. A twinge of discomfort tugged at her. Should she respond to that? She sighed. What did it matter? "Yes, sir. He did."

"Going through his personal things must be difficult. Have you begun that unpleasant task yet?"

"A little. I've been very busy at my shop. I'm not sure when I'll get around to his condo. Although I'll have to before I can sell or lease it."

"Hmm. What about his files? That must be a daunting chore." His eyes gleamed with an alertness Susan hadn't noticed before.

Unease stabbed her mind. Why was he grilling her? It was apparent he was trying to find out something without actually asking straight-out. But why?

"I believe his attorney has stored Uncle Albert's files in a safe place until I can go through them."

A frown crossed his face. "I see. Well, I would be more than happy to take care of that for you with the help of my assistants. After all, I'd be more likely to know what needs to be done with certain things."

"That's very kind of you, Senator. I'll let you know." She rose. "I hope you won't think me rude, but I need to go. Coffee and pastry shops open early."

"All right. The valet will bring your car around." He pushed a button and the door opened, revealing the man who'd escorted her to the room.

All the way home, she ran the short conversation over in her head. It had seemed more like she was being probed for information than a casual meeting. And she'd begun to rethink her first impression of the senator as a kind old gentleman. He'd wanted something from her. But what?

Maybe she was being paranoid. After the accidents and the unexplainable attempts to buy the run-down mansion, she was suspicious of anything out of the ordinary. And this evening was most definitely out of the ordinary.

She glanced at the clock on her dash. Eleven thirty. Was it too late to call Vince? Probably. After all, he was an early riser, too. Maybe when the rush was over in the morning, she'd head over to Falls Church.

Chapter 8

The door shouldn't be open," Vince said over his shoulder to Carl. "Mary's on her way to open up for us."

He pushed the heavy oak door the rest of the way open.

"I've got your back." Carl's voice was low and deadly calm.

"Thanks." He motioned for his three laborers to stay on the porch and stepped inside with Carl close beside him.

He stopped just inside, drawing in a breath then letting it out with a whoosh.

"Stinking vandals!" Carl growled.

Wallpaper hung from the walls in shreds. In the kitchen, cupboards were flung open and drawers lay in pieces on the kitchen floor. One cabinet had been completely ripped out.

"I don't think so." Vince's eyes narrowed and his lips were set in a grim line. "Looks to me as though someone was looking for something and didn't care what they destroyed in doing it."

"Mercy! What happened here?" Mary's voice rang out. Vince went to meet her in the foyer.

"It appears someone went on a very destructive hunt for something." He peered at her. "The door was open when we got here, but it seems whoever did this is long gone. You didn't see or hear anything during the night?"

"No! Don't you think I'd have called the police and Miss Holland?" The frown she threw his way was indignant to say the least.

"Of course you would've. Sorry, Mary." He sighed. "Well, guess we'd better check the damage upstairs."

"What do you want me to do about the crew?" Carl asked.

Vince stood for a moment in thought. "We can't touch anything until Miss Holland gets here and the police check the place out. Tell the men they can go home or head over to the Jenkins place to help Eddie and Frank. Give them their choice."

While Carl headed out to talk to the crew, Vince followed Mary up the staircase. This had been her domain for twenty years. He wasn't about to usurp her authority.

The second and third floors showed more of the same devastation. He left Mary on the third floor and took the back stairs up to the attic. Thankfully there wasn't a lot up there to tear into. The few boxes that were there had been dumped and the contents scattered.

Vince pulled out his cell phone as he walked downstairs. Dreading the task of telling Susan the bad news, he punched in her cell phone number. It rang several times before she answered.

"Hello." She sounded rushed.

"Hi, Susan, did I catch you at a bad time?" He groaned. It would be a really bad time once he told her.

"Rush is just about over, Vince," she said. "What can I do for you?"

"Can you get away for a while?"

"Sure, I planned to come over anyway. I think you'd like to hear about my dinner at the senator's house."

"Sure I would. But I have some bad news for you." He sighed. Hadn't she been through enough lately?

"What is it? Has something happened at the house?" Her voice had gone up a notch.

"Someone broke in and tore the place up pretty bad."

Her sharp intake of breath was followed by a groan. "I'll be right there."

"I think you should call the police, Susan."

"I will. But I want to see the place first. Be there as quick as I can get there."

Carl left to join the other crew.

"This is a sad day, Mary," Vince said as they stood waiting on the porch.

"Yes, but it could have been a lot worse." Mary almost wailed. "When I think about suggesting she move all that furniture up to the attic instead of storing it. . .It'd probably all be ruined if she had."

"I'd say you're right about that."

"Well, I'd best get my roast in the oven. Tell Miss Holland to call me if she needs me for anything. And tell her as soon as the police are finished here, I'll start cleaning things up."

"I think we'll probably need a cleaning crew, Mary. But I'll tell her what you said."

"No cleaning crew can do any better than me. I've been cleaning all my life." She frowned.

"I know, I know. And once the renovations are done, there'll be plenty for you to do. But it would be faster to hire a firm for this job. Then I can get to work on turning this old place into the best B and B Miss Holland has ever seen."

"You kind of like her, don't you?" She grinned and her bottom denture plate rocked in her mouth. She waved and stepped off the porch.

Vince laughed. "How'd you guess?" he called after her. "I like her a lot."

A half hour later, he opened Susan's car door and walked inside with her.

As she walked through the first floor, her face scrunched up and then tears started rolling down her cheeks.

"Aw, sweetheart." Without even thinking, Vince put his arms around her and pulled her close, patting her on the back. He let her cry until the sobs turned to sniffles.

She drew in a sobbing breath and shook her head, looking up at him with tear-soaked brown eyes.

"Sorry, Vince. I'm afraid your shirt is soaked."

"Hey, it'll dry." He looked at her closely. "Are you okay now?"

"Yeah, I think so. Do I need to go upstairs?"

"It's just more of the same. Mary and I walked through. There's nothing that can't be repaired, but it'll be expensive and it's going to take some time." He squeezed her hand. "Don't you think you should call the police now?"

"No. I don't want to endure that again," she said. "What could they do anyway? You know very well whoever did this wore gloves. There won't be a print anywhere."

"There might be. You need to think about this."

She took a deep breath. "Of course, you're right." She lifted her eyes to him. "Thanks for letting me cry on your shoulder."

"My shoulder is privileged." He smiled then took her hand. "I'll tell you what. Since I'm the one who found this mess, you go back to the shop and let me deal with the police. If they want to talk to you, they can come to the shop later. After they're finished here, I'll get a cleaning crew over and we'll get busy. But Susan, whoever did this is determined to find whatever they're looking for. They might not stop with destroying property. Please be careful."

Susan finished filling out her order form and placed it underneath the counter for tomorrow. She glanced at the clock. Seven o'clock already. She stood and stretched, trying to work the ache out of her shoulder muscles. She grabbed her sweater and handbag and headed for the parking lot.

When the car didn't immediately start, she reinserted the key and tried again. Nothing. "Come on now, baby. Don't do this to me."

She tried again, but not a sound indicated the motor was cooperating. She sighed and opened the door. Ordinarily, she enjoyed the mile walk from her apartment to the shop, but as tired as she was, the uphill walk was nothing to look forward to. She supposed she could call a cab. She stood beside her car for a minute then shook her head. She could probably be home before a cab would arrive.

She grabbed her handbag, walked to the corner, then started up the hill toward Shirlington. Cherry Blossom Estates was at the top of the hill. Headlights came toward her then whizzed past her on down the hill. Lighted windows announced life going on in the houses lining both sides of the street.

She could hear a car coming up behind her, so she moved over to give the driver plenty of room in case he didn't see her. The car sailed past. She should have grabbed her flashlight from the glove compartment. Oh well, not much farther to go.

Suddenly a motor revved behind her and she jumped to the side. The auto turned into a driveway and pulled back out, then headed straight for her. She dodged aside in the nick of time, but tripped and fell. Her ankle screamed in pain. The car sped away.

Susan sat dazed. Did someone actually try to run her over, or had they lost control of their car?

A door flew open in the nearest house and a woman ran out and knelt beside her. "Are you okay? I saw the whole thing. Sorry it took me so long, but I had to call my son inside to watch the younger children. He's calling the police."

Susan shook her head in an attempt to clear away the fog. "Do you think they lost control of their car?"

"No way. He tried to hit you from behind, and when that didn't work he turned around and came at you from the front. It was deliberate, okay. Do you have enemies, lady?"

"None that I know of." She tried to stand, then fell back down, her ankle throbbing.

"Here, let me help you to my porch before that nut comes back for another try. My name's Betty."

With help from the Good Samaritan, Susan managed to hobble over to the porch and sit on the step.

"Should I call an ambulance?" Betty eyed her with concern.

"No, I don't think it's sprained. I'll put ice on it when I get home." She dug into her purse and retrieved her cell phone. "I'd better call someone to come get me. I don't think I can manage that hill now."

Ten minutes later, Vince pulled up right behind the police car. He rushed over to her.

"Are you all right?" He stooped down next to her.

"I think so. I just twisted my ankle a little. My nerves are shot, though." She held out her shaking hand. "See?"

The police came and took her statement and Betty's.

Neither she nor Betty had gotten the license number or even a good look at the car. Susan was too busy trying to avoid being hit. They agreed it was black, and Betty thought it was a four-door.

When Betty ducked inside to check on her children and the dinner in the oven, Susan told the police about her fall down the stairs and the bullet that barely missed her. She also mentioned the break-in and vandalism of the mansion.

The police left with promises to let her know if they had any leads.

Vince bent over her. "Put your arm around my neck and I'll carry you to the car."

"No, no, I can walk. Just let me lean on you."

"I'm sure you could if you had to, but why should you?" He reached down and swung her into his arms.

"Well, in that case, okay then." She couldn't prevent the giggle that escaped her lips. She leaned her head against his shoulder and let him carry her to his car. Betty rushed ahead and opened the door. Vince set Susan gently onto the seat and went around to the driver's side.

He smiled at her as he started the car. "That wasn't so bad, was it?"

Should she be honest? "Actually, it was nice. I haven't been carried since I stepped on a nail when I was seven. It's a very comforting feeling. Thank you."

"You're very welcome. Now let's get you home and get ice on that ankle."

By the time he left two hours later, Susan was stretched out on the sofa with her foot up and an ice pack in place. Vince had made omelets and toast for them both and they'd eaten in the living room. A half hour later, he brought her car, while his brother drove his. He'd discovered a detached battery cable. It was impossible to tell if it was deliberate, but Vince insisted she report it, so she did.

At least, finally, the police believed her about something. She went to bed, snuggled into her down comforter, and slept like a baby.

Chapter 9

Susan carried the last of the file boxes into her apartment. If Senator Noble was so interested in these files that he'd invite a perfect stranger to dinner simply to talk, there must be something important in them.

With an *oomph*, she dropped the box on the floor in front of the sofa with the other twenty. Her living room looked like a box factory.

Kicking her shoes off, she went to the kitchen, favoring her ankle. After two weeks she still got a twinge now and then. She poured a glass of iced tea, then returned to the living room. This was going to be quite a job. Especially since she had no idea what she was looking for.

Three hours later, she leaned back, discouragement ripping through her. She should have had the attorney go over these with her. Or even one of Uncle Albert's business associates. Her stomach rumbled. No wonder. She'd forgotten to eat anything. She ambled into the kitchen, stretching her shoulders and neck as she went.

Carrying a plate with a chicken sandwich and a glass of milk, she headed for her bedroom, where she sank into her deep-cushioned armchair. The files could wait. She'd consult with the lawyer tomorrow. Surely he could recommend someone trustworthy with the knowledge to check those files.

Her meal finished, she took her dishes to the kitchen and went back to her room. She got ready for bed and crawled in between the cool sheets, looking forward to the soft downy covers. She reached to turn on her alarm, and her gaze rested on the little drummer bear that stood on her bedside table.

She smiled and picked him up. "Hi, Tailend. Do you miss your family?" She rubbed his furry back, her hand running across something bumpy. On closer examination, she found a line of stitches. Strange. She didn't remember the little fellow ever being torn. Maybe it happened after her last visit. She shrugged and set him back on the table.

She turned off the lamp and yawned as she lay back on her thick pillows, stretching her legs as far as they'd go.

"Good night, Lord. Sorry I forgot to pray before I came to bed. I promise I'll do better tomorrow."

Her eyes closed and she began to drift. She gasped and sat up, wide awake, nearly knocking the lamp over as she turned it on. Grabbing the bear, she jumped out of bed and headed for the kitchen. Now where had she put those little scissors?

She threw open her small pantry and lifted a shoe box down from the top shelf. She seldom sewed anything for the simple reason that she'd never learned how. But she kept it for last-minute button emergencies and so forth.

She picked up the bear, giving him a shake, then squeezing his furry body. She didn't hear or feel anything. Maybe it was just her imagination. No, in the first place her imagination wasn't that big, in spite of Officer Stanton's judgment of her. She laid the bear facedown on the table and went to work on the stitches.

At first she couldn't see anything out of the ordinary. Determined to make sure, she began pulling stuffing out. She caught her breath as her fingers touched something that felt like paper. Withdrawing it, she held a folded paper square in her hand. Her fingers trembled as she opened it to reveal a single sheet.

The ink was a little faded, so with her heart thumping wildly, she carried it to the living room and sat on the sofa, turning on the reading lamp.

To Whom It May Concern: If you find this, I'm probably dead either by natural causes or by foul play. I have evidence of a murder. My life has been threatened if I report this, and frankly I don't wish to die just yet. However, they aren't likely to kill me if they know I have hidden the evidence.

On February 7, 1976, the body of a foreign dignitary, one Ivan du Pres, was found floating in the river. It was unclear at the time whether the death was murder, accident, or suicide. I can assure you, it was murder. I was an unwilling witness of the deed and although I couldn't prevent the act itself, I managed to take two photos. If you will dig a little further into this little fellow's stomach, you'll find them. In case the perpetrators are long gone or unrecognizable in the photo, I will include a list of their identities.

Following was a list of five names. The first name on the list was no surprise. Senator Anthony Noble. The next three were unknown to Susan. But the last name brought a gasp. She closed her eyes against the truth, and tears poured down her cheeks.

"No," she whispered. "Oh no. Uncle Ollie."

Vince sat next to Susan on the sofa, comforting her. If only he could take away her pain. There was no use skirting the issue. If Lionel Oliver was one of the murderers, he was also likely involved in the attempts on Susan's life. He was pretty sure that thought had crossed her mind as well.

He handed her a couple of fresh tissues. She blew her nose then looked up and took a shaky breath. "Okay, I'm ready to go now. Just let me wash my face."

When she returned, there was little trace of her tears left. She gave him a tremulous smile that turned his heart over.

Vince had notified the police they were bringing the evidence in, so at the station, they were immediately escorted into the office of Detective Briner, a bulldog-faced man with a shock of curly white hair. He smiled and pulled out a chair for Susan, motioning for Vince to sit beside her.

His lips tightened as his eyes scanned the letter and photos. "And you found these where, Miss Holland?"

She handed him the drumming bear she held on her lap. He eyed the damaged toy and nodded. "From the reports, there was obviously something fishy about this case. These photos leave little doubt that the statements in the letter are true." He glanced at a file on his desk. "And we'll also check to see if this is connected with the accidents you've been having."

After the detective thanked her and assured her he'd be in touch, they left.

"Do you want to stop for something to eat or a cup of coffee?" He hated to think of her grieving all alone in her apartment.

"Thanks, Vince, but I just want to go to sleep. Anyway, we both have to work tomorrow."

"You're right. But I have another request." He took a deep breath. "What are you doing for Thanksgiving?"

She blinked and darted a glance at him. "Uncle Albert and I usually went out to dinner. Now that he's gone, well, I hadn't really thought about it."

"Well, I have and I've decided it's time for me to introduce you to the family I promised to share with you. How about coming to Thanksgiving dinner with us?" He almost held his breath waiting for her answer.

"Really? Oh no, I couldn't do that. What would your mother think of a stranger barging in?"

"First of all, Mama doesn't let anyone remain a stranger more than two minutes. And second, she's the one who extended the invitation." Practically ordered him to invite Susan actually, just as he'd hoped she would.

"Oh, you told her about me?"

He grinned. "Of course. You're an important part of my life."

"I am?" Her lips turned up at the corners. "I sort of like you, too, you know."

"You should. I'm a nice guy."

She laughed. "And you're the first to say it, huh?"

Their laughter rang out as they drove up the hill to Cherry Blossom Estates. And after they'd said good night, Vince couldn't erase the smile that was planted on his face.

He loved the woman. No denying it. And he was pretty sure she felt the same. It was time he did something about it.

Susan opened the box of freshly delivered donuts, still hot from the fryers and ovens, and placed them neatly in the glass cases.

She glanced around to make sure she hadn't forgotten anything. She grabbed the paper and a mug of pumpkin spice and sat at the counter. Ten minutes to relax before time to open. It had been a busy week and she was glad it was Friday. Tonya was in back giving last-minute instructions to Amy, the girl Susan had hired the week before. Between employees and the overload of customers, the place was about to come apart at the seams.

Cleanup on the mansion had gone swiftly, and Vince and his crew were hard at work replacing and renovating, but she knew it would be awhile yet. But that was good. She'd need time to hire a manager to take over this location and hire a couple of waitresses. Conrad wanted to stay, but Tonya was eager to make the switch to Falls Church. Susan was impressed with Tonya's progress.

She glanced at her watch. It was time. She opened the door, and chill air rushed into the warm café, followed by the waiting line of people.

Midmorning, the phone rang and Susan hurried to answer.

"Miss Holland, Detective Briner here. Do you have a few minutes?" His booming voice indicated the answer had better be yes.

"Yes, Detective, do you have any news yet?" It had been two weeks since Susan had found the incriminating evidence.

"Yes, I'm happy to say I do. One of the men on the list is deceased, but the others are in custody. Preliminary hearings are scheduled for later today." He hesitated. "We have one signed confession. I thought you should know."

"Uncle Ollie?"

"Yes, Lionel Oliver." He cleared his throat. "Some of it concerns you. If you'd like to come to the station after work, I'll discuss it with you."

"I'll be there." Susan's voice shook. She hung up the phone and took a deep breath. There were still customers waiting.

Later that night Susan sat in her living room and told Vince the details of her meeting with Detective Briner.

Uncle Ollie's confession had eased her heart to a degree, in that he wasn't involved in any way with the attacks on Susan. In fact, he'd actually prevented a few incidents that could have been fatal for her. But it chilled her to hear the details of the cold-blooded murder conspiracy. He'd been younger then and a great deal of money was involved.

Senator Noble had been so desperate to find the evidence, he'd sent someone to search the mansion the day the will was read. That person was the one who shoved Susan down the stairs. At this point it was uncertain whether he had instructions to get rid of her or was simply afraid she'd seen him.

She attempted a smile. "Uncle Ollie's statement exonerated Uncle Albert completely of any part in the conspiracy or the actual murder."

Vince nodded. "I suspected that suspicion might have crossed your mind."

"Just for a moment or so. I never really thought he was involved. My uncle was always a champion of right and justice." She smiled. "Still, it is a relief to know for sure."

She blinked away the tears that flooded her eyes. "Well, it's over now. Or almost. I may have to testify, but they don't think it'll be necessary with Uncle Ollie's statement." She smiled. "I'm ready to leave it all behind me."

"I'm glad to hear it." He rubbed his thumb across her hand and a thrill ran up her arm. "My family is excited about meeting you next week."

"I can't wait to meet them, too. I've never celebrated a

holiday with a big family."

He laughed. "You may never want to again."

"Oh, I doubt that's true. They must be wonderful, if you're any indication of what they're like."

His eyes lit up. "If that's flattery, keep it up. I like it." And there went that thumb again.

She laughed. "Go home, Vince. And don't call me early tomorrow. I'm sleeping in."

Chapter 10

Susan didn't know if she'd ever laughed so much in her life. No sooner would she catch her breath than one of Vince's brothers would say something so funny she couldn't help herself from exploding with laughter.

She'd discovered very quickly the whole family loved to tease. And tonight, she and Vince were the main targets.

"Now stop that." Mrs. Martinelli frowned at Frankie and wagged her finger in his face. "Frankie Martinelli, you should be ashamed of yourself, teasing the poor girl so. Now you apologize right this minute for your bad manners."

"Yes, ma'am." Frankie winked at Susan and bowed from the waist. "Please forgive me, Susan, for my bad manners."

Susan covered her mouth to stifle a giggle.

"Ah, Mama. Leave the children alone. They're only having fun." Mr. Martinelli smiled at Susan. "She knows they don't mean any harm."

Susan nodded. "I'm not one bit offended."

Mrs. Martinelli patted her cheek. "You're a good girl. Just what my Vince needs."

At that the whole room exploded with laughter. "Mama! And you scolded us."

The elderly woman's eyes twinkled. "But I'm not teasing."

The dinner table was piled high with traditional Thanksgiving food, such as turkey with stuffing and cranberry sauce, as well as traditional Italian dishes. Susan tried everything.

She took a bite of a salad-type dish and her eyes widened. She took another bite.

Mama Martinelli's eyes sparkled. "You like the *caponata di pesce?*"

Susan smiled and nodded. "What is it?"

Vince's mother drew her brows together in thought then said, "Oh yes. Fish salad."

"Well, it's very good."

"Vincenzo likes it very much, too. I teach you to make it."

The dinner ended with three different desserts, fruit, and cheese. Susan took a bite of each to be polite, but by now she was stuffed.

After dinner, someone rolled back the area rug in the living room and the furniture was pushed to the walls. Music filled the room and Susan had her first experience with an Italian folk dance.

One of Nick's brothers-in-law pulled Susan into the mix, and when it was over she collapsed into a chair.

Frankie jumped up from across the room. "Okay," he laughed, "time for the tarantella."

"Don't you dare, you bad boy." His mama frowned and swatted him on the arm.

"But Mama. It's for Susan and Vince."

"No! I don't like that dance and neither does Jesus."

Frankie laughed. "All right, Mama. No tarantella."

Soon the party broke up, and couples and families began to leave. Vince brought Susan's coat, and she thanked Vince's parents for sharing their holiday with her.

Vince's mother took Susan's face between her two hands. "I hope you will come again soon. Very soon."

Susan leaned back in the car and sighed.

Vince chuckled. "I'd like to think that was a happy sigh, but I'm afraid it was a sigh of exhaustion."

"Mmm. Both. I am tired, but it was a wonderful evening. Thanks so much for sharing your wonderful family with me, Vince. I'll never forget."

"I hope you'll share many more."

She smiled. "So do I."

Vince parked the car and they went upstairs. She stopped at the door and turned to face him.

"Do you mind if I come in just for a moment? I promise not to stay long."

"All right." She handed him her key.

They went inside and she kicked her shoes off. "I don't know how I danced in those things. I think I'll wear more comfortable shoes next time."

His eyes crinkled up. "I should have warned you."

"Would you like something to drink? I can make coffee."

"No thanks. I just want to talk to you about something." He cleared his throat.

"Nothing's wrong at the mansion, is it?"

"No. Everything's going fine." He glanced at the sofa. "Can we sit down for a minute?"

"Yeah, I think we'd better. Before you fall down. What is it, Vince?"

They sat down and he took her hand.

"Susan, I'm in love with you." His voice shook with emotion.

A thrill went through her. She knew he cared for her, but

had hardly dared to hope those feelings went this far.

"Oh Vince. I feel the same. I mean, I love you, too."

"You do? Are you sure?"

She laughed. "Of course I'm sure. Why? Were you hoping I'd say sorry, I don't love you?"

"Oh no. Please don't do that." His smile took her breath away. "You'll marry me, then?"

She stared at him, too overcome to speak.

Concern washed over his face. "Am I rushing things? I know we haven't known each other long."

"No," she whispered. "I don't think you're rushing things at all. And yes, I'll marry you."

The joy that shone on his face matched what was filling her heart. He reached into his pocket and pulled out a small velvet box. Her breath caught at the diamond that sparkled against an exquisite setting.

He slipped it on her finger and slowly lowered his head until his lips met hers.

Finally she pulled away.

"I'd better leave," he said, his voice husky with emotion.

She walked him to the door. "Hey, your mama didn't tell you to ask me to marry you, did she?"

"Sure she did. But I'd already bought the ring."

Susan laughed, and then her lips met his in a long and tender kiss good night.

FRANCES L. DEVINE grew up in the great state of Texas, where she wrote her first story at the age of nine. She moved to Southwest Missouri more than twenty years ago and fell in love with the hills, the fall colors, and the Silver Dollar City. Frances has always loved to read, especially cozy mysteries, and considers herself blessed to have the opportunity to write in her favorite genre. She is the mother of seven adult children and has fourteen wonderful grandchildren.

A Letter to Our Readers

Dear Readers:

In order that we might better contribute to your reading enjoyment, we would appreciate you taking a few minutes to respond to the following questions. When completed, please return to the following: Fiction Editor, Barbour Publishing, Inc., P.O. Box 719, Uhrichsville, OH 44683.

1. Did you enjoy reading *Cherry Blossom Capers*?
   ❑ Very much. I would like to see more books like this.
   ❑ Moderately—I would have enjoyed it more if _____
   _____
   _____

2. What influenced your decision to purchase this book?
   (Check those that apply.)
   ❑ Cover   ❑ Back cover copy   ❑ Title   ❑ Price
   ❑ Friends   ❑ Publicity   ❑ Other

3. Which story was your favorite?
   ❑ *State Secrets*   ❑ *Buried Deception*
   ❑ *Dying for Love*   ❑ *Coffee, Tea, and Danger*

4. Please check your age range:
   ❑ Under 18   ❑ 18–24   ❑ 25–34
   ❑ 35–45   ❑ 46–55   ❑ Over 55

5. How many hours per week do you read? _____

Name _____

Occupation _____

Address _____

City _____ State _____ Zip _____

E-mail _____

A Wedding to
REMEMBER

IN CHARLESTON, SOUTH CAROLINA

BY

ANNALISA DAUGHETY

Wedding planner Summer Nelson is throwing herself into her work to avoid the pain of her recent marriage separation. Husband Luke knows he made a mistake—but doesn't know how to fix it. When a hurricane traps them together, the crisis just might tear them apart forever.

Coming soon wherever Christian books are sold.